Published by Semiotext(e)
PO BOX 629, South Pasadena, CA 91031
www.semiotexte.com

Cover photo: Hans Georg Berger, "Arnaud, Hervé and Huges collecting herbs, Casino Taddei Castelli, Elba, 1982."

Design: Hedi El Kholti

ISBN: 978-1-63590-119-1

Distributed by The MIT Press, Cambridge, Mass. and London, England
Printed in the United States of America

Written in Invisible Ink
Selected Stories

Hervé Guibert

Edited and Translated
by Jeffrey Zuckerman

semiotext(e)

Contents

Translator's Preface 9

A Note on the Chronology 19

PROPAGANDA DEATH 25

My body, due to the effects of lust or pain... 27

Monologue I: Cosmetic Butchery 30

Monologue II: Photographs 32

Monologue III: Internal Mongolia 33

Self-Portrait in Shards 36

Pillage 40

The Glance 44

A Lover's Brief Journal 46

Account of a Crime 54

Newspaper Clipping 55

Propaganda Death (One Performance Only) 57

Five Marble Tables 65

PROPAGANDA DEATH NO. 0 71

Slaughter 73

An Indecent Dream 75

Pure Fantasy 77

Labial Flesh 79

Final Outrages 81

VICE   83

PERSONAL EFFECTS (Inventory of Bougainville's Travel Case)   87

    The Comb   89

    The Cotton Swab   90

    The Blackhead Remover   92

    The Nose Wipe   93

    The Exfoliating Glove   94

    The Cuticle Trimmer   95

    The Eyelash Curler   96

    The Cat o' Nine Tails   97

    The Rigollot's Paper   98

    The Tongue Depressor   100

    The Ether Mask   101

    The Gloves   103

    The Daguerreotype of a Dead Child   104

    The Teddy-Bear Vial   105

    The Vibrating Chair   106

    The Neck Brace   108

    The Static Electricity Machine   109

    The Flypaper   113

    The Vacuum Machine   114

A ROUTE   115

    Regulation   117

    The Hammam   118

    The Planetarium   123

    The Museum of the École de médicine   126

    The Palace of Desirable Monsters   128

THE STING OF LOVE AND OTHER TEXTS 131

The Sting of Love 133

The Knife Thrower 136

Posthumous Novel 142

A Screenwriter in Love 149

For P. Dedication in Invisible Ink 153

Vertigoes 164

Obituary 169

SINGULAR ADVENTURES 175

A Kiss for Samuel 177

The Trip to Brussels 182

The Desire to Imitate 190

MAUVE THE VIRGIN 213

Mauve the Virgin 215

Flash Paper 227

Joan of Arc's Head 241

A Man's Secrets 251

The Earthquake 257

The Lemon Tree 260

Acknowledgments 267

I

The myth of Hervé Guibert is that of the cruelly beautiful man who betrayed his friends, the writer of sex and death who would die of a sexually-transmitted disease. This myth owes its origins to a single book, *To the Friend Who Did Not Save My Life*. The volume was an autofiction: drawing from life while not being bound purely to the facts. But the truth it told was undeniable. It laid bare the symptoms of and treatments for the disease that had just befallen the narrator and author; readers quickly understood that the only reason it turned its gaze upon the philosopher Michel Foucault was to lay bare the reality of how he, too, had in fact died of that same disease. It was a book that did away with secrets, starting with the name of the disease: AIDS. The philosopher had already been dead for six years, reportedly of cancer, at the time the book was published, but his reputation was so firmly cemented that few French readers were deluded by the descriptions of a man named Muzil. As the man was described on his deathbed, there was an outcry among the French public: what right did this writer have to uncover these secrets? But this betrayal of Foucault's confidences were merely the scandal of a moment; Hervé Guibert's most enduring influence has been in ending the silence imposed by the shame and stigma of AIDS.

In the wake of its publication and scandal, *To the Friend Who Did Not Save My Life* would sell hundreds of thousands of copies, and a groundswell of support would rise up for Guibert. He went on to write two more volumes to create a trilogy around his experience with AIDS before his death, subsequent to a suicide attempt, at the end of 1991. The myth around the man was a simple yet seductive one.

It was easy for Guibert's new readers to remain unaware that, before the bombshell that was *To the Friend Who Did Not Save My Life*, he had written more than a dozen other books published by France's most prestigious publishers, as well as having been a photographer with numerous exhibitions and a journalist for *Le Monde* and other outlets. The man behind the myth, unsurprisingly, was far more complex than the myth itself.

It would take more than a decade, and the publication of Guibert's journals under the title *The Mausoleum of Lovers*, for a fuller picture to be anchored in the public consciousness, for readers to look at the words rather than the images. This is how I myself discovered Hervé Guibert: the English translation of his journals came out at the same time that I met the brilliant author Marie Darrieussecq, who had written her doctoral dissertation on his work. As I read the diaries, I picked up several volumes of his short stories. From the outset, Guibert's sentences struck me in their complexity: they were long, sinuous, sometimes self-referential, always designed to implicate the reader somehow. Again and again I tried to imagine how they could possibly unspool in English with the same elegance I saw in the original French, and even though I could sense the scope of the challenge, I couldn't shake the thought of translating his words myself.

This first story of his I attempted was "The Knife Thrower"; it turns out to have been one of his earliest-written stories. As I untangled its long, convoluted sentences, I found myself inexorably pulled in by Guibert's particular trains of thought, the way his sentences looped around and interrupted themselves before arriving at their endpoint. It was a style that made me want to stretch the English language to accommodate the strangeness of the original French. I paged through other stories, translated them to see if I could somehow replicate Guibert's baroque phrases and decentered clichés. All the strangeness and violence and viscerality of Guibert's depictions were wonderfully harnessed by his carefully deployed words. There was a man beneath the myth, but the myth wasn't entirely wrong: his beauty was there, and so was his cruelty; his raw honesty was there, and so was his intense devotion to the subjects of his scrutiny. They felt, if anything, like the photographs he had taken: carefully composed, strikingly blunt, but undeniably bewitching.

II

In Guibert's photographs, the human body recurs again and again. Clothed or naked, whole or squared-off, in flesh or in wax . . . Even when what is photographed is a simulacrum of the real thing, there is no denying that the body, with all its expressive potential, is the true source of inspiration for him.

Such imagery is indicative of the intense physicality of Guibert's stories. He makes no secret of how his own life steered him in such a direction: while his mother was a former schoolteacher, his father was a veterinary inspector who examined the abattoirs of Paris. As such, his childhood in and around Paris was marked by the sight of his father's blood-stained clothes, of beef tongue wrapped in newsprint for them to cook, and by Hervé's own medical condition of a concave chest. If most writers' debuts deal with autobiographical concerns, then it should come as little surprise that Guibert's very first book, *Propaganda Death*, was filled with the images of slaughterhouses and hospitals. The kinship he had already declared with Sade, Bataille, and Genet is made gruesomely visible as he articulates the human body in extremis, culminating in a scene where he describes his own body, dead and on a laboratory table. It was published in 1977: he was only 21 years old at the time. He could not have known that he would die fifteen years later, but here he was already considering his own corpse at length. An early draft of *Propaganda Death* is written as a screenplay; there are headings, directions, bits of dialogue. Not much space is given to interiority. Even when his attention turns to the erotic, he remains visceral: the hookups and street fights he describes with other men are harsh and violent, not so much a series of bodies coming together as bodies crashing against one another. Foucault described the book in an interview with Bernard-Henri Lévy: "Guibert opens with the worst extreme—'You want us to speak of it, well, let's go, and you will hear more than ever before'—and with this infamous material he builds bodies, mirages, castles, fusions, acts of tenderness, races, intoxications . . ."

Interiority would come more and more to the fore in Guibert's later stories, but the entire time I translated these stories, I was unable to forget the words of Nathanaël, the translator of his journals. The greatest difficulty of working on those notebooks, she said, was "in *duration* . . . to be called upon, in a sense, to exhume, repeatedly, Guibert's body, was exhausting." Looking back at the corpus of Hervé Guibert's shorter works, I sense this same heft that is more than the weight of the stories themselves. But somehow this heft is reassuring, as if making my way through his literary career through his stories, his various perspectives on himself and the people around him, had been a way to take the measure of his self. It felt all too appropriate, then that the last story I translated by Guibert, and the last one in this volume, should be "The Lemon Tree." It opens almost photographically, with the narrator staring at his friend's hand in admiration, and closes with one of that friend's fingers down his throat and with "an immense calm" that I myself felt upon typing the final sentence.

Many of Guibert's stories end with unanswered letters or indeterminate images or even just ellipses: a trailing-off, not a sense of closure. It was with the shock of recognition, then, that I read the words of his widow, Christine, who he married so that the revenue from his books would go to her children and so that his estate would be handled suitably: "At the beginning of our friendship (from 1976), every time I read his books, his short stories especially, I had the feeling of something incomplete, as if he didn't know how to finish. Now, I see his work as a closed space, fully constructed and whole."

III

Men are everywhere to be found in Guibert's texts. In a conversation with Edmund White, who had known Hervé early in his career, I was surprised to realize that Guibert's particular stance toward other men—that is, open, unashamed, yet not brazen homosexuality—was not meant as a provocation. It was, however, a quietly revolutionary stance in line with his particular brand of rebelliousness, in which, to quote a line from the end of *Ghost Image*, "secrets have to circulate." If homosexuality was one such secret, Guibert refused to keep it, whether in his life or in his art.

Still, Guibert's stories are in no way utopian. Curses and snubs and physical attacks crop up frequently, almost always borne out of homophobia. But there is a solace to be found in how the narrators and protagonists of these stories refuse to see themselves in the wrong; they love each other, tease each other, suck each other off, and betray each other just as easily as any other couple might.

And just as these stories pose a particular way of living life, so does a particular life inscribe itself in these texts, populated by men Guibert knew intimately. The Vincent Marmousez of *Crazy for Vincent*, for example, is also present in "The Earthquake." The playwright and screenwriter Patrice Chéreau eventually shared a screenwriting credit with Guibert; their relationship is allegorized in another one of Guibert's stories. Early in his literary career, Guibert welcomed Roland Barthes's attention, and they maintained an epistolary friendship. While Barthes does not seem to be directly described in any of the stories included in this collection, he did ask Guibert to write the text that would become "Propaganda Death no. 0"; their relationship ran aground as a result of the conditions that Barthes imposed on its publication.

The best-known man emblematized in Guibert's œuvre is, of course, Michel Foucault, who was not a lover but, first and foremost, a neighbor and a colleague. While their friendship is most clearly illustrated in *To the Friend Who Did Not Save My Life*, the man is also revealed, more obliquely, in what is perhaps the most powerful and unforgettable of all Guibert's stories, "A Man's Secrets." It was written quickly and out of intense grief, as he said in an interview published in 1992: "the day after his death, I wrote a text about his burial. It took me two or three years before publishing it, before even having it read. Then I disguised this character, my thoughts of him were of absence, of lack. Were unbearable. His very image became wholly evanescent. I so needed this friendship to live that, when he was dead, I had to forget it."

There are anonymous men as well, most noticeably in the stories of *Singular Adventures*, and the passions they inspired seem to have been no less memorable. Guibert ends his story "The Trip to Brussels" with a retrospective gaze that transcends nostalgia: "The words we spoke made an apocryphal story that was perfect: faded, singed, written in invisible ink, buried and unexhumable. Nothing could reconstruct these words, they were like a treasure lost in the depths: intimidating, undetectable." The image of a story written in invisible ink is a powerful one, doubly so when one realizes that the original French is *encre sympathique*—the adjective connoting not secrecy and subterfuge but kindness and closeness.

IV

When I began this project, all of Guibert's translated novels were out of print—even *To the Friend Who Did Not Save My Life*. At the time, it felt symbolic yet saddening: if gay rights were moving so steadily forward toward equality with the broader population, why preserve this particular, liminal past? Indeed, such an unprecedented nationwide—and even global—sea change in attitudes toward gay marriage and adoption risked effacing the long struggle that came before it, from Oscar Wilde's trials and Alan Turing's cyanide-laced apple to the Stonewall riots and the ACT-UP movement. Guibert's autofictional writings, by weaving the autobiographical facts of his life with the fictions of his imagination, exist simultaneously as works of art and as records of a particular moment in history that otherwise would—indeed, *has*—become forgotten. But as my work in selecting, translating, and polishing these stories wore on, it became clear that this shift was not inevitable, nor even permanent. As the pendulum threatens to swing backwards, reviving the past and its images, and laying it out for a new generation of readers, seems all the more essential; it is a great credit to Hedi El Kholti and Semiotext(e) that this work of publishing and republishing such an essential queer writer is happening now.

Translating Guibert's stories meant digging back into the history of gay slang, and resuscitating particular eras. "Invert" has not been used to refer to gay people for several decades now, but in Guibert's time, it was still an acceptable term. The word *minet* is still in common currency in France today, but its current American equivalent, "twink," was not widely used in the seventies, so I have had to dredge up the older, blander term "pretty boy." Other examples are strewn throughout this volume.

There are plays on words as well, most memorably in *Propaganda Death*. As Guibert furthered his writing career, however, his prose shifted toward a more classical mode. One particular exception stands out: in "Mauve the Virgin," Mauve himself is watching a boy crack his bones almost seductively, and thinks to himself in French: "quelle os-tentation!" *Ostentation*, in French and in English, implies showing off; *os*, however, means bone, and *tentation* means temptation. The solution I eventually arrived at was a small miracle: "it's almost as if he wants me to jump his bones!"

Any translator of Guibert also has to be wary of the stray word that, with its lexical or semantic shift, seems to knock a whole sentence off-kilter; the challenge, in English, has been to find words that do the same work without seeming like translationese. Guibert's choices are generally deliberate: he worked for many years as a journalist, so it is reasonable to assume that his resistance to telegraphic prose should be reflected in English—even when it forces a reader to do the hard work of following his train of thought. As such, I've often aimed to preserve the continuity of Guibert's sentences, and refrained from rearranging clauses unless comprehension was hindered in English.

In looking at Guibert's manuscripts at the IMEC, I was struck by how clean Guibert's handwritten pages were. He rarely crossed out or revised his sentences; they flowed almost fully formed from his mind. To see his pen speed up is to see when the words were coming almost automatically; to see his pen-strokes formed slowly and carefully is to see when he was deliberating about what thought should come next. The day I spent looking at these manuscripts, after completing drafts of all the stories contained in the volume, feels like the closest connection I have had with this long-gone writer; it was well worth the trip across the Atlantic, and the crack-of-dawn train out of Paris to the abbey in Caen where Guibert's papers are stored.

In "Posthumous Novel," my favorite of all Guibert's stories, the narrator describes a meadow that has become irradiated and allows passersby to uncover letters and words and sentences thought by the people who had passed by.

I ask the reader to imagine me, for a few seconds, during my various wanderings, like a visionary, or like a preposterous butterfly hunter, busy following these grim railroad tracks, and, every few meters, setting off these sodic explosions so as to detect, in the nighttime landscape in fusion, the strongest concentrations of thoughts, disentangling them, photographing them, then magnifying them, and recognizing his turns of phrase (the thoughts preceding his death already had a literary shape, they were all oriented toward this dream of a novel) and then setting them in the silence of the library where I worked and where I returned every night, because it was the only place large enough to welcome all the loot I poured out, and which came back together into long strips of sentences repeatedly interrupted, stuck together, and then undone.

To collect and translate Guibert's short stories is to perform this same sort of gathering, to search in the night of a foreign language for the words that can be brought back and disentangled and rendered into English as sentences that are "repeatedly interrupted, stuck together, and then undone." To be this wanderer or visionary or preposterous butterfly hunter is the strange and beautiful task of any translator. And this act of exhuming Guibert's words exhumes not only Guibert himself, but a historical moment, an œuvre, a life we otherwise would not have in English.

— Jeffrey Zuckerman, New York City, January 2020

A Note on the Chronology

The question of which texts in Guibert's œuvre should be considered short stories is a vexed one: many of his books are classified as *récits*, a French category of novels that highlights their brevity and the attention they draw to the circumstances of their creation. But there are distinctions between the books with many chapters but a continuous narrative, most notably *To the Friend Who Did Not Save My Life*, and the books where the chapters or sections were relatively discontinuous and self-contained. This latter category fits more naturally in the Anglophone world's conception of a short-story collection, and so *Written in Invisible Ink* is chiefly drawn from a corpus of five books of discrete short texts composed between 1975 and 1988: *Propaganda Death*, *Vice*, *The Sting of Love*, *Singular Adventures*, and *Mauve the Virgin*.

The first of these books, *Propaganda Death*, was written between 1975 and 1976, and published in January of 1977. It is included here in its entirety not for the quality of its prose—it bears many of the imperfections and excesses of any author's juvenilia— but because it shows how Guibert's obsessions with the body, illness, sexuality, discontinuity, confession, and other men were all present from the outset. It is, unquestionably, a very difficult and deeply unpleasant text to read. In one of Guibert's notebooks, stored at the Institut mémoires de l'édition contemporaine (IMEC), he writes: "Why is this text terrifying? What makes it so off-putting ('I can't read it,' 'it makes me puke,' 'it makes my balls pull right up into me'), most of all to myself?" and then answers his question: "First, it's a prose that does violence to the body. Then it's a prose that subjects fantasy to horrific treatments, that literally dissects it, tears away its flesh of fancy, skins its bark of haziness and vagueness to leave it bare, raw, skinned by our sight. It's no longer draped in dreams, my gaze is unsparing, and I detail it from its bones down to the smallest fibers, I sum it up completely, almost clinically. Fantasy: the body of still-warm desire that prose dissects and chills?"

Upon its publication, Guibert sent copies to three men whose influence upon his career would become indisputable: the painter Francis Bacon, who had an exhibition opening in Paris the same day the book was published; the philosopher Michel Foucault, who was already Guibert's next-door neighbor and would eventually become a central figure in the younger writer's life; and Roland Barthes, who quickly grew besotted with the ephebe. The latter man exchanged letters with Hervé and urged him to write a follow-up text (begun in 1976 and completed in 1977) that Barthes would have published with a preface of his own. But, according to Guibert in a 1991 interview with Didier Eribon, "he would only do so on the condition that I sleep with him. And that wasn't possible for me. Back then, I couldn't have a relationship with a man of that age." This refusal angered Barthes and drove him to write "Fragments pour H." even as the follow-up text in question, "Propaganda Death no. 0" was shelved. It would remain unpublished until 1991, when Guibert, having completed *To the Friend Who Did Not Save My Life* and preparing to move, came across the stories he had penned early in his career and decided to have them finally published in a collection of juvenilia and early writings. These circumstances around the text's creation make it, despite its relative obscurity, an essential addition to this collection.

Vice was written after these texts: Guibert's papers stored at the IMEC include a journal from 1979–1980 containing much of the first section's text. Interestingly, other papers at the IMEC show early drafts of *Vice* as having included the title story of *The Sting of Love* as an incipit, followed by the "Inventory" and "Route" that are present in the final published version of the book. The first of those two sections is included here in its entirety, while a selection has been made from the second. The original French edition, notably, contains nineteen photos by Guibert in between the two sections. In a 1984 interview, Guibert provides a reason for the book's seemingly sterile and flat affect as he mentions "*Vice*, which was an inventory of places and things, mixed together, meant for vicious acts, without those acts being described. But [it hasn't yet] been published." If *Propaganda Death* was meant to flay imagination from reality, then *Vice* could be understood as presenting this reality with no hint of imagination—thereby leaving readers to invent the eponymous vice themselves.

The Sting of Love brought together, posthumously, twenty-three short stories and three critical texts mainly written between 1979 and 1984. Many had never been published; those that had run in magazines had never been collected in any other volume. As such, they are not unified by any particular theme, but they do serve to round out readers' sense of Guibert's literary trajectory.

If I could tell readers to start somewhere in this volume, I would probably urge them to turn to *Singular Adventures*, which sits ambiguously between genres. Guibert himself was fully aware of the fact, writing of the book: "This could, ultimately, be a novel since there is only one character throughout who meets others within. Wanderings, outbursts, travels, passions. But there are also gaps, jumps in time between the stories, and these are rather episodes in a life plucked from the long thread of a personal diary. All that stood apart from a three-year stretch of ordinary life, and that knocked it off-kilter, threatened it . . ." This equivocation, as well as the fact that several of these stories originally appeared in the *Minuit* review, made it easier to categorize these as stories that were written up through, and published in, 1982.

Mauve the Virgin, published in 1988, is the final book to be excerpted here, and it is by far the most polished one. Its back cover, too, draws attention to the continuity of its protagonists: "Might the curious characters of these stories not each be Hervé Guibert, having changed their identities the better to disguise him as a virgin man, a feverish lover, an earthquake victim, or a disciple of the great philosopher who he accompanies to the grave?" And the stories included within are among Guibert's best; it was nearly impossible to choose which to include.

These volumes have been arranged by order of composition, not order of publication. While *Propaganda Death*, *Singular Adventures*, and *Mauve the Virgin* were all published shortly after completion, *Vice* was only published until 1991, after Guibert's rise to literary fame—he mentions in his 1984 interview that his earlier publisher had originally refused it—and *The Sting of Love* came to French readers in 1994, in accordance with Hervé's literary testament. In the former case, Guibert had had his very first publisher, Régine Deforges, publish his earliest, mostly unpublished writings up, and through 1978 in a volume titled *La Mort propagande et autres textes de jeunesse* [Propaganda Death and Other Juvenilia] with the years of composition for each text noted in the table of contents. In the latter case, his uncollected writings from 1979 through 1984 were collated in a file for later publication as *The Sting of Love*, and the year of composition was included at the end of each text. That information is also included in this present collection so that readers can see where these texts fit within the arc of Guibert's career.

By all evidence, and the attestation of Christine Guibert, Hervé did not write any further stories after 1988. The leading scholar on Guibert's work, Jean-Pierre Boulé, notes that his time working on his short stories coincides with his time working in journalism; in the final three years of his life, his literary output was focused on longer, more cohesive books as well as his photography and the film *Modesty or Immodesty*. This present selection, then, serves as a portrait of the artist as a young man, still honing his tools and learning how to use them to greatest effect—to cite the copy for *The Sting of Love*, "a prose not yet marked by illness." The result, in his final stories, is rather breathtaking, and doubly so as one realizes that all the seeds had been present from the very beginning.

Propaganda Death

My body, due to the effects of lust or pain, has entered a state of theatricality, of climax, that I would like to reproduce in any manner possible: by photo, by video, by audio recording.

As soon as a distortion arises, as soon as my body goes into hysterics, start the transcription mechanisms: eructations, defecations, ejaculate from jerking off, diarrhea, phlegm, oral and anal catarrhs of the mouth and ass. Try my best to photograph them, to record them. Let this contorted, flickering, screaming body speak. Position a microphone inside my mouth, filled as with a cock, as far down my throat as possible, in case I have an episode: contractions, brutal ejaculations or defecations of shit, groans. Position another microphone inside my ass, for it to be drowned in my tides, or dangled over the toilet bowl. Alternate the two noises, mixing them: stomach groans, throat moans. Record my vomiting, rooted in the opposite extreme of orgasm.

My body is a laboratory that I offer up as a performance, the sole actor, the sole instrument of my bodily frenzies. Musical scores from the tissues of flesh, madness, pain. Observing how it functions, recording its performances.

My different methods of jerking off are expounded. The action takes place in a disarray befitting this pleasure, or this revulsion (it's an anarchic text).

The way in which I extract a blackhead from my skin, some sperm from my balls. This flood that slowly builds up and pushes through my body, from the prostate through the seminal vesicles, and then discharges, gumming up, in the cockile trachea.

Every one of my bodily expressions. Everything I can squeeze out and everything that can spurt out, squirt out. Everything that nimwits me.

Every transformation: surgery, tattooing.

Film my ass in operation, being invaded, forced open by shit or a cock or my fingers or any object, along with the operations of my cock.

At the end of this sequence of expressions, the final distortion, the final falsification, death. We gag it, we silence it, we try to drown it in disinfectant, to suffocate it in ice. But I want to let its powerful voice ring out and sing, a prima donna, through my body. This will be my only collaborator, I will be its performer. Don't lose this source of immediate, visceral spectacle. Kill myself on a stage, in front of cameras. Put on this extreme, immoderate show of my body, in my death. Decide its terms, its process, all its props.

Have my decomposing body filmed, day after day, exploded within the fire, strewn, nailed, exhibited, miming the hundred-fragment torture in a game of Chinese masks. Dissect my member and my ass under the camera's lens. Make the fibers fly, the nerves dance, spray. This performance, more beautiful than a horror movie, more tragic than a virgin saint's sacrifice in a tiger's jaws, will excite. No visual effects, no pomposity. An actual body, my actual blood. Take and eat; drink from it (my paranoia, my megalomania). I'll empty it furiously, tipsily (before that, the heroine's hot blood will pulse in my veins), butcher it, and make it burst like a sack.

The audience will be overcome with convulsions, contractions, revulsions, erections, vibrations, ecstasies, pukings of all sorts. And its general body, in turn, will start to speak. This wide-open eye sunken in its socket, this vitreous, white cleft will make it black out as well. Guts and brains will splatter, their ecstatic fetidity stippling a mist. Hollywood and Babylon could be reduced to the space of an attic bedroom, with a single attendee. Who would actually want to produce my suicide, this bestseller? Film the injection that gives the slowest death, the poison that penetrates with a kiss, flowing from one mouth to the other (my name is Fatality)?

MONOLOGUE I

Cosmetic Butchery

Stand in a dissection room and slice up an ass. Autopsy this part of my body that penetration by a cock, the fingernail of a callused finger writing and masturbating, rapturously gouging my intestinal walls, or the roughness of a hardening tongue, makes me get hard, orgasm, spurt cum. Separating the two white cheeks, slicing through the muscles with a scalpel, pinning the shredded fibers down to the table's cork in order to get to the hole. Laid flat on my back, covered by a sheet all the way to the head, legs folded over the stomach, the two hands dexterously maneuvering spatulas, curved tweezers or diagonal pliers, round scissors. Unfolding, once the hole has been reached, the pink folds resembling the slats of a fan from czarist Russia, voluptuous ostrich feathers caressing the rosette. Start with enlarging the hole by inserting a finger, then the whole hand coated in Vaseline. No fear in making use of a bone, the tibia, as a dildo. Armed with an ophthalmologist's glasses, a game of microscopic mirrors, science in service of eroticism, strobe the distended tissues. The head, the groin sniffing between the two legs. Small beam of electric light replicated through the glasses' mathematics and infiltrating the ass. Put the tongue there, introspect the miniscule abyss as its rosaceous walls tremble at the scalpel's touch. With a small pair of scissors, cut through the inside, the edges, these divine pipelines of shit. Loosen the tight folds clockwise, turn them into ribbons, long scarves of pink galantine. My rosette becomes a fashion prototype:

I have a lyrical ass. Inside are complex labyrinths, pouches to puncture, membranes, tunnels, anal glottises. Feel it fully gutted, pierced by the efficacious iron. Make it disgorge, leak, spit. Hear it shit semen through every drain, convulse. Bear no resemblance to a white mouse, be elegant all the way down to the cork slab.

MONOLOGUE II

Photographs

Massive belly on display. Prominent shoulders. Sunken chest. Asymmetrical curves. My lordotic position as a man being fucked. My face is ravishing, luminous, sharp, fair-complexioned. An unfashionable assemblage. "You look like the kind of sixteen-year-old girl with wooers." "Do I have to woo you?" "Are you bored?" I'm fond of hats, veils, clothes-hunting nostalgically, romantic fetishism. Showing up dressed in black leather pants one evening, I slowly strip, shouting "olé!" as I undo the zipper of my gleaming, shiny pants to reveal fishnet stockings, garters, tassels, and a plastic rose where my genitals should be. Ankle boots with stiletto heels offering the delight of mixing zebra hide, pleather, ocelot faux fur, and manufactured ostrich skin. I'll photograph my cock from every angle, soft and tepid, hard and hot, full-on, from the side, sheathed in every manner: hands, wool, leather, oil, mouth, soap, an elephant's foot of a split, vulvaed sponge, rag, piss, shit, and then your ass, this hole that drives me crazy.

MONOLOGUE III

Internal Mongolia

This period when I started to photograph my excretions. Diarrhea, defecation, violent splatters of shit on the toilet's white porcelain, tiny bursts and squirts, to reproduce them. To enumerate them: defecation #1, #2, to tally them up. As the toilet isn't flushed, they've increased, accumulated. Suits, not of white lace. Teeming superimpositions, synthetic proliferations. This results in magical occurrences: perversely staring at liquids changing colors with successive evacuations, multiplying (plants), making strange arabesques. I stayed there for hours, kneeling as at an altar, with all the more interest since these wonders are wholly mine. I adored them like holy relics intoxicating me, sacramental wines infused with decay. What an aroma! They were secreted away in the shitter like one of Bluebeard's rooms, a narrow cabinet holding white, feminine flesh engirdled at their thinnest spots, wrists, the bodies' geometries arranged with a painterly eye, necks, wretched tones spurting over their excavated eyes. I kept the keys. It stank. Secret laboratory with frozen, white walls that I tainted, my eyes half-shut, arrested by the pleasure of liquid, burning shit ruining my anus before bathing our bellies. I came in all dressed up, brought out my undone, contorted, raving body. I set off these violent evacuations, swallowing various fats, prunes, pig testicles. Soft, decaying matter, rot on these vertiginous walls I had driven stakes into at night in order not to fall. My eyes blindfolded, my fear of vertigo and the bright red meat that, with its tubes and curves, provided the substance of my intestines. The other defecations deserved no altar, going straight down the trash chute, I sat on the dark lip, dilating my hole so that it would swallow it up, I spat my solidified, stinking snot into it. The wind swallowed it up, and it fell into the nothingness, straight, making a thunk, never veering even slightly. I photographed my snot in the sink, extracting them from their nooks with my tongue, the greenest ones, the darkest ones, the shiniest ones. Sections, vivisected mollusks, invertebrates. To those I added some piss splattering over them, soaking them, making them float in a translucent mess through which I could see the bottom of the sink, inexplicably bluish, the only possible receptacle for these still-living offerings. Flagella enveloping the jelly. Plasma. An eye. My hand. Or simply, a bone. The runaway snot's delightful, untrammeled vertigo, nasal sphincters released just like assholes, swallowed up by the toilet's black, yawning hole occasionally bisected by the rails' blue gleam. My foot on the pedal to let the wind caress the slit. Like the drool that has slipped in my sleep from who knows what dream to end up on the pillow and to wake me up with its chill on my cheeks, a revealing remnant. The other ejecta were quick to darken and harden. After six hours, the water dirtied by the shit reddened. Then blackened, subtle inks that, by transforming, become poison. To plunge my head in, intoxicate myself, my face in the cesspool of my marinade. The first thing my parents remember me doing was swallowing my own shit, my mother, in my stroller. And my mother seeing me like that, filthy, full, belching, happy.

Scraping my jellies off the test-tube glass. Observing, after twelve hours, these floating splatters. My ass's catarrhs. Everything covered with a thin, greasy film, everything visibly darkened, become opium-poppy, turned dark red. Various substances are visible: greasy matter, ketchup, scales, appearances, commingled on every surface. Afloat, aloft. Some clots, lighter clumps. Magnificent journey.

Circular movements, circuitous waltzes, rising tides. The second day: on the surface a yellowing crust that sometimes splits open with tadpoles (birth).

Self-Portrait in Shards

Raw the red meat back when it was on display in the butcher's stall. Sawdust on the tiling, sawdust to send flying with my shoes, to nudge into heaps. What is sawdust made of, anyway? It looks like what we feed rabbits, like bran. I thought: can you eat that? I would have tried to. I shifted it around while my mother talked to the butcher about stupid stuff, blathering about how she hadn't had a good fuck in ages because my father was no good in the sack and how the butcher was a total stud with huge muscles under his white smock that got her lace underwear so wet she had to wash it every night in the green plastic washbasin along with my father's boxers, which were just as droopy as his package. The liquid was about to drip down her stockings, making its way past her starched tulle slip, soiling them, soaking them, she must have felt it, she was ashamed, she clenched her legs together, not wanting me to see it, the sawdust at her feet soaking it up, as she wore a schoolteacher's gray slip. Was the sawdust for keeping the rats away? So they couldn't gnaw at the butcher's trimmings, reproduce too close to the contaminated meat. My mother grabbed my hand, trying to keep me from touching the sawdust. She flattened the heaps, crushing my plans under her soles, but it wasn't easy work due to her high heels, which could only move a bit of sawdust at a time. I snuck off to make more heaps, sawdust getting into my shoes, into my socks, it was cold, itchy, it got in between my toes, at nights, when I was on my bed and my father pulled off my socks while undressing me. He rubbed them away, stuck his stiff tongue between each toe. Then he hiked up one leg of his pants and made me look at and touch the scar on his leg, telling me about the first itch, then the operation he'd had as a child, after it had swollen, his fear of the doctor, the porcelain bowl, the gas he had to breathe until he was unconscious, his memories while he was knocked out, of shifting hallways full of blood. He came back from the bathroom with cotton in plastic bag, (light) cologne in tiny bottle, funneled from the bigger bottle to save. He scrubbed me gently to make me happy, he was the only one allowed to, I wasn't, soaked cotton wet on my toes, my skin, then stinging slightly. The butcher shops, with their sawdust scattered across the floors that had to be cold underfoot, like bathrooms except I had shoes on, I pushed sawdust where there wasn't any, I spread it around, I wanted to get all the sawdust out of the butchers'. No more sawdust now, no more raw meat hanging from hooks, no more flies buzzing nearby, indicating their presence and the rotting, blue meat incubating, furry under the microscope, within the clean-cut, red meat just put on display. It's dirty, my mother said, don't touch it. No more sawdust nowadays, only disinfected, sterilized tiles, maybe it had just been there to make sure we didn't slip on blood, didn't skid on these viscous humors, no more flypaper, only frozen meat hiding its horrors. It's not the same anymore. We can practically taste detergent and liquid bleach in the veal liver when we eat it. I had a friend at school, he asked me: what kind of meat do you like best? And I said, I don't know. And he said, I like veal liver best, because it's the most expensive meat. Then I said, yes, that it is. At school, over the months, we played different games in the playground at different times, as if there was a calendar of them that had been set, by who? there was no way out. There was the month of playing marbles, the month of toy soldiers, the month of making lanyards, the month of cootie catchers, the month of yo-yos. There were the urinals with water running down the gray slabs, they were humid, they stank like pee, we drank that, we stuck our heads in to see who could drink the most. There were also the shitters, the big ones, we were scared of going in there, they were dark, and besides I never really needed to use them, except when I was going to poop my pants. My mother told me, very clearly, don't poop at school, it's dirtier than here, don't pull down your pants for any reason, it's better if you poop here at home. She made me go every morning at the same time, around seven thirty, so I would be clean and not have to use the bathrooms at school. She forced me to, there was no way out.

She told me, don't touch your behind, don't put your fingers there, it's not clean, you'll put your hands in your mouth after that. I still wasn't able to pull back the foreskin from my dick when it started oozing pus, and my father washed it every night by inserting a pink rubber bulb that he filled with boiling water with some disinfectant mixed in. In the shower, behind the plastic curtain, I had to be careful not to get hard so that my mother, who was washing me, didn't see it. One time I saw my mother's huge tuft of curly black hair, I thought that was disgusting, I didn't have any, and I thought only women had that.

The water got under my foreskin and ran into the plastic sink which my father also used for his dirty, greasy pee. Then I pulled on my skin so hard it gave way and showed the bare, raw head of my willy.

I steal some of the balls of yarn my mother uses for knitting and at night I can't wait to pull down my pajama bottoms and push my dick into the mass, I rub it with the yarn, it's warm, I fall asleep with it, and I make sure to hide it before she wakes me up.

My mother doesn't like being wasteful, so she tells us not to take the soap into the shower, instead we rub our dry hands on the soap first and then we get under the water. And to make sure we don't use too much water, there's a single bath for the whole family, on Sundays, and I always go last and I have to submerge my body into the iron basin where the soapy water that had already been used to clean my father then my mother then my sister is stagnating. And it's disgusting to sink into this blackish water that has already cleaned these bodies I hate. My mother says: if you keep getting in fights, ruining your shoes like that, you'll have to go to school in your sister's high heels. She's serious, my feet are bouncing around in these polished shoes that are too big and when I'm at the playground, wearing shorts and holding my mother's hand, I'm ashamed.

Pillage

The building is black brick, the elevator goes up but not down, its door clangs shut immediately, there's a basement, each floor is a hallway with doors in long rows stretching to infinity, each one next to the last, all of them shut, gleaming black, no noise, the corridors are poorly lit, often completely dark because a bulb has burned out, there are definitely old people in this building.

I'm back after a week away, as I walk in the cleaning lady grabs me, she says, didn't you hear, your upstairs neighbor's husband died last night, he's still there, she's watching over him, I say something vague back.

I go up, I put my suitcase on a chair, the elevator had been making hellish noise before, the light bulb overhead is rattling, every time I'm convinced the elevator car is going to drop down the shaft, I can't ignore the shaking.

I'd forgotten to leave the window open, the room smells musty, it's night now, there's a corpse upstairs, the dust swirls when I move around, the old papers, the pantry all smell musty, I turn on the radio, it crackles, a woman sings, it's unintelligible, I don't listen, I turn it off, I go into the kitchen, I turn on the lights, it's blinding, I see a cockroach in the sink crawling out of a pot I didn't wash, I don't try to kill it, I look at myself, the mirror is hanging over the sink from a hole in the wall, I notice I'm expressionless, my skin is rather red, the travel, the heat, the waiting, there's no noise, the air is impossible to breathe, I'm suffocating, I go to open the window, outside it's even steamier and muggier, the air is fetid, I shut it, feeling afraid something might come in.

I go back into the kitchen, I run the water to make some noise, I see the yogurt jars gone moldy since I left, I hadn't washed them, I hadn't wanted to take them down to the basement, it's against the rules to throw glass down the trash chute, I tilt my head and my nose a bit closer, the rancid milk doesn't stink anymore, I can't smell it anymore, the water's still running right next to my lowered head, I feel my skin on fire, the water isn't running cold, only warm, I turn off the faucet, there's a stool, I sit down, I pull off my shoes, my socks, I scratch my feet, then my head, I'm fine, I'm not taking a shower, I stay seated a minute, I go to open a cabinet, I'll have some whiskey, there isn't any more, I take out my keys, I put on my shoes again quickly, I go out, I don't leave the light on, I hear the noise of my shoes on the tiles, I walk quietly, it's already late, I'm in the alcove just off the corridor, I've turned on the light, the bulb on this floor still works, it's the one on the fourth floor that's burnt out, none of the doors are open, a noise makes me jump, I'd slowed a bit, I go down the stairs.

The night chill hits me like a bastard, I can't avoid it, I inhale it, I walk, I look around, I go down different streets, to the right, then to the left, I don't see anybody, I don't want to stay at home alone, Bertrand lets me in, he's by himself, he's not asleep yet, he barely says anything, he's wearing shoes with pink tassels, a bit odd, we have a drink, we listen to the radio, it seems like something dead, passé, broadcast from far off, bringing us news from the past, the whiskey skins my innards, I haven't eaten, it mixes with some bile, twists in my stomach, almost makes me belch, I tell him we're going out, I'm out on the street again, I have to think about every movement, we talk loudly, there's Bertrand singing but I can barely hear him, the chill stings my eyes, we had too much to drink, we end up in front of my place, I tell him about the old woman upstairs, her husband is dead, that was last night, I wasn't there, I forgot to ask how he died, it's weird that she didn't tell me herself, she usually does.

The old woman hates me, I always get home late, I probably make so much noise, she can hear everything, she stands guard all night, she says she doesn't sleep, she tries to guess who's come with me whenever she hears me talking, one morning she came and yelled at me because I'd held the elevator the night before to go back down, she said she hadn't been able to go down, but she never goes out, she tried to peek past my door to what my place was like, she said she was going to press charges, she said, your fucking is fucking me over.

I tell Bertrand all that even though he's not listening to me, we go into my apartment, then I get the feeling that the old woman upstairs is sleeping, or she's watching over her husband, I slam the door shut, Bertrand and I talk loudly, she's moving, we heard her, we wait and listen, we hold our breath for a minute, there's a corpse right above us, we lie on the floor, we look at the ceiling, he's lying just like us, maybe on the floor just like us, that would surprise me, the ceiling could collapse and somebody would come crashing down on our heads.

The wife must have woken up because she's walking, she had to be asleep, no better escape than sleep, no better way to forget, she's gone right back to her husband's body and begun sobbing, she had to have forgotten it all. We were yelling and laughing while her sobbing started up again, she must have forced herself not to yell as well.

We were up the whole night, we didn't sleep, and she didn't either, dawn came, as crappy as always, breaking through the shutters, we felt like vomiting, but even shoving our hands down our throats only brought up a bit of bitter bile, our bitter saliva, the whiskey's effects had worn off, we shivered, half on the floor, I pulled him close and I tried to fuck him but I couldn't get hard.

An alarm clock goes off, someone gets up and leaves for work. I open my mouth, something slips in, it's liquid, it's Bertrand crying, we hug each other hard, we clutch each other, we're suffocating. I push my knee into his thighs, I tense up, I push him uselessly, blindly, he won't move. I squeeze him. His face is buried, covered in clumps of his hair. He's chewing on them. In the middle is his tongue, stretched out. I take it between my fingers, like catching a fish, it's hard, it's dry, I can feel the individual taste buds sticking straight up, like coarse velvet. I try to cuddle him in vain, I'm cold. My teeth start chattering uncontrollably, without warning, they bite into his tongue, he doesn't say anything, I can feel by the way his tongue's contracting that it hurts, a grimace has contorted his face against me, something's irradiating the insides of our mouths, rinsing them. I pull a bit of cold meat from his mouth, unswallowed from dinnertime last night, and I start chewing on it, it's already half-chewed and I feel myself swallowing it.

Two hours later we're standing at opposite ends of the room, looking at each other, the shutters are still closed, we hear people coming and going in the hallway but it's muted.

I don't make coffee, I don't have any. Bertrand asks for some, I can't give him any. There's a sudden, violent itch on my feet and I start scratching hard, almost scraping off my skin, blood drips out, it makes me feel good to see something come out. Then my hands, I claw my hands raw red, the veins nearly burst through the skin, they could burst if I wanted them to.

We barely talk. Bertrand said I'm going. I went with him, I came out. It had to be noon, the cleaning lady didn't say the woman upstairs had died, as I'd momentarily thought.

It was beautiful outside, he told me all he could think about was when spring would finally come.

The Glance

He comes hard in the toilets, it's his shit pushing his anus wide open pulling his sneer right off his face. The toilets are orange. He shits. He doesn't scream but his ravaged sphincter rattles his intestines. He throws his head back. A determined voyeur has invented a strategy. Not only does the door have a discreet hole at vulva level when it's open, but the window hidden under a layer of paint and facing an inner courtyard has cracks in several places. The shattered glass, right behind the seated figure, allows him to be observed in full, to be seen through the window as he shits. First he has to open a window facing a corridor, climb through, and crouch on the ledge to reach this window. Then he can look his fill. He presses his eye up close. His eyelashes are pushed into the crack. A mirror facing the seat reflects his face orgasming as his shit dilates his anus, and the eye in his back, dilated exactly like the ass to behold and be filled. He watches himself cumming, his eyes jerk around, meet the eye through the crack watching him, and immediately panics. Panics as well and gets up, shit in his ass, the dangling cock with its foreskin pulled back, out of proportion to his dwarf's body. The eye disappears. He jerks off again. The eye comes back, has shifted its position. He hears a window clicking shut, being carefully shut to muffle the noise. Now the hole in the door is where the eye's starting to dilate due to the bodily changes. He presses up, prostrate against the divider. Excited by the eye's determination to amass pornographic material. Pants pulled down, briefs stretched around his thighs. Watching. He'll come again, the first orgasm having been paused, by impaling his ass with two fingers. He cums, spurts everywhere, uncontrollable slime. Is the eye looking around? Who's watching? A trail of perfume arises and spreads through the hallway, lingering like a solvent. He hears a noise like leather squeaking while kneeling. The eye inhales. He aims his cock at this sucking *maelström*. It jumps, heats up in his hand, ready to tighten his ass with every tremor. It spurts. The eye gets hit, goes blind. The semen covers its iris and drowns it. Hanging off the ledge again, he loses his footing and falls. His shoes skid on the stone. He sees the eye falling. He pulls his pants back up and opens the door after making sure that getting out is feasible. The voyeur has disappeared, letting the window rattle with every tremor. It's raining outside and the wind rushes into the stairwell. He goes out, inhales the fans' warm air into his mouth. He goes up to a mirror and goes through the motions of washing his hands, checks how bad his acne is. Footsteps marked on the wooden floor show him which way to go. He's obedient. Is this a train station, a café, or a movie theater bathroom? He walks into the crowd without bumping into anyone, his head hung low. Several shoes match the footprints seen earlier, stand on top of them, cancel them out. Women's shoes, shiny polished black. The path to follow seems circular. He notices that the footprints aren't going anywhere, they always come back to where they started. It's starting to smell like urine again, it's acrid, it caresses his nostrils. The body's upper half, above the legs, twisted from the waist up, must have seen the lowered head. A black leather skirt, quite short, and a green mink jacket. Heavily bleached blonde hair. The gleaming leather, possibly pleather, had squeaked while kneeling. It's a woman. "And the Holy Virgin descended upon me like the softest velvet you ever touched. I got something on my gums, at least I didn't get it up the ass." Listening to the drunkard rambling, he lost sight of the woman, who had fled in a reptilian glance.

A Lover's Brief Journal

14 May '7... Tuileries, around 10 PM. Name: Hervé X., 6 ft, 21 y/o, bookseller. We went to my place.

A big, well-built fellow, nothing off about him. Small cock. Sucks me with an intensity and determination I've never seen before. Hot mouth, swallowed me completely. Makes me cum twice in a row in his mouth, swallows it all. Jerks himself off, the second time he asks me to jerk him off. We don't cum at the same time. Doesn't scream and doesn't say a word when he does cum. Nothing special, except it takes him a really long time to get hard, even though he keeps saying he wants to fuck me. Rims me before. Stuck his tongue way up my ass, I've never had anyone go in so deep. He's licking all around and it's hot and wet. It feels like a dog snuffling my hole. The first time, half-hard, he flipped me on my stomach and tried to push into me. His cock didn't get in as far as his tongue, which says it all. The second time he tried to take me, my legs crossed over his shoulders, I tried to sit on his cock while he was sucking me off. He couldn't make it work, not so much because my ass was too tight as because he wasn't hard enough. He pulled out and whispered: "I can't do it." He was embarrassed. Whereas I kept getting hard so he lay on his stomach and I went for it. My dick was still covered in saliva (since he'd already sucked me off) and so was his ass, my fingers carrying it from my mouth to his ass. It lasted for ten minutes, at moments I went soft in his ass, my dick being too tense. I didn't come then. He asked me to pull out of his ass, saying

"Hurry up and cum, it hurts." And then I told him, I was starting to go soft: "No, I'm not going to cum like that." I went to the entrance to pee in my sink, then wash my dick, so he could suck me off after. I thought, he definitely could suck me as I was, but what good is that, swallowing a dick that's just been up his ass? He agreed to suck me, but not to let me suck him, he said: "I want you to stroke me," he prefers masturbating. He finished jerking himself off right when I was cumming. He left really early in the morning, he set the alarm for seven thirty, since he had to go to work.

(My mouth is wide open to make all your cocks cum, my cock is rock hard to make all your asses happy, my ass is stretched so that you can stick in your dicks. Come in! Let's have a ten-way! Let's have each of our mouths swallowing two, three cocks at once! Let's spread our asses for inhuman cocks, animal cocks! Let's swallow them and crush them with our holes! Let's get soaked in everybody's cum! Let the pleasure drain out, let's cum until our balls break! And then let those last spurts flow over the city, over the heads of decent people, like a downpour of ink! Let's fertilize everything! Let's dance our legs off! Let's wreck our asses, tear them bloody, make them burst open! Let's suck each other up! Let's intertwine our tongues until we swallow them and shit them out so we don't keep anything for ourselves! Let's deck the city's walls with our dismembered cocks! Make the rain bloody! And let's discover, let's triumphantly show off our syphilis, our gonorrhea, our abscesses, our birthmarks! Let our pus flow over the entire city, over their filthy mouths! Let's plague them! Let's birth-mark them! Let's infect them! Let's open abscesses in all this stupid flesh! Let's infect all these too-healthy dicks! Let's look upon this city darkening under our commingled pus! Let's love ourselves and hate them! Let's orgasm as we pull our heads from our bodies!)

Can you feel me? Can you feel that? Happy?
That's nice!
That's nice, that's top-notch, that's majestic!
Spectacular!
Mommy!

Ramming my throat with their cocks, two of them in my mouth, almost tearing it, slashing my throat with razors and cumming there, their filthy cocks with the foreskin half pushed back in the slit, fucking me through their cum all mixed together, ramming my face twenty times in a row, not bothering about my pleasure, spitting phlegm into my mouth, rubbing their cruddy eyes over my face, farting in my mouth, knocking me unconscious, stealing my clothes, selling me off after leaving their fecal odor of camel mud all over my body.

As soon as my glans is in, a guy whispers the word cop, and I have to pull my foreskin back over it right away while shoving my cock back into my pants, it's all messed up, I follow the man who tried to fuck me, we step out of the gardens for a moment, the cars are going past, he doesn't realize I'm following him, three men are there, Arabs, the man I was following has walked past them, they're talking to me, I don't realize that I'm still walking, they ask me if I've got a five-hundred–francs, I say no, one of them grabs my sleeve and pulls me, the others have followed him, he's short, he says we can check, then I understand, I'm going to give them my cash, six thousand francs in my coat pocket, and a few coins too, six or seven hundred francs, I'd rather only give them the coins, my hands are covered in blood, they ask me if I've got anything else, they pound my face, everyone does their part, the first one punches me in the face, another kicks me in the balls, right after that a third guy takes a running start to headbutt me, I fall down, I get back up, I shout for help without thinking about it, they run off, I run in the other direction, I turn around, I see one of them hurrying to pick up the coins that fell out of my pocket, hungry, greedy.

I make my way back to the man I was following, a policeman whistles, the man asks me if it's because I yelled, we run off, those idiots, he says he should have been the one to take the beating, I look at my bloody hands, I pull a tissue out of my pocket, I feel the six thousand francs, I put it in my mouth, it feels like there's something weird on my lip, the upper one, the tissue turns pink, the blood dries quickly on my hands, it practically disappears, I touch my lip, it's dangling, I ask him where I'm bleeding, if it's my lip, he says yes, when we get back to my place I wash my mouth, the first thing I do is look at myself, I had no idea I was covered in blood all the way up to my eyes, they might have had knives, that would have been just as horrible, no time to look carefully, it's too much, I take a sheet of paper to write something, I got completely undressed, I write and that gets me hard, I jerk myself off with one hand, one of my teeth feels like I could yank it out of my mouth, there's blood on the paper, not romantic blood, filthy, discolored, bubbly water, I can't taste it anymore, except for the gash in the middle of my dangling lip, I have another face now, I go soft, he had appeared in the middle of the bushes, and was now leaning against a tree, I had followed him, a few feet behind, I stop because he's turning around, I don't know if he wants me, but he smiles and waves at me, I take a few more steps, he turns around properly and starts rummaging for my dick in my pants, he shoves his whole hand down my underwear and feels around for my ass, he sticks a finger in, I'd be happier if we sucked each other off, men are coming, he waves them away, I rub his dick through his pants, I kiss him, he sticks out his tongue and I suck it into my mouth, I unbutton my coat, he opens his as well, he doesn't have any underwear on, he pulls down my pants, he has a beautiful cock, long and thick, we jerk each other off, he turns me around, spits on my ass, and tries to push in his cock, hard as a rod, his head splits my hole, I scream, I tell him to get out of my ass, it hurts too much, the cold is making everything contract, a man says here's a cop, we pull up our pants and zip our flies, I've soaked two tissues now, he says do you want me to walk you back, he says they took everything you had, I say yes, I follow him, he has a tiny car, I tell him where I live, he keeps looking in the rearview mirror, at a stop light he leans over to me and licks my wound with his tongue, it's sweet, and it hurts, my mouth is really hot, with one hand he unzips his fly and pulls out his dick, with the other he pulls my head down to his chest, he pushes me under the steering wheel and masturbates his cock with my mouth, he makes the wound open up, it really hurts to swallow when he pushes too hard, he runs his hand through my hair, the light's turned green, he starts and keeps me from pulling my head back up, at every turn the steering wheel rubs my head, I look at my mouth in the mirror, it's like raw meat, there's a huge chunk dangling that might fall off, I take some sleeping pills so I don't stay awake, we get to my place, he gives me a little slap on my thigh, he asks me if I'm okay, he gets out with his cock exposed, hanging between the two sides of his raincoat, gleaming again with my saliva under the streetlamp lights, it's drizzling, my shoes full of mud, every time I go out this is what happens, my mouth won't close properly, I feel like part of my lip has come loose, the man is handsome, I see him under the street-lamp light, he pushes me back behind a door and kisses me, he strips my clothes off, he makes me squat and makes me suck him off, he nearly chokes me to make my throat clench around his cock, his semen dribbles out as he cums deep in my throat, I belch, he crouches down, brings down one of his hands and starts jerking me off, he says suck me good, you slut, feel my package, see how much you like cocks, swallow the whole thing, I'm cumming, keep going, take it all, bitch, you're almost there, his hand moves faster on my cock, it's swollen red, engorged with blood, I'm going to cum, he stops stroking me immediately, I hear footsteps in the hallway, he winks at me, bares his teeth with a cruel smile, and goes to open the door, I have some friends to introduce to you.

(I'd like to smear my gonorrhea over the entire world, infect the planet, contaminate dozens of asses at a go, it'd be fun to coat every seat in the movie theater with my pus, spread it everywhere, drip it all over the bathroom seats, pustules popping up all over the place, Queen Syphilis walks in on platform heels, and if I'm also bleeding from my ass, I'd like to open up abscesses on the skin of strangers, my bed every morning is a field of carnage, a slaughterhouse, I tattoo cocks on my thighs with the nib of my Waterman fountain pen, my blood stained the bed sheets, not just the pillow but the middle of the sheet as well as the foot, anyone would think that my body had flipped over in the night, that my body, while my soft, white dick was leaking pus, folded up on itself, and, if I'm not just bleeding from my mouth, had been magicked within Fu Manchu's suitcase.)

(My family bathtub is where I started exploring my ass. Methodically, studiously, when I was nearly sixteen. I was careful at the beginning, just the first half-inch the first couple of times. Then I kept going deeper, my pointer finger coated in soap, until it disappeared completely, my ass's geology almost supernatural, penetrating the opening, pushing apart the insides, searching inside, descending in a basket down these abysses, ophthalmologist's glasses on my forehead, to uncover my body's prehistories.)

Saturday nights: just like everybody else, I stay home on weeknights and go out on Saturday nights. So I end up next to all the filthy working-class guys at the bars, the filth is what arouses sociable inverts, the bourgeoisie who puke at the smell of velvet. At the place du Palais-Royal, I go up the avenue de l'Opéra all the way to the rue Saint-Anne. I go into the dive bar where everybody pays fifteen francs to get their cocks fondled. I'm holding an Old Fashioned, and I'm swallowed up by a horde of fags all packed together in the darkness, an idiotic teeming horde. Quickly find one guy in this glum place who's sleazy and glassy-eyed enough to get me hard. His drool flows over my tongue, thick and heavy, connected in long strands back to his mouth. I make him suck me off and jerk me off over and over before spraying across his tongue, down his throat, and all over his taste buds. As I pull my pants back up, he spilled all over my leather belt and my jeans. The Marshal's nephew moans "You came all over me!" while trying to wipe the disgusting glaze off his jeans. "Just tell your family it's sauce gribiche." I said "See you soon," and went off. I walked out of the place without a second thought, my balls completely drained, with some shrimp salad in my belly. No irony in saying it was a delicious Saturday night!

I'm still hard, I'm dripping, I've got a huge dick I love shoving into pretty boys. I stick it down their throats, I stick my fingers up their asses, and then I use my dick gleaming with everything they've spit up. They shut their eyes, they cum, their tongues hanging out, choked by pleasure. And then, in the night, they release splendid farts that I inhale happily, pushing out my jizz, spitting it out of their mouths and asses. My dick, having been sucked off, hoovered up, nibbled on, explodes in joy. I lick the head of their dicks. I like rubbing two, three dicks at once over my face, my eyelids, they're magnificent jewels. I wear them. Suck this, swallow everything, I like your mouth, I like it when you gobble up my dick, you have a beautiful dick my boy, it's huge, I like sucking it off, what a beautiful dick you've got, I'm sucking it like crazy, you like that, does it make you horny when I suck you off, kneeling in front of you, like a snuffling dog, getting it all wet so it's dripping with this hot drool that gets you hard in my mouth, teasing your frenum, cum in my mouth, shoot all over me, get it all inside me. I love gulping down your bitter semen, your glorious gravy. I love your muscular ass when it swallows my dick, it's always hungry for a fuck. Your ass feels even hotter than your mouth. You're lying on your back and your legs are wrapped around my neck. I'm on my knees. I take my dick in my hand and press it into your hole. Your ass, I love your ass, my boy, I love fucking you, your ass is amazing, ahh your ass, I love your ass, you like it when I fuck you. Your insides are clamping down around my dick, squeezing it, it's an insane tunnel. I'm fucking you so hard I'll split you in half. I'm going in so deep I can hit your balls.

I cut my head off to suck on your huge dick, it's so red, excited by the spur I've dug into your ass, the fleshly ordure you'll have to shit out. I suck with my eyes shut. I fuck you. I love your ass, your ass is amazing. You take me. It unloads, sharply. I slobber all over you, my eyes bugging out, my retinas blinded by the orgasm. My head falls back down, I suck your dick with increased intensity, I jerk it at the base as well. I want to see it shooting far, spurting thick globs all over my mouth. I pull out of you. The sweet aroma of your shit.

Account of a Crime

In the early hours of March 7th, 19—, H.G. was found dead, lying in a pool of his own blood, in the middle of his messy room. Death had silenced him.

His chest was compressed until his heart burst out, until it puked itself. His body was cut up in strips and pieces which were put on display, nailed to the walls of his room. Then his bones were boiled in a huge tin pot in order to make various jellies, which were subsequently dyed and enumerated.

Newspaper Clipping

At first it looked like the victim had staged this macabre scene, but there's no denying the impossibility of such actions. This horrible crime, this repugnant feast therefore has to be the handiwork of a sexual deviant who, considering the victim's proclivities, may well be his own accomplice. Empty Polaroid SX-70 film cartridges scattered around what remained of the body would suggest that the monster had taken a number of photos throughout his act, before disappearing into the anonymous night, without leaving any trace or print. The police are on alert. Everything, especially the autopsy encumbered by the poor condition of the corpse, points to the murderer being a close friend of the victim, perhaps even his lover.

So it has to be a sexual crime, or a moral crime.

"He was wearing black velvet gloves, not to prevent leaving fingerprints, but to hide the scales growing on his hands. And a cardboard ruffle to hide the hole in the middle of his chest."

Some overly wagging tongues insist that this declaration has to be one of the dead person's ultimate jokes, as he had actually spent his life, or a large part of it despite his very young age, developing then building a machine for self-butchering (and self-pounding, since his anus was violently battered): a multipurpose machine, an egocentric robot, some would say winged, as if intent on flying out the first window to be opened . . .

But aren't these stories, which would set the imaginations of some horror-filmmakers or horror-storytellers aquiver in excitement, themselves a result of perverted, fanciful thoughts inspired by this crime, of a story begging to be amplified with apocryphal details?

Let's come back to reality! The police are currently investigating a small traveling circus that includes a knife thrower who, oddly enough, disappeared the night of the crime and whose description closely matches the one given by Mme Vichnou, H.G.'s cleaning lady. But everything, for now, remains purely hypothetical.

Propaganda Death
(One Performance Only)

Declining these heavy, overburdened dreams, which take me into these imagined places, these sites yet to come, these crime scenes that my desires secrete, this practically acrid dampness, the fourth floor of a huge hotel in another country, a whole wing in gloom, deserted, massive, something has to happen there, the first time I go there, an intense yet secret and silent excitement, a gathering of gay men, every time I go back I find the space empty, or rather, I can't find the place again, or I've gotten the floor wrong, or I've gotten the hotel wrong, or it's not the right time to come. I wander. I keep on hoping to find someone behind a door, or in the closed-up shitter. But the place remains deserted.

These ascetic brothels, these sealed-off saunas where boiling drops of water keep on dripping from the ceiling, where the walls split into shards.

I look at you. It's on your cheek, right next to your left nostril that I press on with the sharp point of my scissors, which I push in to pierce, and I start to cut through your cheek clockwise, like a ground beef patty straight out of the presser, a zucchetto. Or I cut off your whole nose with a single snip, at the base, with a gardening tool for snipping flowers.

Not to have genitals anymore. No lonely genitals, no genitals without you. Maybe you'll get a heavy, huge set of genitals in the mouth, swollen with semen that's been building up for two months and that I refuse to release. Genitals at once drunken and dead.

I'll force-feed you my fuck jelly, make you swallow my lumps one by one.

We connect to each other, center to center, sucking our ends, mouths made for cocks, mouths made for holes, two twins together top-to-tail in the matrix jelly.

Everything wears away in living. In the toilet that only my family used was some red, my mother must have been on her period, a red decoction heavier than the water, decorating it, this morning I jerked off while waking up, I had to get up to put a washcloth under my stomach, right where the semen will drip as it doesn't spurt, because it could get on the sheets and we're not at home, we're renting, my mother dislikes stains and rings on the bottom sheet, to stay hard I breathe through my slightly loaded breath, and once I'm filled up, I shift, I imagine it's your breath in my mouth, that the dick I'm pulling back and forth in my hand is yours, the body folded over so as not to stain the top sheet, I can't bring it all the way down since, with my head buried underneath, the dome protecting my dreams, keeping me from losing that breath.

I jerk you off and I watch the way your balls move, swell, retract, contort, lively as jellyfish. I swallow your package and lust after the head of your cock and its reddish corona spiked with small white granulations reminiscent of beef tongue.

Your semen impregnates my ass, inseminates my shit, coats the walls of this pocket your dick-lusciousness has just banged around, right where I make my own fuckjuice, discoloring my fluids. Comes back out as phlegmy water, in small bursts, a sputtering trumpet. Inside me your curdled, congealed sperm ferments. Rather not shit it out and keep it inside me, let it soak in, penetrate, and fertilize, so that it can increase and fester. I keep it in, force myself to, fortify myself, stopper my hole, tense up my guts to keep it from slipping out or leaking out, from dissolving in the toilet water. I burst from your juices, they fill me up, poison me, get into my blood. Your semen, your phlegm, your yellowed blobs permeate my brain. Inhaling these live particles from you into my body and getting high off them faster than if I'd snorted cocaine. In the heat of my body they don't die. Feel them rise up in my throat, getting past my glottis into my mouth, taste them, keep them from slipping out and getting spat out, and even a scowl of disgust, of pleasure, that my body is more than an oven, a waffle iron, a bakery where my matter transforms yours, reingurgitates them, the ecstasy of your secretions, the absorption of your sap.

Ersatz: the fifty-franc white plastic dildo bought in a Pigalle sex shop. Slathered in extra virgin olive oil made by the Cifréo brothers, it splits my ass, countersinks it, bores into it, fills it, widens it, drains it. It has only one speed, the three-speed model costs an extra ten francs. Battering my ass with plastic, making it vibrate in my mouth, sucking it and sliding it over my cock, my frenum, around the head, holding it between my ass cheeks so it tickles my balls, making them spew. I pull it back out and wash it clean of its remnants of greenish shit, malodorous greasy sludge, bits of leek vinaigrette and pineapple kirsch.

The school's gray bronze urinals, flaking in spots, a constantly-flowing curtain of water, three stalls cheek by jowl to allow leering, beneath the water changes in the metal's color, slate, sometimes yellowed, it reeked of urine and our faces pressed against the water's flow we drank the water, which tasted like piss, the goal was to drink the most.

A story already told a hundred times, the first ejaculate in my hands, my father's, come back from school, getting up to throw mandarin peels in the yellow bucket, behind the kitchen door, inexorably attracted, fascinated by the detritus, a bizarre object, a small plastic wrapper drenched in viscous matter, a transparent jelly, touching the rubber and sliding it between my fingers, not understanding anything and understanding everything, fascinated and disgusted, etc.

Never before nor since such an intense impression of death in my joy. Because my dick in, by your ass is decapitated and cut off, starts to gush in globs, three four long spurts, like some blood draining out of me, chicken's head chopped off and blood pouring, dribbling in momentary waves: he eats it off, bleeds me dry. Because in your ass, beyond the folds, the pockets, the craters, the tongues, the tentacles, some scarlet spots. Those, soft as silk, as chopped-off breasts, and these, ringed, pigmented, roughened, sandpapery. Chopping my dick gleaming with paraffin oil.

Your ass is made of rubber that girdles my fingers.

Through my window screen I hear soldiers hurtling down the street, huddled together and laughing together, their guffaws, I spy on them and make them climb up a rope ladder hanging from my window, because my parents had locked the door downstairs.

Further off the helmeted watchman with his rifle on his shoulder is unmoving, doesn't see a thing. Their thick, short hair, their unwashed cocks stinking of shit and the previous night's ministrations, their white pustules swelling their pores, beneath my stiffened tongue roving over them, two teeth grinding against each other to burst them, and the pus spurts over my face, I rub my dick, splatter my palate and drench my eyes, coat my face, a primal soup to swallow.

Because, each one of them hunched over my stomach, their pants pushed halfway down, they came and jerked off their cocks over my mouth, and discharged them while calling me a whore.

The little girl says:

"Four knife thrusts, four stabs, and she was strangled. Oh, she was so very adorable. Her picture was in the paper. A little nine-year-old girl. Her friend wanted to kill. She was practicing her somersaults."

Because, when I kill you, there's a club or a howitzer or the sharp remnants of a mirror that's just shattered or my fingers gripping your throat in your sleep or my tongue which has transmitted a death to your own without your realizing it.

Defense of the criminal sentenced to death.

Since my body fills with water, a spout by my derriere, swells my stomach, my intestines, bathes my shit, an inverted tide that becomes tinged by the bile salts it touches, and makes me shit liters of black water that carries and ejects fibers, creases, intestinal residue, scales.

My seminal vesicles discharge and deflate. I cum.

Since my lips have a bit of mollusks and a bit of vulvas to them. The lower lip has the shape, the consistency of this gelatinous and slithering tongue, of the moist, drooling, resinous coating on stones, pterodunculars, on snails or slugs, suctioning your ass and imbibing your tides as if at a ciborium, on your knees.

I'll find some octopus in your belly when I open it up, some shaggy vegetal tentacles that once extracted and unfurled on your throat, your sawn-open sternum, will make for beautiful frills, red jellyfish-like ruffs. And once your throat is opened, your neck yawning, your sweetbreads removed will result in goiters, two lips, a slit I'll kiss tenderly. Your flesh will stick to my ribs.

In your wide-open mouth a lever of sorts, a spacer that separates your jawbones, I fill your mouth with ice cubes of ether piled up to keep your tongue chilled, to facilitate its extraction, and it's in your mouth, as I maneuver scissors and scalpels to manipulate your fibers, retractors, chisels, tweezers, hooks, handsaws, gouges, and curettes to scrape your bones and extract your inserts, that's where I come to drink, sucking the ether ice cubes and your tongue, which has hardened and gives my own this cold, headache-inducing liqueur that goes straight to my brain. And out of all this transparency, your body's transparency, the ice's transparency, I exult.

And out of your bones I make finery. Your cut-up, jagged skin forms intricate hats, veils, tulles for you that cover your face and cling to the circumference of your skull.

I examine your gentle throbbing, open you up, tear you apart, hack through your sternum, use both my hands to separate your reddening gills under your shirt tinged blue by slivers of flesh, the enterotome cutting open your intestines lets out roundworms swarming in your gut like vermicelli, moving you around in the refrigerator's chill, shoving in my hands and then my head, inhaling what remains of your fecal matter, which almost crumbles apart.

Pink silk ribbons to decorate the faces and skeletons of decorative dogs. With both hands I pull apart your drapery, crawl, sneak in, peer in fascination at your machinery, use the nocturnal transparency to observe your shit factories, your bony and mucosal assemblages, your sacs, your tubes.

Your hand on my stall. Under your muscles are blades, pincers, pins traversing and supporting them, forming refined architectures. Unfurled they resemble the sails of a boat. And your nerves are floating, dancing.

On your torso the scalpel traces tattoos of death, opens your lips just about everywhere, geometrically. There, as in a tree's whorls, they might represent aerial images, cupolas, rivers, aquatic animals surfacing and shifting and swarming around your stomach. There I discover your fascias, your serous membranes, your subcutaneous tissues, all these translucent tissues covering your cavities which I smooth out, peel away from the muscle, methodically pin down and tie together. (No need for candles to brighten this night of your body; its internal transparency illuminates all.) Then I reach your parietal pleura, then your visceral pleura, I unfold them and they're softer than silk and they can be used to make large clothes for you, and I cover your face and your body with them like a transparent shroud, a sort of secretion that would have taken, then I tie them together to make myself a cradle, a hammock, and I lie in it and curl up in it, I caparison myself with it, I pull it around me, I snuggle in it, and fall asleep in it, and your juices trickle, coat me, seep into me, and dissolve me.

And if I'm crazy, they'll drill my head, they'll cut through my forehead, they'll trepan me. Or they'll force me to drink a potion that makes me shit out all the demons occupying me.

So death benefits from a costume ball to complete its depiction, its double remains seated, inert, its head lolling on its stomach and it looks like he's still alive even though it's only a shell and death, draped in white cloth, keeps on, drawing sniggers out of a bow woven from your hair and pulled tight on a tibia, posing as a mask: the sagging bodies looking as if they were drunk, the faces eroded by disease hidden beneath giggles of glued cardboard. Children's paper hats: legionnaires' caps, Russian toques, woven Chinese bonnets, fakirs' turbans, etc.

"What's that in your hair?"

"A fog monster, those little critters that suck out bad blood."

And also toads, lizards, guanacos, and, imported from Brazil in a ship hold, those things that look like huge cowardly yet dangerous maybugs. As soon as one of them stops, another one jumps on it and devours it. And those pink millipedes that swarm after torrential rainstorms, cyclones?

"A very small snake, but if it bites your finger, even if it only hits bone, you have to cut off your arm with an axe right away, or burn the bite with a flaming ember. We put it in a jar to watch it and we gave it fleas to eat, spiders, lizard tails. It swallowed everything right away, and with the fleas we only found legs and wings after. One day we picked up a maybug and gave it to the snake. The next morning in the jar there were just bones, the snake's skeleton. And the maybug flittering around, whirling, whirling . . ."

Five Marble Tables

Five marble tables, aligned parallel to each other, five sinks, at the bottom the shower hose, for power washing, the table slopes concave to let everything flow into a furrow, some daylight streaming through high windows, heads and feet swaddled, the foot sticks out, tight around a steel wire, three-hole-punched paper with a number written on it, they ritualistically scribble something specific, they bring a mirror up to my upside-down face, my mouth, for that single purpose, they sever an artery to see the color of my blood, darker almost black, to see if it's still spurting from the heart, no, it flows, slowly, it stagnates, a rag soaks it up, they clean up my yellowing body, with rags, rags, birth, and soft, natural sponges, they spray high-pressure water into my body, through the slit, my intestines float, swell, then silt up, the water diminishes to a rivulet, he breaks apart my ribs with shears, he has just nervously raised the sheet covering the head, seen the head, and set a finger right below my eye, pulling the skin toward the cheek to see the gash, stuck together, white, my eye suddenly appears with its iris, blue, before falling into the skull, unhooked falls, to start he cuts the entire front of the body, from the pubis to the trachea with a single snip, it doesn't make any noise, like slicing a caramel flan, the bottom of the body had to be washed with a cloth, between the thighs, shit, urine, salts were ejected without my feeling anything, he can't go too high with the knife, since nothing absolutely has to be seen, I should be clothed again, a tie should be knotted just so to hide the top end of the incision, to show me to my family, the work clean and properly done, just a little autopsy, closing everything up I find a part of myself removed, the delight of feeling myself becoming aquatic again, floating in the alcoholic jelly of a jar, I infuse, I transfuse, I have my heart in a washbasin, it'll be put in a jar and it'll sink like a stone, it's what I use to love you, I feel good, my body dispersed, multiplied, exhibited, they number it and it no longer smells like shit, something more insidious, persistent, takes everything, goes everywhere beyond all the padding, eating into the disinfectant that would silence it, obscenely it becomes manifest, acrid in summer, sickly sweet in winter, death, it's my body, it's pallid like broth at the beginning of illness, like crushed aspirin in strawberry jam, it's treacherous, it's soft, it's yellow, spineless, chlorinate, floral, everything floats, I float, I swim, I shut down, I reek, I force him to breathe, he cuts, his white-plastic apron girds his lower back, he slams his genitals into me on the table, he has a white balaclava on, white boots, white gloves, I see his eyes, I'd like it if he at least made an obscene gesture, even with the scalpel, on the neighboring tables to the right and the left, an old woman with brown skin, whose body teems and splatters, whatever was holding her hair back has broken and her long white twisted locks, liberated from their braids, fall from the table, on the other side a child that had been murdered, twelve or thirteen years old, his skull cracked, his stomach bloody, disemboweled, the child had committed suicide, his head explodes under the pressure of gunfire, his own hands shot a bullet straight through his face, no more than a cloud of smoke, the man taking pleasure in slashing his throat with a knife, this child is close to me, on the other table, farther off is a young Arab along with the old woman and the child who committed suicide we communicate through the room's icy silence, in all this whiteness that we continuously produce, produce our souls, produce our humors flowing down the channels, our waters, our bloods merging and forming a thin blackish torrent, through the man takes the same metal from one body to another, mixes us together out of clumsiness, within me the kid and the hag, fibers that fell, detached from the blade, went flying, ended up elsewhere and intertwined in an upper layer, cupola, fifth arch, the kid the hag and I each embrace the others, we dance.

We know these gurneys well, we understand that they are for the dead, they're tinged differently, screech differently, they echo as they meander, ghosts of marble and rusted steel, they impress and inspire fear, the electric elevator doors close upon them with an authoritative clang, they carry away the smell, the ineffable smell of morgues and autopsy rooms, women have trouble scrubbing them down, the most powerful hoses have trouble erasing these corpses' memories, macabre traces of temporary tattoos, all his instruments are beside him on a little shelf, he handles them lovingly, caresses blades and scalpels before twisting them in our flesh, having cracked our drumsticks with the blow of a hammer then extracted, all the bodies are there right next to each other, shrouded, almost anonymous, the gurneys dragged over here, shoved next to each other, end-to-end, crammed together or spaced apart, solitary, my hair is still beautiful under its covering, cloth embroidered with letters that spell out over my face *Hôpital de la S.*, the hag laughs, bares her teeth in her decayed mouth, without making any noise, just to show her grimace, she's insane, locked up, died at the hospital, I'll be closed back up with a stapler, they'll leave my body empty, with nothing in it, only the bones of my spinal cord will remain, visible from above, the marrow hardens, this hole in my stomach, and my belly, get filled by a cardboard ruff attached around my neck then covered with a shirt, it's the usual outfit, the child latches onto me, he doesn't want to let me leave, with all his fibers, his blood, and his humors blocking mine in the channel, I tell him that my body is done, nothing particularly interesting for the one who had handled me, all that needs to be done now is throw it out, the heart is over there, reddening, obvious, transparent, tinting the solution, my skin gets stapled with the metal implement, five big staples, no time to put in stitches, too much flesh, they finish by knotting this black, severe tie, they put the lungs back in, mechanically they took a bit of intestine lingering in a sink, not worth the hassle of using a jar, they're all the same, less valuable than the heart, less decorative, they threw in the hacked-off ribs which clinked against the other bodies' bones, red particles pulled out rather than peeled off, no time to scrape the bone, all that in a huge black bag made of watertight plastic, Venice's trash stinks up all its canals, strange neglect, strange remnants, body matter, memories, words, carcasses and music, it all flows, commingles, it's eaten, regurgitated, and it corrodes, all his life photographing the moon, a snapshot every night, tertiary and quaternary, distraught I am, distraught I cobble together my suicide contraption, tonight when the moon didn't appear, a machine for self-butchering and self-pounding, I watch myself doing it, seated upon a bidet on wheels, in front of a mirror, I watch myself cutting my throat with a single, slow cut, smoothly, I arranged, along a huge kitchen knife, various razor blades, and with that, I watch myself sink the zigzagging point of a gouging machine into my ear, I plug it in and it immediately vibrates, corkscrews its way in, but it's heavy and my arm falls, its point skids onto my jaw, the bone sprays a haze, I start again a bit higher, right on the temple, the eardrum bursts and it

bores its way into the brain, crumples it up, I watch myself in stupefaction, I don't feel anything, the bone and blood are bursting, I
don't see anything in the facing mirror anymore, facing the scene,
it's stained, filthy, I fall back to the ground with a dull thud, the
too-short cord has come unplugged, it's not vibrating in my head
anymore but remains inert at an angle, fireworks, the machine
sticking out of my skull with my body slumped beneath makes for
an odd picture, I'm sitting in my Meccano chair, plugged into the
huge telescopic spectacles beneath the dome of an observatory,
inspecting my brain, the armchair spins in spite of myself, it's not
held in place, this has to be delirium, I look at the moon and the
beautiful black clouds racing past and shrouding I'm blissfully
happy, riddled with holes looking at my head, in my head, it's just
unbelievable all these eyes turned inward, connected to this
swirling flood, toward this red polar chaos, toward these icebergs of
hot guts slipping and shifting, clogging my arteries, making them
swell and burst, I explode, croak, splinter scarlet, it's beautiful, all
my organs lodge in my head, white, monitoring, broadcasting my
heartbeats, echoing in me in this sudden calm edged by tiles, I
empty myself the best way I can, through the tube, I fill as I like, I
take in, they plug reheated toad, alligator, and rat blood into me to
bring me back to life, two cannulas come out of my nostrils, I'm
connected to a machine that breathes for me, the tube drains my
juices, another in my trachea, my head reconstructed, resoldered,
the horrible machine thrown in the trash, you did something very
stupid, I'm sewn back up to my throat, it'll knit back together, it
takes, long needles, dripping devilish drops under the skin, everywhere on my arms, interfering, I fall, fall again, fall, hitch, unhitch,
I'm stippled, flooded with other liquids, other cells, lamented upon
other skins.

The gurney goes into the elevator covered with a sheet, I'm alone with a man whose reddened face is shredded under his skin, corpulent under his shelf, at six o'clock in the morning before starting these cadavers' incineration he eats a boiling oil-and-garlic soup, he drinks some red wine, red wine straight from the bottle, my emptied-out body goes into another refrigerated room, dead at the hospital, once again next to other bodies that are unknown, anonymous, numbers tied to their ankles, my arms are next to my torso and my legs are aligned with my pelvis, it's easy, I won't let go of my body, I cling to it, I push out everything I can inside but it all stops immediately, I'm clean forever now, my muscles tear apart, I can't go back into myself anymore and I leave this deserted place, all the fight gone, all fury slain.

Propaganda Death Nº 0

Slaughter

As a child I dream of pleasure rooms. There's a check-in counter at the entrance, we go down into an underground space. All the customers are men. They get undressed then find each other naked in the damp of a huge room with rusty zinc and slate walls, cluttered with pipes, boilers that water and fire flow through. Without touching or talking to each other, the men take their places in stalls of sorts, open compartments where the powerful and sputtering yet liquid and soft flame of a gaslight bathes their bellies and their crotches. I wait for an empty compartment and take my spot in turn in front of the fire that showers me and engulfs me in wellbeing, I'm the only child there.

My father works in slaughterhouses. He brings home blood-stained overalls that my mother has to clean, beef tongues wrapped in newsprint. One morning he wakes me up at dawn to take me to see for myself. We walk past blindfolded animals being dragged, we hear their bellowing, the noise of sagging bodies with legs cut off and skulls shattered on the tiles. My father shows me how the piston being pressed to their foreheads works, shooting an iron bar through their brain (the fillings magnetizing the meat). We aren't like those Jews who bleed them dry, my father tells me. In the gray, damp morning (all the tones are uniform, gray or dirty blue, the sky, the cobblestones, the slaughterers' overalls), all that flows down the gutters is the animals' blood, blackish red, this thin yet dense torrent we walk along.

In the morning I return to the abattoirs to get my hole punched in by the slaughterers, the animal-fellers, the strongmen who haul the carcasses on their shoulders. They squeeze my ass and from their bloodstained overalls they haul out their winey dicks and make me suck them, I'm hunched down in humors, gelatins, clots, they stay ramrod-straight, belching, manhandling my body like an orifice. A steer snatches my belly and, with its hot, massive, slimy tongue, eats it up, wrestling away from death.

An Indecent Dream

The dream can be full of ignominy. It conceals a geography of pleasure, an itinerary with its impasses, its openings, its stairwells, its gulfs, its forbidden directions. Desire is there, alone, idealized, freed of all materiality. But we often get lost in its labyrinths before reaching pleasure.

More than in the site of pleasure, my dream walks me in front of its sign. I feel its nearness, its extensiveness, without being able to find it. For example, I walk in front of a stairwell that could lead me to it, but I'm unable to go down it. A sauna or a whorehouse: the place isn't clearly defined. It's an underground, unlit place. My dream might take me there one night or another but deviously skirts it and its sign. It keeps on diverting and delaying the climax, so I never reach it.

That night, finally making my way down a stairwell that might lead me there I happen upon two entrances. One, on the left, is lit up. The other, on the right, is dark. There are no doors. I have trouble locating pleasure and choose the wrong entrance. I step into the room on the left. It's a low, arch-ribbed room bluntly lit despite the lack of windows: the light is a common-room light, a hospital-room light. The room is filled with children's beds, lined up side by side in two rows. I immediately sense that my presence in this space is unusual, that I'm not the expected visitor. In the beds are very young children, sometimes two to a bed, all of them boys, nude, very thin, exposed, albinos in the white sheets. These are just bodies. The ambient heat is a greenhouse's heat, or an incubator's heat. They're silent and soft, numbed, almost boneless, drugged and underfed. They've never seen the light of day, they've never come out of this place. They're half blind because their corneas have been coated with overly acidic eyewash. Some of them have had their eyelids sewn shut. They don't know how to talk, they drool, they groan. Some are in incubators, others are still fetuses in jars. The oldest ones are barely pubescent. All these children have been captured, or bought from their mothers at birth. Women dressed as nurses monitor them, clean them. It's a place to pay for pleasure, like whorehouse or sauna. The customers look bourgeois; the cover charge is very expensive. The men leave their dark suits on the bars of the bed-cages and go lie down, naked and old and scrawny, beside the children under the sheets. They kiss them, caress them, masturbate beside them, fuck them.

I, revolted, could free these children but I can't gather them up, not even body by body. They liquefy immediately. Some parts of their brains have been cut. They don't react anymore. Their anuses have been artificially stretched and deepened and are dark red gulfs anyone could easily stick their hands inside. Put in a vertical position, their orifices release and let out yellow liquid shit, whitish lumps from the bourgeois men who get dressed discreetly and leave after having glanced into the stairwell, making sure that nobody could catch them by surprise.

Pure Fantasy

I know nothing of a woman's vagina. So I dream about it. A rebus, a thing hidden deep in a landscape, an implicit yet essential thing, a thing that has to be identified or reconstituted from dotted points. For me, it's a pure fantasy.

If I dream, it's a woman I want to kill and who's taunting me, baring her breast before getting to work opening up her breast with a small sharp tool. As soon as it's sliced through, the flesh splits in two and unfurls on each side, shiny, palpitating red. I think: the consistency of a Chinese fruit, the resinous, glassy film coating a peeled lychee. Laid out like a fish gill, the striated, symmetrical flesh of a skate. I think: that must be viscous, my fingers will sink deep. The woman takes my hand and forces me to touch her wound: no, on the contrary, it's very soft, unreal like squeezing silk.

Then, as she walks past a mirror, I seize the opportunity to push her whole body against her reflection.

In another dream, it's a boy lying on a bed who's contorted in pain. He begs me to hold his hand, and to squeeze it so that his pain, which materializes as a tide, a current, can escape. The pain flows, passes from his body to mine, but doesn't affect me, I feel it go through me like lightning through a rod. The pain simply empties out of one body into another without penetrating mine. This current that vibrates, warms, and electrifies our hands, makes me hard.

As soon as I'm aware of my erection, the boy metamorphoses into a girl. Still bent over in pain, she pulls my body against hers, presses it close, hugs it, and in her embrace sends us crashing off the bed. Then her hand sneakily takes my erect penis to put it in her vagina. There's barely enough time to realize it. I think: for the first time my penis is in a woman's vagina. I try to define this feeling. But as I'm buried within her, the woman grows older and dries out under my eyes in an unending, accelerated, seamless process. She clutches me tight, keeps me inside her. But her vagina is cold. She's just died. I pull out in horror, leaving her unmoving on the floor.

Another time, it's a shirtless boy I'm kissing. I know him. I think: I didn't realize I had such desire for him. I caress him: his skin is soft, golden, magnificent, dotted with a welter of small black nipples that keep moving around, teeming like bacteria under a microscope. He suddenly tells me not to touch his back. I suspect he's very hairy, and that he's ashamed of it. He turns around: thick black hair, like a monkey, falls from his shoulders. But that's not all: his back, an accumulation of growths, wounds, hollows, vegetables, is a veritable field of monstrous animality. He's split in two from top to bottom by a suppurating wound. But his desire hasn't cooled. Confronted with this, I almost feel normalcy.

Labial Flesh

It's at the anatomical wax museum in Florence that I had the revelation about women's vaginas. Segments of bodies in wooden boxes, sumptuous cadavers with gleaming organs lie on white silk sheets trimmed with silver thread. The layout is a result of the artistry, the determined and manic attention of an eighteenth-century anatomist. The women are open and outstretched, in wigs as they take on the poses of saints, dissected as they rear up in half-mimed ecstasies, gleeful at the sight of their extracted organs, coquettish with their viscera. An array of women's underbellies, their thighs sawn off, realistic to the point of reproducing, within the wax, the handsaw's movements through flesh, then bone. The vitrines are low and the schoolchildren walk past, crouching down to see the barely mauve lips of those open vaginas pleated in the wax, these spread-apart, ringed vaginas that an eye can venture into and lose itself within. For the process of erections, swollen dismembered dicks with protruding, nearly purple veins held at their base by bowknots, shredded pink silk ribbons. The woman has to push to expel and that explains the openness of her vagina, from one vitrine to the next the fetus develops, hair appears on its scalp, its entire body is bathed in a honey, a thick substance that preserves it in the egg, alveolar shapes, sticky pleurae layered like Moroccan pastries, twins nice and cozy in the organ jelly, all around this barely mauve labial flesh the bulging belly, the egg, and stuck on a bandage directly atop the wax hair all around the lips, real hair, or animal hair, or hair cut short to give an illusion of hair, curly hair, abundant hair just beneath this ornamental orifice the small tongue of living, varnished red flesh, the erect clitoris. The schoolchildren press their noses against the glass to see up close this magical, dangerous object, frozen in the wax yet still warm, welcoming in dreams, to be expelled back into the body, to go back within and cocoon within the egg ready to sprout (the exhilarating, childish project of putting lentils or beans in damp cotton in order to watch the seeds hatch with each passing day, white then stalks that grow upward and die, or that have to be grafted because they're over-grown), I too crouch down the better to see, it's a woman, a mother, the schoolteacher clears out the room full of uproar, laughter, whis-pering, gasps, sudden blushing, nascent fantasies.

Final Outrages

Bottoming delights me, everybody makes such a big deal about topping. When I fuck, I lie unmoving, soft, malleable, unconscious, I let myself be covered. I'm like a corpse. I hide areas, I put on my clothes of light. I like to imagine myself a blonde, too-pale little girl, an Ophelia dead in a sanatorium, stolen away in the bloom of youth by an ailment gnawing slowly at her interior (while making her exterior radiate!), a sleeping beauty unburdening herself in the humus-scented darkness of a coffin, virginal, her hands joined together in prayer letting fall a rosary of blessed boxwood, sighing at what eternity is offering, as a mercenary body-snatcher comes and takes me on my virginal bed, as a hunchbacked, reeking maniac sends the nails of my coffin flying before cutting off my two long blonde plaits to keep them between his shirt and his heart at all hours of day and night, as a medical student comes and finally demonstrates his love for one of these women he's in the habit of dissecting, as my little prepubescent brother who secretly pined for me comes and kisses my icy lips and wets my eyelids with tears, grips my fingers so tightly with his hands that he nearly breaks my bones, as this man too spineless and too gutless to love the living prefers the odoriferous company of the dead, as this masked man reveals, within his black frock, a gray cock that he pounds my belly with, as this wild child escaped from an insane asylum makes the cemetery's gate creak and, while the moon projects its dwarf shadow over the slabs, sets his crystalline laugh echoing among the chrysanthemums, raven-hops on my grave, as this man with such a contorted gait, with such a swollen eye (from having seen so much because the other is dead!) looms in the paths along the tall cypresses to pay me a final outrage (a final homage!), disinter me from my painful cavern, disembowel me with a six-blade knife, and hang up, while dancing a wild saraband, my intestines, like Christmas garlands, from one cross to the next.

The maniacs, the dead, and the convicts are trapped in water. As in Venice, the cemetery is on an island. We circle around it in a pirogue, using the fog to berth without catching the watchman's attention and waiting until nightfall. We let the boat drift. Hordes of cats and lizards fled the mausoleums at our approach. As we take stock of our tools, pickaxes, cords, sheets and candles, ether, we dedicate our prayers to the moon, begging it not to betray us . . .

Vice

He was walking down the street.

He suddenly wanted to be transplanted into a bath of vice (settings and act).

He was willing to pay to be in a vicious atmosphere, but he found porn films wanting . . .

PERSONAL EFFECTS

(Inventory of Bougainville's Travel Case)

The Comb

The comb is a piece of ivory or tortoiseshell, of horn, originally made more clumsily out of picks set in a stub of wood, and serves to smooth out hair, to divide it into distinct masses on opposing sides of a part that lays bare the hairs' roots, the skull's palest leather. The comb becomes a useless object of pure nostalgia for bald men, who generally melt the ebonite in the fire or, conversely, hold onto it even more zealously, like a relic, a souvenir of a happy, fertile time. The comb is thus locked up in a small case that perfectly sheathes every tooth. Bald men only attach so much importance to preserving the teeth of the comb because they see the breakage of one of them as an even more foreboding omen than alopecia is.

The Cotton Swab

The cotton swab, which is used to extract these small, yellow, smooth, waxy, slightly bitter secretions known as cerumen from the ear's inner cavity, is made of a wooden stem and, rolled around its end, a small quantity of cotton. Cotton swabs are sold in boxes of a hundred each in drugstores and supermarkets. But some families prove this purchase's uselessness, its purely extravagant nature by making cotton swabs themselves, with the help of a broken matchstick or a lollipop stick notched at their ends with pocket knives, the better to bind the cotton to the wood. The single-use brand-name Q-Tip and the family-made cotton swab more or less perform the same service, which is cleaning one's ears, and can bring about the same pleasant irritation of the auricular labyrinth's tissues through repeated frictions if they're pushed into still-unexplored canals, increasingly close to the fibrous, translucent membrane that transmits sound, can even set off a small spasm in children should the maneuvering be especially deft. Some women also use cotton swabs, dipped in alcohol, to clean their children's belly buttons, or even, dipped in nail-polish remover, to scrub away the varnish that sneaks onto their skin as they paint their nails. Some people insist that using cotton swabs is thoroughly dangerous: not only do they risk puncturing the eardrum, but they also push all the auricular discharge into distant canals, resulting in small grains that harden irrevocably until they fill in and block the passageway connecting the middle ear and the inner ear, causing the perception of sound to be lost forever. For cotton swabs, our great-grandmothers simply used the unfolded iron strips of their hairpins.

The Blackhead Remover

The blackhead remover is a flat, thin tool made of hard material, iron or metal, open on its wider end so that, when pressed against skin, it can extract, sometimes in a long twisted white coil, the small plug of sebaceous material that had taken root in one of the dermis's orifices. The blackhead remover often has a sharper, triangular-shaped end, hardly an effective substitute for a nail file, meant for scrubbing nails while in mourning or cleansing them of their desires, but it's hard to see what more perverse use there could be for this unbeautiful little instrument.

The Nose Wipe

The nose wipe is quite simply the profane, parodic name for a hand-kerchief (nose wipe: snot rag). It also designates, in a distant land particularly preoccupied with hygiene, a small portable machine, designed like a milking machine, that single men can affix at any time to the terminal organ of their lower abdomen, in order to extract and grind, and transform into a fine, volatile powder, the recent product of their seminal vesicles.

The Exfoliating Glove

The exfoliating glove is principally a glove one puts one's hand in, although it is made not out of silk or lace, but of a rough cloth, potentially an agglomeration of twine, which scrubs away the outer layer of the skin. One rubs in some eau de cologne or camphor while extolling its anaphrodisiac virtues, so as to warm up an aching muscle, to slough off already-decaying skin. The exfoliating glove is a fairly masculine instrument, intended to strengthen the body, but some women whose skin cannot bear running water or alkalis willingly use them.

The Cuticle Trimmer

The cuticle trimmer is next to the brush, the polisher, the nail file, the scissors, and the nail varnish in the nail-care box, a small case intended for the care of fingernails and toenails. It's the sharpest instrument: with its two honed points which clamp together harshly with the squeeze of a palm, it breaks and severs, through repeated clips, through consecutive small angles, all around the nail, because its actual shearing mechanism, which acts through the flexion of a lever, is superficially very narrow. To harmonize, to even out these successive trimmings, and thereby render the cuticle trimmer's work invisible, requires resorting to a nail file. Having been thus wronged, the cuticle trimmer hints at the threat that it could, at any moment, slip and nick the flesh around the nail to leave a more enduring trace.

The Eyelash Curler

The object most similar to the eyelash curler, which women and some inverts used for brightening their gaze, is the escargot tongs, or the curling iron. The eyelash curler is composed of two rings in which one's fingers can fit, but the movement they imprint isn't one of shearing, because the end of the arms are made of two parallel curved pincers that pinch the upper lashes, then the lower ones, while curling them gently, and of two flat blades that clasp together over the cornea of each side of the eyelid the better to open the eye. The eyelash curler has never been effective, except for depigmenting the eyes they're intended to outline, and for creating permanent gaps between eyelids.

The Cat o' Nine Tails

The cat o' nine tails has been hung, among the cobweb dusters, from ceiling hooks, in the dim backroom of the hardware store. It carries within itself, in its unmoving straps, the screams of battered children, it exhales the pleasure of perverted lovers.

The Rigollot's Paper

The Rigollot's paper, or mustard paper, is a strip of cloth, tulle, or paper, packed with linseed flour or ground-up black mustard grains, which the mother floats first in the cold water of a soup bowl, immersing it every so often with her fingertips so that the powder, thinning out, forms a sort of plaster. The child is lying in bed, he has opened his pajama top to bare his thin little chest, he dreads the moment when the strip of cold, damp tulle will be pressed onto his skin, and will soon warm up his skin, sting, then prick, and burn until he begs his mother to remove it. She has carefully pasted the poultice on the child's chest and protected the pajama top, which she returns to button up again, with a layer of cotton wool, she looks at her watch, but there is no prescribed length for using the mustard paper, apart from extreme irritation, unbearableness. She tells the child: "Think about something else," "Think about vacation," "Your father keeps it on all night without any trouble, he sleeps with it on," but the child focuses all his thoughts on that point on his chest, on this heat and chill, this itch, this bite. The mustard paper's effect is revulsion, it draws out the blood trapped in a diseased, inflamed, or congested organ, it reactivates circulation. The child is about to cry, fortunately his mother has set a small container of baby powder with holes in it on the nightstand, and soon the cruel bloodsucker will be nothing more than a horrid little ball of sodden green paper in the trashcan, and the mother, will open his pajama top to dust his reddened chest with a cloud of talc that she will spread, like a caress, with her soft hands. Immediately after, the child will fall asleep. The Rigollot's paper, which takes its name, quite simply, from Professor Rigollot, who invented it, has, like the cupping glass, the cat o' nine tails, or the thermogenic cotton strip soaked in vinegar and placed on one's lower back, become an outdated remedy. It's practically never used anymore, except in increasingly luxurious simulacra.

The Tongue Depressor

The tongue depressor in its various forms, as simple flat strips of sanded wood or as metal paddles, is found alongside some small scrapers in the kidney-shaped bowl during the medical examination. The tongue depressor is used to open the mouth properly, to prevent swallowing and biting, to examine, with a beam aimed by a headlight at the center of a basin of mirrors set on the otorhinolaryngologist's forehead, the veil that coats the throat, and to discern, beyond the uvula, potential tonsils, small almonds full of lymph that hamper children's respiration. The tongue depressor imposes a rather disagreeable pressure on the tongue, an ever-colder, ever-harsher contact with the taste buds' velvet, and, to avoid it, it's enough to promise the practitioner that one knows quite well to open one's mouth properly, one's mouth quite wide.

The Ether Mask

Disassembled and empty, some parts wrapped in silk paper, the bulb, the nose clip, the snorkel, and the central part, a rubber or tin ball, kept separately in a wooden box, the ether mask gloomily waits for its moment in the otorhinolaryngologist's glass case. Intended to alleviate laudanum- and mandrake-based anesthetics, which were often followed by a definitive fainting fit, the ether mask was originally composed of a silver case in which an ether-soaked sponge was placed, connected via a tube to an inhaler, a mask that cleaves perfectly to the gums beneath the raised lips, and which the child, who's kept from breathing through the nose with the help of a small metal clip, has to bite while inhaling the anesthetic vapors until complete narcosis results (the ether mask is often used for tonsil operations, for circumcisions). Perfected by Doctor Ombredanne in 1932, the ether mask now comprises a steel or rubber urn, a mask that covers the entire facial area (children are just told to only breathe through the mouth, in order to prevent completely numbing the brain), and a small bulb that the child squeezes himself for more of the ether vapors, until he falls unconscious in the operation chair.

This form of anesthesia only brings about a partial loss of consciousness: the child still clearly feels the scissors entering his throat and the blood suddenly filling his mouth. The ether subsequently causes vomiting, and nightmares that engrave themselves into the child's memory forever. Very few etherists have an ether mask, which certainly might facilitate their doses; they prefer to inhale it directly from a vial, or to drink it. The ether mask is also not advisable for fighting insomnia, for eradicating temporary depression. If it contains too many details, it may be that its mere description can put readers to sleep.

The Gloves

Whether tailored from an animal's hide or finely crocheted, whether mitten-shaped or fingerless, the gloves evidently serve to protect the hands' skin from cold or bad air, from cracking, from infections, they're lined with suede or warm furs, they sometimes hug the fingers' outlines and go all the way up one's arms, as antiseptics they keep the microbes of surgeons' hands away from the opened-up body, they absorb all sweat or, pocketed, let it all escape, they're supple, they're put away in glove boxes, all it takes is a swing of the hand for them to slap louts, but it should never be forgotten that the hands they're keenest to help are those of thieves and stranglers.

The Daguerreotype of a Dead Child

The daguerreotype of a dead child appears to be a small case of sculpted black wood or ebony with two proportionally minuscule hooks for fasteners: it can be hung from the end of a chain, but it's a bit heavy, and not oval-shaped, so it's kept atop some furniture, or in its bag, it's brought on trips, hidden in the false bottom of a brief-case or, more commonly, right on one's own body, beneath one's underclothes, in more intimate, noble locations, the heart, the throat, never the stomach, held by strings or ribbons, it's looked at frequently, sheltered from every prying eye, it's the reason to step away, it's kissed respectfully, a few tears are shed over it, the heavens shouted at. This small box's lid, when opened, reveals a carmine velvet cushion in which an inscription, a dedication, a vow can sometimes be read, amid flowers, topped by a cross. When held in one's hand and seen with one's lowered eyes, the first thing to be seen is a mirror, a smooth silvery plaque that reflects back one's gaze in the oval frame embedded with gemstones and engraved with fili-grees, and it takes a careful tilt to make out, captured on this plaque of silver bromide on glass, the immobile depiction of the dead child, lying on a small bed, dressed for church, with eyes shut, arms crossed, pale cheeks hollowed by illness, a ribbon or a bow tie around the neck to hide the blue mark of the hands that had wrung it.

The Teddy-Bear Vial

The teddy-bear vial appears to be a stuffed animal, with a light brown coat, of very small dimensions: it's sitting, it's smiling, it's a charming and very benign animal. A woman could easily keep it in her purse, a child in his pocket, or hidden in his hand. Anybody who notices it, for the woman, deems it just a trinket kept slightly too long, and, for the child, nobody notices it at all, because it's typical for a child to befriend an animal of this sort. But, the little blue or pink rosette encircling its neck hides, and reveals, upon being untied, a more mortal wound. It becomes clear that the head can be flipped open with the flick of a finger, whereupon there gleams, amid the neck's fur, the cap of a crystal vial. It appears that the teddy bear is nothing more than a lining, a cover, intended to camouflage the slyest machinations. Should a woman's beautifully thin, pale hand demonstrate the stratagem among society, abruptly decapitating the bear she had been playing with to reveal its trick, it would arouse wonder. But the same hand could act more deviously, splattering headier perfumes (Jungle Gardenia), slipping it into an ice tray's water which will soon crystallize to make ice cubes that mete out, in the guests' glasses, a glacial liqueur, that instantaneously seals and freezes their veins. The child generally uses the teddy-bear vial for more inoffensive ends, scattering miasmic vapors in public spaces, packing the vial with baby teeth, plucked-out eyelashes. But, going by this description, it would seem that the only users of teddy-bear vials for poisoning could be women and children.

The Vibrating Chair

This model of vibrating chair is an easily disassembled and transported replica of the colossal vibrating chair that the dukes of Pomerania had installed in their sitting rooms, akin to their physicians' and electrostaticians' cabinets of technologies: at first it was nothing more than an economical device for catching lightning, a sort of prehistoric lightning rod, until the dukes of Pomerania, whose easy morals and feelings, whose appreciation of dance and extravagance was notorious, took pleasure in it, and ordered more frequent artificial lightning strikes from their electrostaticians. The basic model of the vibrating chair (of which the electric chair, made in America, is merely a sinister perversion) was quickly refined: first they covered it completely in smooth, silky fur, the shining hides of wild cats, cassowaries, and ocelots, so that the potentially nude body could sit as luxuriously as possible with thoroughly adjustable switches and levers ultimately added on. One could be seated or reclined there while the body, run through by a delicious electrical current that breathes life into every limb, sways and rolls, and while its blood is shaken like milk in an immense agitator. Several virtues have been found in the vibrating chair that surpass the pleasure gained, it would give new life to one's body and new vigor to one's weakened limbs, it would brighten one's blood, eliminate one's humors, expel one's seminal discharge. The vibrating chair has been, even more recently, perfected: padded with a waterproof cover beneath the fur to reduce the number of incidents, and outfitted with straps, leather and rubber strips to keep the body from being thrown at high speeds. The vibrating chair was, in the home of Pomerania's dukes, an outright attraction: people came from all the courts of Europe to experience it, and the dukes occasionally, by hiding the wires connecting their boudoirs to their electrostaticians' cabinets, took pleasure in making it look like a haunted chair. Women swooned in it, and it was forbidden for use by children, and even adolescents, because one of the last dukes of Pomerania had met a far too luxurious death there. Hidden from the public are all the instruments that he had assembled himself, without his scholars' knowledge, to revitalize the machine: the iron collar that closed around his neck with its studs pressing lightly into his skin, the leather belts binding his wrists and ankles to the fur, and which he had replaced with reeking rat hides that hadn't been cleaned of grease, and with an even icier marble plank that he enjoyed all the more, the rings and straps that pulled back his hair, and this long, flexible, black-colored member that protruded from the chair and quickly swelled up in his anus, under the pressure of a valve, until it took on the dimensions of a stallion's erection, all these flasks that surrounded his head, like a crystal helmet, and instilled in his brain, through his nostrils, total narcosis, the heavy vapors of decoctions of hell's seeds and devil's hair, all these objects reside half broken, burned, crumbling apart, in the crates of the subbasements of the palace of the dukes of Pomerania, where there is displayed, in the museum's rarely visited rooms, just the classic model of vibrating chair, like an extravagant object from another century, a duke's caprice.

The Neck Brace

The neck brace is a leather bandage punched with holes, a case with steel fasteners, like those of a briefcase, which hugs the neck and the nape perfectly, sometimes even the shoulders, and props up the chin, right where bones are absent, right where the cylinder of the neck, wholly softened, weakens and wavers like a flamingo's. This circular support is typically open in the front, like an arrow slit, to let through air, of course, but also to let through a tongue or a dagger, because the youngest ones afflicted with this congenital vice feverishly seek out this crimson contact of taste buds or cold steel. And, when, after nightfall, the precious case is opened, having been hidden by a knotted scarf or a too-high ruff, betraying a face's stiffness and a gaze's sternness, the head then has to be held in one's hands and in a cloth, because it rolls, it turns, it falls backwards, and from this finally-freed mouth that drools, it's possible to do whatever one wishes, the blood spurting from the heart stops in one of this innumerable knots, the protruding small muscular callus that purportedly indicates masculinity bobs up and down endlessly like a mechanism, and the subject dies of exhaustion, suffocates if abandoned in the void, if left unsupported by one's palms on both sides, like the rarest of illuminated tomes.

The Static Electricity Machine

Originally it was noticed that yellow amber, after having been rubbed, attracts light and dry bodies: this was explained by saying that this rubbing gave a soul to the amber and that this soul attracted light bodies as if by a breath. Then a scholar by the name of Guillaume Gilbert recognized that the property of attracting light bodies, after prerequisite frictions, was common to agate, diamond, sapphire, ruby, opal, amethyst, aquamarine, rock crystal, sulfur, mastic, resin, arsenic, talc, and other substances. Moreover, he saw that these materials attracted not only stalks of straw, but also wood, metal filings or sheets, stones, dirt, and even liquids, such as water and oil. But it was the illustrious Otto von Guericke, burgomaster of Magdeburg, who achieved the honor of having built the first electrical device by means of a sphere of sulfur: "Take a bowl of copper, or as it is called, a phial, the thickness of a child's head; fill it with sulfur crushed in a mortar, and heat over a fire to melt the sulfur, which must then be stored in a dry place. Next, pierce this globe in such a way as to pass an iron rod through it along its axis . . ." With this rudimentary machine, Otto von Guericke was able to see, while working in darkness, the luminous phenomenon that accompanies the rubbing of the sulfur globe, that is, the electrical spark. The gleam he obtained was very weak, comparable only, in his own words, to the phosphorescence that sugar presents when it's ground in a dark room; to hear the spark's fizzle, he had to hold his ear very close to the globe. In the attractions and repulsions the sulfur globe had successively exerted upon the light bodies placed in its vicinity, Otto von Guericke thought he could see phenomena analogous to the attractions and repulsions the earthly globe exerted upon the bodies within its sphere of action . . .

The British physician Grey was the first to electrify a man's body. He notes that if a child is hung horizontally on horsehairs and if this child is brought into contact with a rubbed glass tube, the patient's head and feet attract light bodies. In his articles, the Frenchman Du Fay distinguishes between two types of electricity: vitreous electricity and resinous electricity. The former is characteristic of glass, rock crystal, gemstones, animal hair, or wool. The latter is characteristic of amber, gum copal, shellac, silk, yarn, and paper. The nature of these two electricities is to repel one another or to attract one another. In an experiment that aroused widespread interest, Du Fay drew electrical sparks out of the human body. After isolating himself by hanging silk cords from his office's ceiling, the physician lay on a small platform held in the air by these cords and had himself electrified by coming into contact with a thick glass tube that had been rubbed. The patient's body only had to extend its finger for a spark to surge. Out of the darkness had come a luminous emanation . . .

Hausen, a professor in Leipzig, built a machine which is depicted in a book published in Paris in 1748, Guillaume Watson's *Expériences et observations sur l'électricité*. A young abbot turns a handle that conveys a rotational movement to a glass globe. The role of conductor is played by a child suspended in the air by silk cords that isolate it. Through its feet, the child collects the electricity developed on the globe's surface; the fluid follows its body and is transmitted by its right hand to a little girl atop a slab of resin. The little girl holds her left hand out to the patient and, with her electrified right hand, attracts gold foil set on an isolating side table.

Finally, in 1768, the British optician Ramsden institutes a significant change in the machines currently in use: he substitutes the glass cylinder with a tray that turns between four animal-hide cushions stuffed with horsehair and pressing against the glass by means of a spring. It's interesting to notice that the reason that, in electrical machines, the glass globe is replaced with a cylinder or a disc is the relatively considerable number of accidents that this globe had caused: it exploded suddenly and sent dangerous shards flying at the experimenters. Discs might split in two while they filled with fluid, but at least would not detonate, and their use was harmless. Thanks to these machines, it was possible to simulate fire raining down with water flowing from an electrified fountain; shooting stars were successfully produced by electricity in a metallic disc rotating very quickly with many spikes equidistant from the center.

But, of all the phenomena that were discovered at this time, the one that aroused the greatest curiosity and attracted the most attention was the combustion by electrical spark of inflammable materials. Doctor Ludolf, of Berlin, lit ether with sparks excited by the approach of an electrified glass tube. By drawing out a spark with his finger, Winckler, in Leipzig, lit not only ether but also eau-de-vie, cow horn's liquor, and several other liquors. Watson, in England, repeated and extended these experiments. He lit, in addition to more or less concentrated eau-de-vie, various liquids containing volatile oils, such as spirits of lavender, sweet spirit of nitre, turpentine, elixirs and styptics, peony flower or lemon or orange or juniper or sassafras essence . . .

In her novel, *Pauliska or Modern Perversity*, published in 1798, Révéroni Saint-Cyr shows us how the breath of pretty women is converted into fluid, how love can be communicated, like rabies, by a bite and how, by rubbing the skin of children or women, a rejuvenating magnetic source may be obtained . . . And on a parchment in red letters:

"Love is dog-madness, it can be communicated, as this malady here mentioned, by a bite. (Diet.) Burnt turtledove bones, camphor and snakeskin. (Operations.) Repeated bites.

"Love is the physical union of two beings in order that their masses become one, thus you must give the atoms impetus. Irritate the fibres with ashes of the operator's hair and eyelashes. Intense penetration through the pores; increased friction on the skin. For a draught, the operator shall give his breath converted into fluid."

The Flypaper

The flypaper is a spiral of slightly sticky cardstock that quickly yellows in the air. It unfurls like a streamer, or like a Christmas wreath, absolutely gruesome for flies' feet. Enticed by the delectation of the jam that its varnished surface promises, the fly lands on the paper, a glue it cannot extricate itself from: the roll thereby strewn with wings and slow suffocations, famished and mute supplications, is, once it's completely packed, subsequently thrown in the trash. A minuscule and unnecessary object of torture, the flypaper, which used to attract flies rather than repel them, has been replaced by ultrasound.

The Vacuum Machine

Composed of a glass dome set on a piece of marquetry and connected to a system of pumps, valves, and wheels through which the air drawn out of the enclosure is evacuated, the vacuum machine is inexorable in the sense that it creates an unreal space, denuded of any particle, unlivable for any sensitive thing. This machine, in comparative-physics demonstrations, has become a parlor trick: under the glass dome is set a living bird, then it's closed shut, taking care that the strips and rubber discs designed to guarantee a perfect seal are positioned correctly, the bird flits around panickedly beneath the glass cage that all the participants' sleazy eyes are stuck on, and when the gaunt, acid-bitten hand of the physician starts turning the wheel and the air compressed by the pumps thins, the bird doesn't even float in this space void of all weight, it can't fly anymore, it's immediately flattened against the marquetry below, its heart and the small ivory balls of its eyes burst, the fragile skeleton of its keel breaks apart, and when the dome is taken away, in a hiss of decompression, all that is left is a small powdery, bony mass of feathers, slightly liquid as well.

If the enclosure of the vacuum machine is enlarged to human dimensions and the pneumatic system is activated after having sealed in a nude, blindfolded man, the same process results: the skin immediately turns blue, and the man is crushed, nailed by the mass of the void, all the skin on the surface of his face and his body bursts, bored through as if under an acid's violent flow, soon there will be nothing more than his skeleton, like a thorn stoked to a white heat.

A ROUTE

Regulation

The city, the State will now need to set aside a particular number of vacant spaces, for the sole purpose of small, libertine initiatives of vice truly luxurious in the waste of time they will inflict upon citizens.

Some props, some scenery will be set down along particular streets, in abandoned lots, houses being demolished, theaters that haven't really been abandoned, that have secretly been maintained. False nights would follow false heatwaves, temporal eccentricities, and various latitudes, creating within the city a truly devilish, wildly variable route. Other spaces created out of nothing would vanish as soon as the vice had been consummated: these would be like spring-loaded traps, but traps of pleasure; some amateurs would build them illicitly in accordance with their own fantasies, and would hide, waiting for someone to step within and redeem their inventiveness. Vice would become a free public service. The State would run competitions that would recognize designers of establishments and machines of wickedness never before seen.

The Hammam

The woman, behind her glass check-in counter, amid her eau de chypre and de violette, her jars of brilliantine, her faded price tags for gloves and cupping glasses, her discolored plastic roses, stares a long while at the visitor and asks him blandly if he's been here before. She's reading a romance photo-novel. Hammam V is a typical sort of establishment, marked on the street by a sign, at the far end of a courtyard, its mosaic façade centered symmetrically between two lanterns, the shattered pane of one covered by a plastic bag. A placard at the entrance shows the opening times, the days reserved specifically for men and for women, because the hammam, ritually, is a place where men come to relieve their bodies of fat and their souls of vice. Innocuously, the establishment, for baths, massages, and relaxation, as the signpost enumerates, is composed of cubicles evenly spaced along both sides of a corridor. These cubicles stay empty. Right in front of the pane is a frosted-glass door where *Steam Room* is written, immediately past which is a long stairway that abruptly reflects back one's image, hunched because the archway is low, in a triangular-shaped mirror pocked by specks of silver, fogged somewhat by water vapor. The slightly bitter and salty accumulated smell of steam, exudations, soap, and arches of marinating feet freed at last, is quick to irritate one's nostrils. At the bottom of the steps, the visitor loses himself among several prospects: frosted-glass doors hot water seeps beneath, the showers' roar, a screen through which a dark room of white shapes sleeping on mats can be seen, a Moorish-style bar counter with red-and-yellow accents, and just to the right a changing room where the same colors recur. The man at the bar takes the little ticket with *Hammam* stamped in blue ink, repeats the check-in lady's question, like a password, to the unfamiliar face: "Have you been here before?" then holds out a white bathrobe and a warm cloth towel and snatches his tip. His skin is dark, one of his eyes is caved-in. The visitor undresses in front of a locker, having chosen the number himself, among these lacquered red- and yellow-colored strips, scattered by mirrors where, in the shadows, crouching men are already watching him. A nearly black hand with a gleaming golden ring grips the door to the toilets without revealing anything of his body, other than his outstretched, bare feet.

The foot's arch moves indifferently from a slightly sticky black linoleum to the cracked white tile, inclining to let the water flow; the contact is rather disagreeable, might even set off a few shivers in imagining how easily mushrooms, greenish mosses could take hold on these surfaces. The showers, even with the floor, stretch down the hallway, parallel, all along the central room bordered by a basin of green water, adorned with several rocky stones upon which a glass wall's soft light falls. Above the body of water where nobody swims but on the edge of which are sitting men who wink at the visitor while blatantly groping their crotches and smiling to show him their golden teeth, rises up a tall metal spiral staircase. The men shower in rows and in the nude, their hands pulling a metal handle that releases the water, lather their heads, slowly soap their long brown members. At the back on the right of this central room, its walls broken up by transparent glass screens through which can be seen the relaxation rooms and the neighboring rooms where people can scald themselves, is another frosted-glass door that leads to a black room filled entirely with thick white steam cut through only by a lamp's shaky yellow gleam, and at the center of which stands a pyramid of steps bordered, on each beveled side, by an iron ramp. At the very top of this pyramid can be seen the shapes of two men standing, facing each other, one of them shaving with a small hand-held razor. The walls are peeling all over and smeared with handfuls of excrement that someone had tried to get rid of. But the cylindrical outlet that diffuses the steam, and burns the fingertips of those who approach it, is adorned with a delicate painting of a heron catching, with the point of its beak, a fish.

The pale, effeminate man, standing behind the bar counter, amid several old bottles of aperitifs and a wine press with lever, whispers tales of luxury at Hammamet while running his palm over the lacquered waves of his hair. A small numbered board with various drink orders kept in its cubbyholes is framed by plastic roses. Black and white lozenges make up the paving, and the arcades are adorned with Christmas wreaths, on the walls are painted yellow desert dunes, a moon, and on the mirrors, in finer brushstrokes, to hide the joins, a few palm trees. Above a white plaster angel, a twin to the one in the entrance, no longer spurting any water, is a television up high broadcasting the wedding of Queen Elizabeth, then squadrons of military planes. Men girded in white loincloths are reading magazines as they recline gently upon their chairs' red pleather and drink orangeade. Between the bar and the showers a shelf framed by mirrors is embedded in the wall and holds large snail-shaped hair dryers as well as small red plastic brushes. One of the men, sometimes dressed, sometimes not, might smooth and finger-wave his dense black hair.

The various rooms, broken up as has been mentioned by glass screens, cannot hide anything, they barely dampen the noises: as such, in the dry-steam room where a glass wall's light falls on the wooden slats worn nearly gray and a squat, prone body folded over a curved mat sunken like a hammock, the man in the bar can be seen, just above a squalid sink, through the glass, bent over his counter, but what he is saying about the crudeness of Arab mores cannot be heard, and on the other side, in the darkness of the relaxation room, the pale, sleeping forms are visible again. The white cloths hung on the wood seem to wrinkle immediately, crumpled by the acrid, salty steam.

The metal staircase rises above the basin's murky runoff and appears to be endless until it reaches a long hallway, also red and yellow, daylit, lined on each side with slightly open doors behind which are men lying or sitting, alone, each in a small room, winking as they see the visitor walking past, their grimaces invariably revealing one of their golden teeth and groping their crotches. Other men, who kept their long bathrobes, are leaning against partitions, and waiting indefinitely in the silence. Some wear their towel around their neck as a scarf, or as a turban on their head. They don't talk to each other. Each narrow room has a wooden plank covered with a red-pleather mattress, a small marble ledge set in the wall where an ashtray rests. Each room is sealed by a frosted-glass window and locked. Through the doors can be made out an eagle tattooed on an arm, or even a gold chain bracelet encircling a thick hand (the gold, too, gleams constantly among the smiles and the silent invitations). Some doors are shut. A white, fleshy man opens one of them and slumps against the doorframe, sweating, disheveled, clutching his bathrobe in front of him like a woman hiding her breasts, his wrists covered in colored, loose bracelets. The dark-complexioned men's circumcised members are often speckled with small spots of whiter skin.

The visitor goes back to the bar to ask the man with the caved-in eye if he could open the door to his locker for him, and to pay for his drinks. As he leaves, he examines, behind the glass check-in counter, the arrayed small bottles of eau de cologne, de chypre, and de pompéi that only cost four francs and must have been low quality. He decides to buy one that the lady holds out to him, the plainest one, the eau de pompéi, and once he's back home, he cuts himself, as if deliberately, in opening the small steel cap that seals the flask, in several spots on his hand, he nicks his skin, the steel slips under his nail.

The Planetarium

We had just entered the cupola, this circular space where the walls displayed the city's silhouette as a shadow theater. In the center a huge black machine rose upward, mounted on a wheeled platform, like a two-headed robot, immobile but with downcast arms boding movement. I asked the man in charge how he got this machine and he answered that it had been given to him by some German engineers from the Zeiss company, who had traded it to him in 1937 for his stock of pumas. He took his place by the control panel (he was a man with a shaved head and small round glasses who I had only ever seen in white coats), but I didn't have time to make out the levers and joysticks, because it was already getting dark and the children accompanying us all had their necks craned back against the tops of their chairs. A melody arose: I recognized the opening of *Tannhäuser*; the night swelled and the stars imperceptibly imprinted themselves one by one on the celestial vault. I heard the machine's motor, its mechanisms whirring, in the darkness I tried to pay attention to each movement: the two black swaths dotted by a multitude of stellar fluctuations. Suddenly we were in pure darkness, and the children whispered to each other, afraid that bats might cling to their hair.

Finally, the man's amplified voice rang out. He launched into a popular lecture on astronomy, equal parts scientific and fantastical, unfurling a gleaming vocabulary I instantly snickered at. Using a tube pointer, he indicated the stars and planets and, like a will-o'-the-wisp, the little green arrow darted between galaxies and nebulas, constellations and Pleiades, marked out hazy objects, globular clusters, double stars, and, in this labyrinth of lights, among these three thousand stars, traced imaginary lines, delimiting a number of geometric figures, letters, and symbols. We beheld animals' heads, we saw the light of Gemini. The man apologized: the moon had burned out.

Suddenly he seemed to have lost control of the whole machine: it spiraled out of control and the sky spun vertiginously around us, and the days and nights raced past each other, seasons, equinoxes, particles slipped into space, ribbed with flitting stars, and the ropy nebulas were shot through by gaseous currents, dust clouds bloated and burst, strange spheres appeared, aurorae borealis, and the stars underwent contractions, explosions, they descended on us all. The children let out shrieks. The thrumming machine kept on running, and we heard the platform's wheels clanking against the protective wall. The expert, whose slip of the hand had thrown the universe's course out of joint, tried to calm us down: "Don't be afraid," he yelled, "what you're seeing, here and now against this celestial vault, are just the appearances of objects whose light took millions of years to reach us, and which have long since moved from their original positions!" I wondered whether this celestial dome sheltering us wasn't actually a cranial dome, and this spectacle the effect of an embolism, an abrupt clot lodging in a particular hemisphere, or insanity resulting from some hallucinogenic.

We exited the planetarium. To make up for this mishap, the man invited us to witness a demonstration of static electricity. He undressed two children with long, silken hair. And he placed them in a wire-mesh cage, barefoot on a metal base. Then, encircling the children, shooting through gleaming and crackling tubs, from one pole to the other, lightning stuck all their hair on end. Finally he gave them each a small stick to point at the other. And for a long while, from one body to the other, the boys exchanged electricity that was now attractive, now repulsive.

The Museum of the École de médecine

At the end of a hallway, at the top of a stairway, well past the class-rooms and the amphitheaters, the cold rooms, a dark and dusty door, a sign: *Anatomy Lab*, a bell. Then the face of a woman who appears in an even darker vestibule, and who listens to the visitor, who has come, he says, from the capital, to this province specifically to see this museum, but she doesn't have the right to show it to him, and inter-nally, while continuing to repeat his lines mechanically, he begs, he formulates incantations, he thinks he's enchanted her, and she lets herself be convinced, she takes the set of keys, she leaves him by himself. The door has opened onto a long gallery, like a hallway lined on both sides with tall vitrines and, carpeting the walls, huge dark wooden cabinets where he already sees faces, appearing between white cloths, orthopedic instruments, whole, circular sections taken from men's torsos and variously colored in their jars, fetuses, monsters, skeletons, and on each side of another central hallway, small, low vitrines that display more minute pieces, dismembered penises injected with wax, molds of vaginas, and anatomical preparations akin to those of the museum in Florence: outstretched half-bodies simulated in wax, disemboweled, unfurled, and with its inverted flesh fastened by needles. He trembles, he doesn't know where to go, where to turn his eyes, he almost would prefer to run down this long hall-way, fly through this room and disappear through a broken pane. He notices, specifically, in one vitrine, on the contorted and rachitic skeleton of a dwarf missing his tibia, a small label with partly faded blue ink that he starts to read: this was an acrobat, at fairs, notwithstanding his small size, he made fabulous jumps, then he had sold his body to the Faculty so he could stash away a bit of money, which had immediately been stolen from his trailer, and he had died of disappointment, and someone, no doubt a madman, in the museum's collections, had carried off his skeleton one day in a huge bag hidden under his coat, and he had been found again, several months later, in a public dump, and this is why the dwarf in this vitrine is missing his tibia these days. He goes from one vitrine to the next seeking an anomaly like his own, but he only sees cuts of dissected faces, strips of grandfathers who haven't had their mustaches removed, simply hung, with small clips, on metal rods, and eroded colored-wax molds of penises and anuses, pulled tongues full of holes and pustules, warped syphilitic faces that bemoan themselves and that have had their eyes' color and sadness reproduced in enamel. This long hallway is punctuated at its center with flayed anatomical models sneering, or posing like dancers, one arm in the air, or like Sun Kings, their bodies half bowed over an outsize stick, they're also like infants in their parks, surrounded, imprisoned. It has now been more than half an hour that he's been wandering through this museum, the door at its end still slightly open to a darkness where there cannot be seen the face of the woman who had let him enter, on his own recognizance, in case he set something on fire or he fainted. He takes some photos in haste, but the glass immediately chimes, and the furniture cracks, something unleashes against him. He puts away his camera and runs out. He thanks the woman. It is four thirty. It's the hour when all the little children leave school and, each day, as they go along the river, throw small stones at these impenetrable windows to make the shadows shake.

The Palace of Desirable Monsters

The pavilion is circular, divided into compartments that are just as much particularities. Light penetrates there, but the human beings who leave it must take an oath of silence. The subjects are not studied, they are kept in these places as a simple act of allegiance, of pity. No photos of them are taken, no words of theirs are collected. The beings that delivered them were also immediately doomed to be forgotten, as the disclosure of such conformations incurs the shame of this humanity. Special taxes are levied each year and secretly directed to the teratological pavilion. The problem is not that the beings do not die there, but that they cannot be reproduced.

Here are some of the specimens I, having flouted all the laws, or having myself escaped from my brothers, have been able to observe there.

Scales or moss growing on their skin is the most common occurrence, nobody scrapes them off, because they grow back thicker, I personally have been exempted from this; the scales, however, have a nice effect when they throw silvery or golden reflections, but nobody should ever attempt to detach them because they are attached to the skin more inextricably than fingernails are, and it is said that torn-out scales are just as much truncations of one's soul and one's knowledge. When the moss changes color and attains the thickness of hair, the subject who secrets them is given, purely out of charity, spindles and spinning wheels so that he can weave them . . .

The men with dog's or wolf's heads scare me, and yet they are the gentlest ones; in the winter frosty droplets of tears hang onto their fur, but they grunt and bare their chops to show their teeth, their penises swell amid their fur and nobody can ever be sure that they are truly gentle . . .

For this man whose head is four times larger than his body and has a weight that he cannot support, a circular room was built with a huge ottoman in its center for his head to rest upon. His body could thus have moved around by crawling around the ottoman and following the very slow movement of the sun. When night fell, he lost consciousness, each night he thought he had gone blind. It was said that this man's suffering was immense, but he had never himself seen any other human being, his food arrived through a trapdoor cut into the ceiling, he believed that the hand that operated this trapdoor, and that he sometimes saw, was that of God . . .

*The Sting of Love
and Other Texts*

The Sting of Love

The sting of love is all the more vicious given how anodyne its appearance is, like any curative chemical in a vial: colorless, unperturbed and transparent, without any suspended particles, without the tiniest bubble, and when the vial's neck is broken between two fingers, no vapors, or suffocating or even sharp smells arise from the narrow opening. Too deep a whiff of this product is headache-inducing, but the merest taste, even just a drop on the lips, is immediately sickening; on the tongue or, worse, gulped down and flowing throughout the body, it results in horrible nausea until spasms expel it. Acetone is recommended to trigger this spasm; otherwise, overly rich, absorbent food, butter or chocolate in massive quantities, gingerbreads, will do.

Injecting this beneath your skin or in a muscle doesn't arouse anything, just a slightly disagreeable feeling: usually the liquid comes back out the hole it had been injected into, otherwise it can form small aqueous nodes that harden and end up completely disappearing. It's a liquid that has to go directly into the bloodstream or the heart via a long, ultrafine needle dipped in ether; wholly fluid, it doesn't burn.

Colorless, languid, and transparent, this liquid obtains through slow distillation, repeated and complicated decanting requiring particular material, porphyry, obsidian for containers, fine sieves washed with high-altitude rainwater, dried with greasy leaves that coat the stone with a film for the liquid to decant, the particular materials for these manipulations are selected through possibly useless superstitions, obtains, then, from the blood of two young, energetic animals mixed together, strictly hot blood, drawn right from their hearts at the moment of their first union. This process won't be described further (and actually has long been kept secret from those using the sting of love), because it is dreadful: as they come upon their first pleasure here, and like the erasure of their captivity and of their ribcages painfully pierced by these needles connected to pumps, the two eagles finally set loose beneath the same dome, the two panthers intertwined in the same cage, each drunk on the other's odor, sniffing, licking, the female opening up at last to the male's fervor, collapse at the very moment of their shared joy into an endless, miserable, muted groan, into a string of sounds that tears the soul beyond eardrums, more unbearable than ultrasounds are to moray eels' overly pricked ears. If the sting of love's fluid is allowed to evaporate, on the glass there will appear here and there remnants of crystals recovering their original red color. This glass is said to be able, when raised to specific temperatures, rubbed by the fingers of psychics or those prone to sparks, to reproduce these sacrificed animals' groans.

The sting of love bears no relation to any ordinary hallucinogenic drug injection, to any liquid derived from a mushroom's spores, an alkaloid's decomposition, or an opiate juice. This dose can only be taken alone, because witnessing it results in terrible jealousy, and if two people inject themselves at the same time in the same place, they are both immediately seized with the desire to destroy each other (the fact of the beloved's presence is far more painful than any possible affliction) and the bodies found afterward are, like those after a cock-fight, riddled with bites and scratches, sometimes totally enervated. This infusion simply puts people into a dual bath. To start with, it doesn't put you to sleep, it overcomes all wellbeing, it doesn't cause any hallucinations, it simply plunges you, for hours on end, without any breaks, peaks, consequences, into loving stupefaction. This isn't just something else suddenly projected over yourself, like a hologram: it's, suddenly, in every part of your skin, another skin covering it, in every hole a tongue or a member pushing through, a million kisses, heat radiating incessantly through your body, like a soft and radiant torrent, a loving lava, suddenly the body is no longer yours, your skin is inside out and licked all over, from your mouth to your rectum, only a continual carnal flow, the open body spills, every excrescence molded, sheathed, inhaled by abstract mucoses, as if sealed in a pocket with the invoked body, to which no face can be attributed because it has all faces. A happiness so great becomes unbearable unless one is shackled, or, better yet, in bed, because the effect of this injected liquid doesn't end with any climax, it persists all the way into sleep. It is impossible here to determine the specific link between consciousness and dreams. Anyone who wants to fight against this surreptitious transition with conscious effort, who is afraid because the dream, at first still just as wholly gentle, slowly turns into a nightmare, flickering with swift animal shapes, anyone who wants to prolong this amorous stupor indefinitely with a second injection is struck with melancholy, as with a tarantula's bite, and loses speech, nails, job.

The sting of love, for all its risks, has been sold for some time, through ads in certain publications, between those for small magical stones kept on your breast against misfortune, elixirs and purgatives, hernia belts, and Angel's Water to make hair grow on the baldest of men's scalps. Those who use the sting of love would be defrauded by this pharmaceutical firm's decision, for financial reasons, to cut pure wildcat or vulture blood with chicken blood. And it was finally banned, just as, more quietly, several years ago, lachrymal vials were banned from the joke shops, because they aroused tears far too easily.

— 1979

The Knife Thrower

The small black-and-white photo, its negatives having been destroyed, scratched out first with the tip of a needle and then warped in fire; this photo, which I still have, shows him naked, stretched out on the velvet cover of a high bed with a cross over it, his eyes shut, a legionnaire's party hat on his head that is an exact paper replica of the kepi his cousin is wearing in the framed photograph on the nightstand beside him, his young cousin sent by his father, the Marshal, to Indochina, in 195–, and blown apart by a bomb explosion.

This misleading photo was taken one August night in 19—, the same month I met him, identified by a friend at a bar as a knife thrower and Mademoiselle B.'s famous lover. It was an evening when his aunt, the Marshal's wife, whose place he was staying at, was away traveling, visiting a Carmelite convent in Périgord. The doorman was asleep, he had a key to the house where the shutters were closed day and night. He successively turned on all the lights, and I explored this lair filled with heroic photos, marble busts, crystal chandeliers, and miniature planes, this never-open museum, dedicated to her husband the deceased soldier, and to her sacrificed son. The Marshal was said, after this tragic death, to have become a pederast and an opium smoker. The Marshal's wife had committed spiritually to the faith, and she spent every week giving Vietnamese afternoon teas for young boys chosen because of their resemblance to her son. A., who can be seen in this photo, was incidentally an almost exact copy of his cousin.

I took the photo in the Marshal's own room, where images of his son abounded. How had he become part of this mise en scène? Four years later, I still have no idea. He couldn't have imagined that I would be ready to blackmail him. I still didn't know, that night, how much I was worth to him, how much he coveted me. The truth was that he was the one who had chosen me. And he thought he would easily be able to get these photos back, to use a bit of violence if needed should I refuse to hand them over. We had gone to my place, bringing along these party hats that were the main component of the mise en scène. And I made him drink, thinking that it would make the shoot easier, also believing that he was the only victim of deception, and that this deception would not be mutual. I even put makeup on him.

An almost exact copy of his dead cousin in Indochina, the difference being that his left cheek bore a scar that skirted his nostril, a patch-up after a motorbike accident. Every time he ate, as he chewed, his cheek oozed a heavy, runny sweat, which he wiped with the back of his napkin, hiding it with a semblance of shame. He explained away this liquid by a missing nerve, severed during the operation.

For a month, almost every night, we had dinner together. Our usual friends' absence made this August an empty month. A., dressed entirely in black leather, told me about his adventures with ladies of the night, his misadventures rather, since they got away from him most of the time by refusing his money. When we left the restaurant, he usually insisted on taking me to Pigalle, and he talked to the hookers while pointing at me, talking about how much a double trick would cost. But the prospect of actually doing something with one of these women was never raised.

One day, when he came to my place, on pretext of feeling sticky after a prostitute's ministrations, he asked me to wash his genitals myself in my bathroom sink.

He ended up confessing his strange passion to me: knife throwing, and explained his methods to me, and that night he made me a gift of his first knife, a little knife with a broken handle that, by swiveling around its metal frame, could make a second sharp object. The blade was undamaged. Knife throwing, he told me, shouldn't be considered an art in and of itself, or a mere feat, it had to be incorporated into a show, like an additional trick within a dramatic, musical, or erotic performance. His dream was to put on a show where men in formalwear, in a château, discussed the art of knife throwing over dinner, and gradually, during their discussion, displayed their skill, practicing on the servants, blindfolding themselves, and throwing their daggers all at the same time—this was the finale of the performance—at a woman bound and gagged on the overturned table they had just dined upon, in his fantasy a captive woman these men lusted after and would have broken all ties in order to possess.

The throwing knives, plenty of which he showed me with a sort of pleasure in making me feel their weight, were hunks of narrow, sharp metal, with handles swaddled in leather straps. The knife had to be held by the blade at the moment of its throwing, making a half-turn in its trajectory. A good knife was worth its weight, it had to be several kilos. The throwing performances, he said as if to reassure me, were rigged: first of all, the handle was hollow and filled with balls of mercury which, by a fundamental law of physics, forced the knife to plunge straight and minimized any possibility of skidding; then the wooden plank the steel bored into was lined with magnets that repelled the blade away from the human shape outlined in chalk. He trained in a suburban warehouse, with other circus artists. One afternoon he invited me to come with him, and introduced me as his partner. Small posters were pinned to the walls, with his made-up, over-the-top sadist's face. He performed under the name Zagato.

He wrapped his knives in newspaper. One blade more valuable than the others had its own empty spot in a black-velvet case, like a compass or a musical instrument. He liked to stroke the blade, to feel the sharpness on his fingers' tips, and often kissed it right before throwing it with a flick of the wrist. Then his whole body thrilled, danced fluidly like an animal, dark and gleaming like a puma's rippling fur. He trained on truncated tree trunks, the human outline chalked on the plank still empty beneath the cloth that covered it, like a policeman's marks after a murdered body has been taken away in a stretcher. He declaimed the love he felt for hearing the steel split the air with a whistle, then plunge with a sudden thump, thrumming for a long while in the wood. He took his hot knife out from the cracked bark, and made me feel with my fingers how hot it was, sometimes burning.

The effects of intoxication, as a cover for deception in this unusual affair, have yet to be determined. He invited me to come to dinner with a friend of his, and what a friend this man was, who certainly had a businessman's acumen. At eleven in the evening, he was still buttoned up in a suit, his Adam's apple gripped by the knot of his tie, tapping his fingers against a briefcase. They both stayed sober the better to push me, before I had realized it, into drunkenness. The main problem with a career as a knife thrower, said A., was the lack of partners, the gradual disappearance of these brave women who served as live targets, usually out of devotion or love for their lovers, without whom a knife thrower's performance couldn't happen. Zagato had lost his own several years earlier because of a macabre agreement between steel and magnet to defy their usual repulsions. He had, in vain, been putting classified ads in the professional papers with these words: "Circus artist seeking partner for throwing performance. Good pay, insurance, travel benefits." The candidates fled when he unveiled the heaps of flying steel which their eyes had to confront. Zagato had been invited to represent France at the next international conference of knife throwers, which would take place in December on the stage at the Hong Kong Casino, and he still hadn't found a partner. When he offered me the part, I thought it was a joke, and I let out a laugh as I signed the sheet that the businessman had taken out of his briefcase incuriously, without even reading it. The abrupt change in their looks, which I saw shift from friendly to menacing, made me get hold of myself. I also wanted to get hold of the sheet, but they had taken it away, they were already giving me a duplicate with a relieved smirk, an almost sneering smile.

Starting the next morning, I had to show up each day at the suburban hangar to assist Monsieur A., better known as Zagato, as he practiced for his next performance on the Hong Kong Casino stage, where I had to appear in drag, a live target under an alias I had yet to pick, either Mademoiselle Fuchs or Mademoiselle Calypso. All the travel and insurance costs were taken care of. My monthly salary through December was four and a half thousand francs. After then, I was free to renew the contract or not.

I showed up to the first practices, trying to figure out how I could get out of them. A.'s behavior toward me changed completely: he became violent, he forced me to try on a shiny black lamé dress that had been bought in a batch of things formerly belonging to the Chinese variety-show singer Suzy Wong, and he ordered me to take hormones. For the performance to happen without any problems, he told me, I had to trust him completely. Fear was what made accidents happen. I faced, bravely at first, these knives that he threw at me full speed and which rang out as they hit just a few centimeters from my heart. I forced myself not to shut my eyes, but there was always a single second when I believed the knife had touched me and when I superimposed over us this funereal inscription: "Here lies Mademoiselle Fuchs, shredded on the stage of the casino in Hong Kong by her partner, the famous Zagato." He had grown obsessed with making the feat yet more intricate, he stood just a bit farther away every day, he threw the knife from between his legs. When he made me put on a blindfold after tying me to the board, I fainted. I announced that I had decided to stop, he could do whatever he wanted with his contract with his sleazy booking agent, nothing in the world would make me go to Hong Kong, I would press charges, in any case I was keeping these compromising photos, I threatened to show them to his aunt the Marshal's wife, or to have them published in a tabloid. He came to my place that same night in order to get them back, we punched each other. I refused to give them to him. I reminded him of that night when he turned up at my place, and when he had begged me, oddly, to wash his crotch in my bathroom sink. Apart from these punches, that was the only physical relationship I'd ever had with this boy I would never see again. The next day I ended up meeting with the booking agent who tore up the contract in front of me as I threw the rolls of film into the fire.

— 1977

Posthumous Novel

In 19—, when I was still an archivist, I learned, somewhat by accident, through a photograph published in a weekly, about the person, then the work, of a certain Jean L., who had published five short books with Éditions du Pôle, from the ages of twenty-one to twenty-eight. Shortly after his fifth volume's publication, I wrote him a letter, a long letter. But he never responded, and I had no idea whether he had even opened it, or whether it had ended up in his hands, because I sent it to his publishing house, requesting that they forward it to him, and it hadn't been found while examining the papers in the first three drawers of his dresser, where he kept all his correspondence, at the end of his bed. This letter was lost. Seven days exactly after having sent it, I read in a newspaper a short report of his suicide: he had jumped off a train from Paris that was supposed to take him to A., shortly after going through the V. train station, was what it said on this page of *faits divers*. The same day, his parents made the necessary arrangements for his body to be transported to the Porquerolles cemetery, as he'd requested in his handwritten will. Several times in the following years, I went to his grave, which was beneath a cypress, next to the grave of a father who had drowned while trying to save his son. The father and the son, I read on this slab, and according to the mother's wishes, had been buried in the same coffin: wholly familiar, through his books, with the person who was Jean L., I thought with some pleasure every time that he had to be delighted by this proximity. His books, which very slowly went out of print, weren't republished, and his name was quickly forgotten. He would be for me, too, I confess, and because my rereading and my trips to the Porquerolles cemetery became more and more infrequent, and because my life had taken another turn, growing old had brought me other endearments, other enticements for my heart, when an article in a science journal I read by chance once again gave me renewed momentum. At this point in my preamble I beg my readers to trust entirely in me.

In Holland, a deatomization effort for a particular portion of the countryside irradiated during an experiment had revealed the presence, in this countryside, hanging like clumps off of trees and, broken and sown over the ground, of countless words, incomplete sentences. These groups of overwhelmingly ordinary words only became visible under the effects of magnesium in negative ionic fusion and could only be recorded, during the brief burst of osmosis, on photosensitive film. The distinct photographs, taken by the researchers at varied intervals, revealed that, as if swept by the wind, these sentences weren't immobile, but rather moved every so often, some having disappeared, others meanwhile having agglutinated by sticking to members of prospective sentences, a sort of perpetually transforming puzzle of words. At that point, having made several presentations but finding little interest in this raw literary phenomenon, the Dutch researchers abandoned it.

Almost ten years of stubborn, secret investigation now allow me to confirm the following with absolute certainty: whether a traveler sitting in a train, a driver, or even more so a passenger in a car, or a walker going through a wood or a garden, every living being, under the effect of autonomous or mechanical locomotion (and locomotion, as a purely physical phenomenon, spurs and speeds the flow of the being's thoughts), propels the various movements of this thought temptingly and hurriedly toward this or that part of the countryside; at the exact moment when his or her view, in accordance with the thought, but more or less clouded and blinded, tricked by it, lands on this or that part, leaf on a tree, bend in a path, horizon, the sentence—but it's often a single name, like a romantic incantation—takes root at that spot in the countryside, roadside dust, branch shaken by the wind, setting sun.

The Dutch researchers proved it: not only are these sentences, this primary literary formation, not physically lost, because a single ionic combination is enough to make them legible, but also these sentences are not stable, they move, advance, retreat, dwindle or accumulate, grow prettier or uglier just as they do under the writer's patient hand.

And it's here that I plead with the reader, yet again and more than ever, for his or her full trust: I am a thoroughly sensible man (but doesn't the madman insist that he's reasonable?), who isn't impelled by any whim, and what I'll disclose now should reveal not so much a novelistic fillip as a vital message of what happens in the hereafter.

The sentences, tossed out by the living, perhaps unthinkingly or in the darkest moments of their despair, and the meanings of which offer no help in determining where they settled, are in fact nourishment for the dead, who don't eat, and who spend their time, whether in hell or in heaven, hunting for the rarest sentences, as the bee gathers the flowers' sap to bring it back to the hive, or weeding out the most useless sentences, endlessly and sleeplessly wandering souls spinning around these clumps of words just to gather honey. The sentences are the dead's nourishment and their monuments, they are their works, their novels, they slowly and patiently stitch them together through countless comings and goings, and sometimes words fall from their pockets or their overflowing bags, and they cross boundaries to make baroque combinations, and each point on the horizon and each night's setting sun abounds in these repasts they delight in (the thoughts of the living, or of those who had been). The hardest-working souls devote themselves to clearing the landscape of its filthy or indifferent sentences, but there are dedicated souls focused solely on reconstituting the very first drafts of some great writer's peregrinations. Wonderful works float, inaccessible to us, in the atmosphere and are seen again and again by the most meditative members of the dead's populace. The most tortured or uncertain souls, the ones who never made anything out of their living, go backwards down the path of their lives and their wanderings again, both in geography and in history, and try to regain and recollect the sap of their youth. The awful souls do nothing but drift hopelessly, according to the rules, to rub out, with the erasers of their tears and their worn-out fingers, their tired lips, their horrifically vile imaginations. The animals have all sorts of other concerns (maybe an animist researcher will uncover them someday) but there are some loving souls whose entire work for eternity consists solely of edifying a single word, usually a first name or a sweet yet immense whisper, made from an assemblage of thousands of worn-out or incomplete words the slavish souls had tossed into the vast garbage pit. So it goes for a particular country where wind currents bring wandering souls to a very strange monument made of a single giant letter, a T, which had to be cemented together by breaking apart several previous novels to intermingle the letters.

But let's go back to Jean L., who seems to have gotten away from us ever so slightly. The reasons for his suicide were never fully cleared up, and moreover, in several interviews before his death, he who had never written a novel, and at the same time had done nothing but write, like so many others, in hopes that he might, someday, have written a novel, he had declared that he had just started a work, indeed, which might be a novel. But, among his papers, nobody found anything more than a few scattered and enigmatic bits that hadn't even had enough time to become a draft.

I thought that maybe, by carrying out this sort of investigation, like a dead soul's gathering, which consisted of "x-raying," throughout his final trajectories, and especially the one right before his death—which is to say meandering through the countryside on each side of the Paris–V. line's railroad tracks—the greatest possible number of his thoughts, extricating them, like precious stones from an excavation, from the rubble of all the trivial or ordinary thoughts of those passengers who had followed him on this path, I might both gain information about the reasons for his death, and perhaps reconstitute the bulk of the novel he was planning to write. The circumstances of his suicide and the theme of his novel, which he hadn't been able to write, having been interrupted by death, were thoroughly interwoven.

I ask the reader to imagine me, for a few seconds, during my various wanderings, like a visionary, or like a preposterous butterfly hunter, busy following these grim railroad tracks, and, every few meters, setting off these sodic explosions so as to detect, in the nighttime landscape in fusion, the strongest concentrations of thoughts, disentangling them, photographing them, then magnifying them, and recognizing his turns of phrase (the thoughts preceding his death already had a literary shape, they were all oriented toward this dream of a novel) and then setting them in the silence of the library where I worked and where I returned every night, because it was the only place large enough to welcome all the loot I poured out, and which came back together into long strips of sentences repeatedly interrupted, stuck together, and then undone.

I found, on the side of the railroad, sixty-three kilometers from the V. train station, a pile of particularly condensed and enduring thoughts, untouched, and which can be found here at the end of the novel: I have every reason to believe that these are the living's very last thoughts, because the sentences that burst with the spasmodic pulse of blood from a sliced vein, and like red flowers thrown onto the cortege, these sentences traced an empty space, and where the grass oddly enough had never grown back, like the outline of a bullet-riddled body the policemen had traced in chalk on the ground, a twisted and charred space, smashed in by the body that the train's speed, I had asked some specialists, must have imbued with increased weight. However I wasn't able to find any bundles of sentences around Jean L.'s grave in Porquerolles, the way some of the tombs' occupants give rise to painful posthumous flowers. Either L. isn't this grave's real occupant, which is fairly unlikely, or he fell silent for once and for all to engage in other activities (some sentences visible in various landscapes lead me to believe that the dead also indulge in painting, but I would be awfully curious to make out their motives and their methods, which perhaps will be clarified someday), or maybe he even felt that his novel had had enough time to finish itself by the end of the trip he then had to declare his own death as the terminus and as the end of his novel.

Consequently there are crude remarks in this book, because it wasn't really written, it was stitched together, created from the thoughts of a man right before his death, and there are holes, shifts in tense, superscript numbers that lead nowhere, like a ghost train's stations, and so a blank appendix. There are repetitions, because Jean L., at that extreme moment in his life, got stuck on particular obsessions, and broad uncertainties as he hadn't completely decided, at the moment of his death, on the exact shape he wanted to give his novel.

I haven't added a single word, I've only reconstituted. Maybe I'm completely wrong, maybe this assemblage is completely absurd and L. would have disowned it? The reader can always construct another book out of the material provided, I urge him or her do so with imaginary scissors . . .

— 1982

A Screenwriter in Love

It would be a story, and the characters would be those of a short story, or a failed novel. It wouldn't matter what they were named: the little one and the big one, the youngster and the oldster, the beanpole and the billiard ball, the pursuer and the pursued, the sneak and the sly one, it really doesn't matter. The story would have several beginnings and would just keep on delaying its end: that's why this novel couldn't be written. Such a fulfillment would put an end to that vaunting ambition.

One of those false starts would take place in a provincial town, on the seashore, during one of those early sunny days. The young one is in love with a girl, an actress, who herself is in love with a marquee name, a theater-stage reverie. Love has to follow the principle of communicating vessels. The girl holds in her hand a rolled-up poster, and on the wall, all of a sudden, there unfurl a pale, stripped-down citadel, a dark blue lake with turrets rising out of it, or maybe just one, memory is so easily mistaken. The actress says: "It's *Massacre à Paris*, it's playing at Villeurbanne, we can't go there, there are too few performances, see those footbridges there, the actors go from one tower to the other, the whole scene is performed by the lake, and at the end the performers whose throats have all been slit fall into it, they're floundering in all this blood, it's just crazy." For the first time his name is uttered. She's never seen him herself, she's just read the reports in the papers, but she sends him her photo, and he does the same.

Another of those false starts would be a fleeing of sorts. That Saturday he told his parents he was leaving for school, as usual, but that he might not come back for lunch. He settles down on the roadside, hitches a ride to Paris. That evening, he goes to the Théâtre de la Gaîté lyrique to see this crazy man's play. *La Dispute.* He leaves, amazed. This amazement, however, wasn't pointless: how could he describe it? He had been told a story, he had seen a forest, some nights, and the trajectory of his entire life seemed to have been traced, his heart and his mind, his body and his politics. But there's still something inexplicable there: like a mystery, a breakdown, unspeakability, he doesn't even know how to say why one might remain so attached to a work, just one, for their entire life, like a mirage, and how it would be easier to cut off one's hand rather than sacrifice this admiration, especially when it's at the edge of the adult world: but isn't this mystery just courage, pure and simple? Having the courage to be oneself, to speak for oneself, to present oneself, and to liberate every secret, to invent them?

The final start—because this text would take on the characteristics of infinity, the abyss, and take on the temptation to self-destruct—goes quickly: the young one is on the back of a motorcycle driven by an actor who's speeding in the gloominess, the drizzle. Final day of shooting: a gray-and-ocher factory courtyard, a spliced-in exterior, dogs barking at the end of their handler's leash, an old car, a camera. A quick introduction. A look. Pages to be written on this look.

The actor is in love: so many love stories. A fame-hungry rising star, he doffs Davy Crockett's coonskin cap, sabers champagne bottles like a Polish great-grandfather, jumps in the elevators to break them, one night his car takes him to a moonlit forest lake: he's become part of the performance. One time he says he's an orphan, one time he says he performs because he saw his mother cry the day Gérard Philipe died, always the same story. He stops in front of an immense wall surrounding a building, an orphanage in fact, he says "I wasn't there myself, I was at the boarding school next door, but we ran off, and at recess time it was cigarettes we launched, there was always one lying around." The actor says he doesn't want to perform anymore with that director because he always positions him in the dark and nobody recognizes him on the street, that he got into this line of work to be in the light. Later on, sheer drunkenness leads him to bang like a madman on that same director's door, shouting his name.

The beanpole, too, is in love. He lives in an attic bedroom as long and narrow as a hallway, with iron bars at the end, and he arranges for the director a dinner of white lilies, oysters, and camembert that will starve the starving man. He has him listen to old shellac records. Then he asks him: "May I kiss you?"

One night—everything happens at night—he knocks himself out with sleeping pills, he dozes on his narrow child's bed, he's put back on this faded pink shirt that he used to wear to school for the horrid gym class. A few hours earlier, the other one had said: "I won't see you anymore" or "I can't see you anymore" and slumped down with his sunglasses in the backseat of a cab. He runs at full speed down the steps into the Opéra métro station, he cries, he screams, a voice that he'd never known before rises up from his chest and shrieks through his mouth, and he doesn't care if everyone sees him like this. Sheer chance had put a set of vinyl singles in his hands at that moment, all last summer's hits. He sits on a bench to wait for the métro, he isn't screaming anymore, he's still crying. Next to him sits a Black, whose presence he senses, who's looking down at him warmly, and who takes the singles from his hands to look at them, and with each title he starts singing the tune to console him. He hears some knocking in his dream. It's impossible that the guy could have come back. He gets up, stumbling, disbelievingly, he opens the door: the other man is there, soaked in the rain, he collapses in his arms. The other one carries him to his small bed, they fall asleep in innocence.

He told him the story of the Black with the discs, it's a secret. He'll see that secret told again in a film he hasn't written. The guy betrayed him. Other secrets will be found one day in an article or in a press kit. Together they start telling a story, they pose themselves the problem of betrayal. Of love: the work becomes akin to a visiting room, a cistern where they give up.

— 1982

For P.
Dedication in Invisible Ink

My feelings about this man were skewed: even as I could have said that I loved him, when I found myself before him, at long last, I wanted to go for his throat.

I dreamed that I lived in his apartment, but this dream wasn't murderous yet, I wasn't taking the possessions of a dead man for myself, he had handed them down to me, out of weariness, out of friendship, he had wanted new furniture, and he had left me the old, frayed velvet couch, the too-low, mismatched chairs, the star system hanging from gold rods, his childhood puppet theater, the moth-eaten curtains, the magnifying glasses ringed with dark wood, all the objects dearest to him, the stuffed owl and the bride's coronet with wax pearls, the small empty cushion under its funereal cloche, he had bequeathed them to me, with no regrets, and I was alone, now, in this too-big apartment, sitting in one of those too-low chairs that smelled like rotting roses, it belongs to me but I didn't know how to occupy it, every motion and every step terrified me, I was like the heretical intruder who had tampered with the seals. This apartment which I had paced around so many times, not as a friend, much less as a lover, but as a simple collaborator, walking softly, almost slipping along the long varnished wooden slats that made the floor look like the overturned horizon seen from a sinking ocean liner, was one that I felt I could have paced through many years later without looking, while blindfolded, one that right now, from afar, I could list all the images and all the trinkets thereof, the fiery manes his father had painted, the skinny teenagers, the sensual smokers, Hoffmann's monsters, the skeletons frozen in their dance, all the way down to the repulsive dust tinting the covers of certain books permanently, the never-used makeup bag, the earthenware pitcher and basin, all of a sudden I dropped them out of a window, higgledy-piggledy, so they would shatter in the dumpster full of trash from a cleaning company, rather than kiss them or revere them in silence I threw them into the fire, my dream was long gone.

With my folder, which inevitably grew thicker each year, under my arm, I rushed up the stairs; the huge white steps that unfurled in curves like marble slats of a monumental fan, I took them in twos (and, in my dreams, twice that) with astonishing energy, and I grazed the banisters' corners, as if to prove to myself that I knew this path by heart, and that it couldn't trip me up, even those stormy days that darkened it almost completely, like the racing lanes the athlete has mastered. Upon reaching the third floor, I was panting; standing in front of his door, I allowed myself the time to catch my breath, to present myself to him in the most detached, unconcerned way possible, like a clerk, my breath calm, but also sometimes, on particular afternoons filled with rage, with this sharp resentment that he was already arousing within me, I took pleasure, rather, in arriving with my heart pounding, my breath halting, barely able to say a word for a few minutes, as if to scare him. The huge dark-blue varnished wooden door bore no inscription or trace other than the scratches of the burglars' crowbar that had warranted additional reinforcement, usually no sound emerged (I say no inscription, although I was almost jealous of this rudimentary, illegible graffiti that a key or a penknife evidently caught in the act had left on his door); a peephole, which was never closed, let through a small speck of living light that I expected the moment his steps, which were decisive, always late in terms of the doorbell, and which often were accompanied by the noise of a cigarette being lit, or a cigarillo being relit, came and announced this fleeting shadow who disturbed, for at most a second, the burst of thoroughly infinitesimal light. Then my heart, despite having been calmed, started pounding again, and I hurriedly shifted my folder to the other hand, so that the hand I held out to him wouldn't be damp. Often, in fact, well before he'd had the time to be close enough to the peephole which could betray my movements, I brought my hand up to my forehead in order to push back the rings that could have come loose in the wind, I always walked with my head down as I went to his place. Finally he opened the door, and each time his gaze, which, depending on the day, could be oblique or direct and up to the final visits, directly touched my heart. He saw it, and every so often the depravity of this gaze seemed to be all the more aware of its effect, of dumbfounding me. I held out my hand, dried on my pants, and he, shorter than I was, brought his lips to my face. I quickly stepped past him to enter the room, I heard his voice behind me, and I didn't turn around, I was terrified at the thought that he might make out something ridiculous in how I dressed. I had never been as ashamed as in his presence of a loose hem, of a frayed shirt collar, of a regular stain, even of a too-new watch band that might stick out of a sleeve with a gleam I suspected he would consider vulgar. He himself was, as always, badly enough, or rather indifferently dressed, with drab, ordinary clothes, but he often allowed himself such remarks on my dress, as if to mortify me a bit more. He knew how much I felt physically uncomfortable in front of him, and he took pleasure in it with a teasing irony that was more caring than it was disagreeable. Sometimes he told me, looking down at my pants: "Oh yes, that's a style that I don't like at all, I'd never wear that," sometimes acknowledging my jacket: "Oh but it's been two years that you've been wearing the same jacket, you could just buy another one," sometimes, touching my tie with his fingertips: "What a horror, it's a mourning tie, you're crazy to wear that!"

He was superstitious. Some days, because they were indicated on the calendar by a number that he deemed evil, he didn't see anyone and stayed shut up at home. By contrast he had his chosen days, those on which he began a new project, accepted an order, or signed a contract. He was born on the Day of the Dead.

For a long time, I had held out hope for some Christmas or birthday gift from him. Coming from him, the most ordinary gift would have taken on extraordinary value, but this gift did not come. For years I waited, knowing all the while that should he himself ever suspect my plea, he would have found it vile and pretentious. One Day of the Dead or another, on the second or third year, I don't remember anymore, as if to reveal my wish to him, the other way around, I decided, in the tiny studio apartment I lived in, to choose one of my few things, and one of those, specifically, that I cared most about, and to bring it to him, without a box, without wrapping paper, the better to show its origins, it was this matte porcelain, this snow sleigh full of flower petals borne by two nude angels. He wavered, then went to set it in his bedroom, not far from the stuffed owl, this bedroom, always in half-darkness, which I had only ever gained access to by probing, clandestinely, by noticing, with a skewed glance, socks sticking out of boots, or a towel thrown on a chair. As for his intimate life, I didn't want to know anything, I didn't ask him any questions and when I realized one day that someone had entered this bedroom, and might be able to go into it again, and when, in a conversation, with this truly intense pleasure that consists of talking to a third party about a person one loves, he was on the verge of saying the name, I went deaf by sheer will, and relegated that person to the state of an other, an initial. In front of him, I only spoke of that person as the letter X.

For a long time, we had called each other *vous*, and when his body lay on mine, I still called him *vous*. Then his body no longer lay on mine, never again did so, and years later we were still calling each other *vous*. One day, helped along by some wine, or the joy of a discovery at work, he said: "It's been so long that we've been calling each other *vous*, maybe we could call each other *tu*, couldn't we?"

The response to my gift never did come, and I waited for it in vain, I did not give him another one. But I'm lying when I say that his body never again lay on mine. Every year, but only once a year, like a birthday, on an unforeseen date that he alone was able to set, he only had to say a word, or rather shoot me a glance, for me to give myself up to him, for me to immediately get undressed and lie on the ground, whether it was made of ice or fire, in front of him, for my knees to fold, for my arms to enclose him. I never did get to hold him for longer than it took to climax, he fled again, and I ended up taking these yearly embraces as exams of a kind, tests of availability or blindness, and they revolted me, each time I found them more tepid and mechanical, a tepidness that was horrible and humid. The year preceding the event that I'm going to describe, I pulled back and left him to the depths of his drunken misery.

Often, when I had a meeting with him, always at his place, I forced myself to be overly punctual. But every time at first, he wasn't there, he was delayed by an earlier meeting, or had forgotten ours, or claimed to have forgotten it, and after having enacted the already-ritual actions of shifting the folder from one hand to the other, then wiping off any potential dampness on the inside of my pants, then running this hand through my hair at the very last minute, that of the doorbell ringing, I had to accept the proof that he was absent. But maybe he was at home, busy, or he wasn't alone, I turned around to see if anybody might catch me and I brought my eye up to the peephole but it only gave me a sensation of luminous cold, and ultimately I was relieved, hearing the loud ring of the phone, to notice that nobody picked up. I sat on a step, even in the sharpest cold, and I waited for him, fifteen minutes, thirty minutes, an hour, I didn't move, holding back from taking out the book that was in my folder, I only cursed him, like a premonition of all the curses that I would cast on his head, I cursed him for not having warned me, nor having left a note on his door (I knew without a question that I would have jealously kept the briefest and blandest note he'd written), I stayed seated on my step but mentally I saw myself get up, and attach a wire to the ring that hung at the top of the stairwell or to one of the banister's patterns, and I let myself fall into the void, strangled by the wire that had uncoiled, I saw my body bounce around and I saw him come, quickly, taking off his sunglasses, lighting a cigarette, and I took pleasure in seeing him bump into my dangling feet and look up at my blue face. But he was actually coming and pretended to be surprised, he offered a mechanical, hurried apology, and opened his door. As if out of respect for myself, as if to grant myself this respect that he refused me, I talked and played down how long I had been waiting, I lied and he wasn't fooled, I was freezing cold and he didn't offer me anything warm to drink, we went directly to his work table. Our only interviews played out that way the first years, but from the third year, and for me that was like a slow, insidious victory that at the same time hurt me as much as an excision of what was still dearest to me, this uncommon feeling I had for him, so bewilderingly positioned between love and friendship and admiration, I didn't expect it anymore, I didn't sit on the icy step anymore, I went down to the café, as he had suggested. He found me there, apologized, and we drank a coffee together, he joked, we talked about all sorts of things, ordinary things that we almost never allowed ourselves to talk about on our own. The fourth year, but maybe I'm moving too quickly through this chronology, a little note with the first letter of my first name, and which was ended with the first one of his, was stuck in a groove of the door. I unfolded it with relish, even hoping occasionally that he wouldn't be there, just so that this note, which still bore a minimum of feeling, could be present in his stead. I put it in my pocket and went down to the café. The fifth year, a phone call, early in the morning, usually let me know that the meeting had been pushed back or moved up. One day in the sixth year, not seeing any paper sticking out from the door, and being certain that he would be there, I was stricken to have to ring repeatedly into the void, and I was determined not to wait for him, even for five minutes. Out of fear of seeing him on the street, I rushed to catch a cab to get home. I only left a small note on his door, which he told me was harsh and unarguable when he called me, the ringing preceding me as I was still climbing my stairs, and I knew it was him. I talked to him coldly and took another cab to meet him. He was especially warm. Every time after that, I could be sure that he would be there, that he wouldn't be a minute late. The king of the jungle had been tamed, or maybe it was the lion that subdued its tamer, but one or the other, at this point of submission, attacked the other in hopes of breaking him, and these visits grew increasingly rare. The break-up happened over the course of the seventh year, bit by bit, as if by blows, and neither the assailant nor the stronghold, at risk of breaking their necks, wanted to bow down.

At this time, his apartment which hadn't yet been sold to be turned into offices, was laid out thus: one entered through a sort of large entryway, more of a hallway, which led, on the left, to the kitchen and, on the right, to the always-shut or -ajar bedroom door, then, straight ahead, there was a door leading to three rooms in succession, with windows overlooking the street, first a living room where he received his visitors, but which was also a reading room, a sort of antechamber to the actual office one then walked into, and which was almost exclusively made up, apart from the sculptural bookshelves carved from raw timber covering the entire back wall, of simple planks on trestles covered with old, well-worn curtains where, books and folders for his ongoing work were piled up higgledy-piggledy, and, somewhat in the center, a larger table that served as desk, at the crux of all the other tables flowing in successive rows toward it. His armchair of carved, deep wood, faced the windows, as did the little, wobbly chair in which his four or five colleagues, backlit in the various stretches of time allotted to them, followed one another. It's on that chair that I sat over six years to carry out this unattainable work that we wrote twelve different versions of, before giving it up. It often happened that the hour spent on our work would impinge upon another's, and that two colleagues would see each other, worriedly, one shyly holding out a hand to the other in front of him, secretly enraged to find the chair occupied or, conversely, to have to concede it.

This office, where he sometimes had me listen to a bit of music, or put a photo album in my hands, to have me wait during a long phone conversation, led to an unused library at the very back of the apartment that was more of a stockroom and that he had tried to turn into a guest room, which very soon looked, despite its bed with sheets and covers, like the forgotten bedroom in some horror film that had once been the dear, long-dead person's; on the other side, the office led to his bedroom, and it sometimes happened, during the time set aside for work, that he went either to unplug his phone in one or the other or both of the rooms, or to take the office handset into his bedroom so that, once there, he could indulge in a more intimate conversation every word of which I listened to. If one crossed his bedroom, which I had the chance to do once, my heart pounding, like a thief, when he'd gone down with the preceding visitor (what did such a considerate gesture that he'd never performed for me mean?), one would find oneself in the entryway, which had long remained empty, until he decided to fill it with a table, some chairs, and to buy tableware.

One of those working days, because, as I've already said, and in this respect my account is in danger of seeming like a long thread of jealousy, we no longer had any relationship apart from work, he apologized for being in poor shape, for having little energy. He had had too much to drink, he said, the night before, it was specifically the eve of the Day of the Dead, I specifically held back from pointing out that I'd recalled this birthdate, and as I'd just noticed the presence of the new table and chairs placed in the entryway, he added: "Yes, I was celebrating my birthday, and for the first time here, I had my friends over, it's amazing how nice it is to have dinner at my place." I won't need to describe the effect that these words had.

In fact, the only sign of friendship he gave me was these postcards he sent me from each of his trips, to Rio de Janeiro or Budapest, and the few well-worn phrases on them, which he suddenly wasn't stingy with anymore, became a balm in the general desert.

Each time that one of my books came out, one of those books that I might not have written and brought out if not for him, not so much to prove to him that I could stand on my own as out of fear that he might abandon me one day, in this work that we had undertaken together, and that I clung to at all costs, because it was bound to him, because it bound me to him, to assign it to someone else, someone known and renowned, he simply thanked me over the phone with two or three warm words, which cost him nothing, which left behind no trace. And so I tried, in turn, through my books, to be someone even slightly known and renowned so that my name might one day be connected to his, and in equal measure, like a secret marriage, on some poster, in some paper.

For six years, I put myself at his disposal and I handled his requests before everything, before my own work, which only existed at the outset to fill the voids that his absence and his other projects, like betrayals of our own, made me suffer. I waited for him. He could give me no news for six months, and one day or one night he might enter the fray anew, and insist on dozens of pages from me that he would, under my eyes, set to striking through, underlining, copying out, as if to attribute them to himself through his own writing. He could wake me up at three o'clock in the morning, from the telephone switchboard of the hotel in some foreign country that his work was detaining him at for months, to dictate a list of revisions, which often consisted of moving around commas, and which I had to transfer, no later than the following day, to the next version, which might be the sixth, but which he would decide that we would not have anyone read, and that also meant, even though for four years I hadn't received a cent for this work, completely retyping a hundred pages, bribing secretaries, sneaking at night or on Sunday afternoons into the only office that I had access to with machines capable of the individual characters that worked for him, and paying for photocopies, then sending him the new copy via express delivery, and waiting for his further revisions. And for six years I put myself at his disposal, I waited, if those terms could have some reality, my heart and soul wide open, for him to come and skim off, like a tithe, like a puncture deep within myself, the froth, all the salt on the surface of the drained water, the cream left on the tainted milk emptied of its essences (that milk was, a bit, all my other writing, which even so had to darken the pages of five or six volumes, but in retrospect I had to admit that it was this writing that I originally attached the least value to, the abated writing of withdrawal, that was the most valuable). And in exchange for that, no gratification: I wasn't, and it was rather vain of me to regret it, one of the few friends who would sit at his new birthday table: he often took care to omit my name in those interviews where he was supposed to talk about our work.

However, to soften slightly the bitterness of these recriminations, I have to recall this tacit contract that, from the outset, he suggested to me, and that I accepted joyfully: not to be his ghost-writer, as all the foregoing might lead one to think, but to work together in total freedom, without either of us being paid, to be able to take our work where exactly we want to take it, without any external constraint of time or money. This was possible because each of us, on different levels, had a work that sustained us. But two years after this pact, for the first time, he betrayed it.

— 1982

Vertigoes

The doctor examining me gazed at the back of my eye with a thin beam of light, then used many low-weight hammers all over my body to provoke shudders, nervous contractions, he grasped my lower lip and said "You're suffering from vertigo, aren't you?"

1. I spent the night with T. We got up, I'd already taken a shower, and we got dressed, we went down together to have breakfast at Madame Odile's, then we went back up and T. undressed again to take a shower. Suddenly the phone rang for me and I left T. lying on my bed to go answer my mother in the next room, in my office. My mother's voice was pleasant, she had just spent several days with her sister, we talked about the bad weather that was common to the two places we were speaking from. I hang up and I go back to my room, T. isn't there anymore. I go into the bathroom, where the door is shut almost all the way, maybe I'll find T. there. No, he's not there. I go back into the office, he's not there either. I call his name, he doesn't answer. I think he's hiding, and my worry starts to grow as I look behind each door in vain. He can't be on the balcony, he can't have left the apartment. I haven't heard him and his form, however fleeting in my field of view, would have betrayed him if he had wanted to get to the windows. I go from one room to the next and then I think that maybe he's moving around at the same moment I am, contrariwise, behind my back, right under my nose. My tone turns to begging: there's no chance, given our closeness, that he won't notice the intense fear that's overcome me.

Because, in positioning myself on the threshold of the two rooms, a leg on each side, and swiveling my head from one side to the other, I see that he can't be following me, or preceding me, because he isn't there. Now I know that he can't be anywhere in the apartment. Within a few seconds, I think I've gone crazy, I'm seized by a horrendous vertigo that feels like my own death: I've never known T., because he's not there, because nothing betrays his presence. The nature of our friendship means he would have shown himself a long while ago, he wouldn't have abandoned me in my terror. He doesn't exist, I made him up. Or maybe it's me who doesn't have any existence in these rooms, who's never lived there. I must have been dead for a long while, I'm a ghost, an out-of-place guest. It's T. who is alive, the tenant of these rooms I loved in dozens of years ago, before my death. My hand is close to a glass door and I think I can reach my wrist through to come back to reality, to make my blood and the clamor of glass come to my aid. I scream. But I hear T.'s voice, he's coming out from under my quilt, on my bed (I'd completely forgotten this possibility, as I searched my eyes had glided over this bunched-up shape without the least suspicion), I grab a pile of clothes on the floor and with a yell I throw them at his face, coins fly out onto the walls and fall down again, papers, a marble from his childhood that he always keeps in one of his pockets as a lucky charm. I sob, he holds his hand out to me. I notice that I slipped on the hallway rug, and with my white shirt hanging off a door handle, with the small sheets of paper scattered around, this empty, ravaged field of view, with its rumpled rug, T. being out of sight, is the exact reflection of my terror, of his disappearance. I get up coldly and go into the next room to get my camera, I turn around to sit on the bed where T. is still lying, and I take out the lens, I aim at the empty space, and I say "image of a terror." But before I'm able to take the photo, T. tears the camera out of my hands and takes the final photos of the roll, uses it up. As he puts it back together brusquely, he breaks the camera. I scold him. He cries like a baby and refuses to admit the reason for his sadness.

2. I was with M. in Berlin, we'd set aside a day to cross the border and that Tuesday, as of ten o'clock in the morning, we were in the East. But the art museum where I wanted to find the Leibls, the Liebermanns, had most of its rooms closed. And the two cafés I wanted to take M. to, those two cafés where I had gone with T. two years earlier, were closed: the first one every Tuesday, the second one only opened at ten o'clock at night, right before the time we were supposed to return to the West. With nothing to do, we wandered up a street that was called the Street of Pretty Houses, where all of them were ugly. We went into the Jewish cemetery to walk among the graves, but they were all identical, and unremarkable. M. wanted to leave right away, just as he wanted to leave East Berlin. But at the end of the very long wall surrounding the cemetery rose up a strange tall building, a tower of red bricks bearing the placard House of Youth. Not since we had entered the East had we stepped into any home, other than the museum, other than a café where we had had to get in line behind the other customers, and I decided that we would visit this house before leaving. M. was reluctant, but I was already going up the steps, which were high and steep, strewn with crates of empty bottles. As M. followed me, I didn't turn around: I knew that it would only take him a single word to convince me not to go any further. Suddenly I felt scared, but all the same I pushed open the swinging door and ended up, before I could figure out what had happened, in an immense room completely filled with people sitting, each one older than the last, talking in the silence with their hands and wearing small flat paper hats topped by cubes

that they rotated every so often, as if they were augmenting their conversations with additional signs. On the faces of those cubes, indeed, were drawn different objects or animals, kettles, chickens, vacuum cleaners, wheelchairs, hedgehogs. Everyone turned toward us. I'd already started to take a step back when I tripped over the back of a very small man: he turned around, and not only did he have one of those cubes on his hat, but also, despite his very small proportions, a long ropy beard of black tow corkscrewing down to his feet. When he looked up to meet my gaze, he let out piercing shrieks, barely human tones akin to some words as one might hear from the lips of those who had never been taught how to talk. M. rushed down the stairs at full speed. I left the threatening dwarf. Once M. and I were alone again, in the empty street, at the foot of the building, we decided never to tell anybody the story: nobody would believe it.

3. I didn't know T. yet. I'd been living in Paris again for a while: I was barely eighteen, I was staying in a single narrow room with a window closed off by iron bars. I fell sick and, as I had no friends to come and take care of me, after having endured several days without any real medicine, and as my fever was worsening, I decided to take a train to see my parents. But the five hours on the train were my undoing: when my parents came to pick me up at the station, I was barely conscious. They put me in bed and called a doctor. But the doctor took a while to come, and in my bed, the entire room seemed to spin around me. I couldn't get my bearings anymore within the surrounding space: between it and me there seemed to be an unbearable lack of proportion that meant I would disappear, sometimes the room was tiny and my body too large to live in it, sometimes my thoroughly infinitesimal body drowned in the humongous space. I was scared, I screamed. My mother came to my

bedside. I saw her face hunched over me and I glimpsed something like a life-saving equation in this face. I had to kiss her lips as quickly as I could, or rather she had to kiss mine, this contact alone could restore my place within my room, within my world, within my life. If my mother didn't want to kiss my lips, then all I had to do was throw myself out of the window. I begged her: my delirium scared her, she pulled away, and I saw that, in the hallway, she was saying something about her fright to my father. I couldn't throw myself out of the window: my mother had shut it, she had even pulled the shutters closed. So I got up and went into the hallway, pressing my fists into my eyes, and as I banged into the walls, in this forced blindness, in this darkness streaked with glimmers, trapdoors, radiant monster, I made my way to the bathroom, to the one mirror in this apartment: my mother refused to kiss my lips, the only solution I had now was the guarantee of my own face. I groped around and turned on the light, felt the cold sink against my belly, and opened my eyes again in front of the mirror: I recognized myself and I came back down to the level of reasonable men.

— 1982

Obituary

For three days, I had been waiting for P.'s call (apparently, the proof is in these lines, I was in a rush to insert him into a story). I went to bed around ten o'clock, after having dined alone, a bit sick. I had set pills for my throat beside my watch at the foot of my bed; bending down to turn off the light, I had noticed a heap of dust and hair that I had disgustedly picked up with my fingertips and I had stood up again to go throw them in the trash. I was awakened at eight forty by someone dead. The phone rang, I turned on the light to see what time it was. I immediately thought it had to be P. If I could have guessed, as one reasonably might have, that it might be a colleague from the paper calling me to bury a dead man, I wouldn't have picked up, I would have betrayed my tribe. I was horribly disappointed to hear the woman's voice. I even struggled to say no to the job, but it was an esteemed ornithologist who had died, I felt accountable. I asked what time the piece needed to be dictated, my colleague lied to me, she said ten o'clock. I hung up, it was eight forty-five, I still had an hour and fifteen minutes. I got up immediately, shaved and showered, while waiting for my hair to dry—I knew I couldn't write anything if my head hadn't been washed—I rummaged through the folders on my shelves for some information about this British ornithologist dead on the eve of his seventy-ninth birthday. I pulled out all my ornithology dictionaries and went out, my head still a bit damp, it was nine ten; I brought along, to read at the café, the longest article about this ornithologist written in his lifetime. On the street I came up against gazes I didn't usually meet: those of needy children, and of those red beings who had spent their night digesting horse meat. A man leaning over a trash case plucked out a sheaf of torn-up letters. I tried to sneak up on him, but he didn't want to explain his action, and he peered at me in an askew, vacant, not even bitter way that I was determined to outdo. The idea occurred to me to besmirch the ornithologist's memory, to only dictate falsehoods that nobody would ever bother to check, I'm still the only ornithology specialist at this paper and in this country. I actually get the feeling that some of my colleagues don't know what this word entails despite its commonness, or whether I care more about birds, about insects, about earthworms, about platypuses. But I lingered at the café, rereading my article while chewing on a dry croissant. The fat woman wasn't used to seeing me at that hour, when I left and looked at my watch, it was nine thirty. I had very little time left, half an hour, barely enough time to get back to my place, go up five floors, set the croissant I'd started eating on the mantle of the chimney while thinking that I would finish it once I'd taken care of my obligations, brush my teeth, and start working. I was scared of the stenographers most of all. I'd used them twice, when sent by the paper to distant countries for ornithology events. I'd learned that dictating an article was a huge humiliation: the nasty stenographers made me repeat my name over and over like I was an impostor, accepted the number of sheets I would be giving them with exasperated sighs, tried to get rid of me by transferring me to other stenographers, cut off the call, promised to call me back, forced me to repeat particular sentences, always the most frustrating ones to repeat, making it clear by the tone of their voice just how useless and shameful my stories were, they who were the first to hear about coups, airplane crashes, and the deaths of the powerful. I did my best to dictate commas and to spell proper names, despite their entreaties: I knew in any case that the day after the next I would read an article completely unlike the one I had composed, ignominiously bylined with my name, an atrocious fantasy that the pitiful gazes of my colleagues and the countless letters from unhappy readers would make me regret. Such corrections would make me suicidal: each clarification brought me even lower in the eyes of these jealous beings. I would rather say that, yes, it was I who wrote that stupidity. Spending time, if such a phrase can be used, with the stenographers had instilled, within my writing, a sense of uselessness, a hatred for repetition. The time I spent with them was so painful that it had ceased to be a matter of beautiful sentences, of parentheses, of subtleties or flights of lyricism, and was now one of pure information, of a style that was rightly called telegraphic. When, having set aside my dictionaries and my press clippings, I finally set pen to paper, I saw one of these characters resembling their voices, a grayish, furred face, the telephone operator's helmet crimping their thick hair to show a streak of bare, flaky scalp. It was nine forty-five. I didn't have the time to write something serious. And in this old article I'd just reread, I'd already written, without realizing it, an actual obituary: it would be enough for me to dictate it again, nobody would figure it out. But I forgot everything I had known about the man and immediately launched into a ridiculous, non-sensical confabulation. I described how this scientist had secretly been a monomaniacal collector of birds, that he had recorded them, had stuffed them, had imitated them, had dressed up in their remains, and, behind his wife's back, had indulged in ornithomancy, that method of divination through the song or the flight of those celestial creatures. I was still a bit feverish. I finally specified the cause of death, because after all he wasn't so old: joining his mouth to birds' beaks, eating feathers, drinking shit, sleeping on a small cushion padded with the thin bones of pigeons, he had ended up catching ornithosis, that infectious avian disease that was transmissible to men, in which it took the form of pneumonia. He had expired while chirping a single word: beauty. It was ten ten, I knew that my article was no good. But I had never dictated an obituary, I didn't know that this kind of article, in the stenographers' eyes, commanded respect and might finally allow me into the pantheon of grave-digging or cremating journalists. The article flew like a letter by post: the stenographer didn't stop me at any word, she paid attention to each comma and at ten fifteen the article was typed in sextuplicate, copies of which were sent by pneumatic tube or a copy boy to the copy editor, the editor in chief, the section editor, the layout designer, the proofreader, and ultimately archived as proof of their dutiful service and our lies, in their stenography archives, on onionskin paper, the time stamp being admissible proof in case of retraction. I imagined my article making its way through the five floors, I counted once again the number of people whose hands it had to pass through: there were five of them who could unmask me. I forgot the croissant on the mantle, I was daydreaming a bit. At heart, why did I insist that I wanted to love P.? He wasn't a bird. I had only known him for three days. He would have been more like a cat, and I was allergic to cats. This old love, which I'd given up on, had flared up again unexpectedly, after a year apart, to show him to me again, as if certain of the effect he would have on me. And his neck was so thin, I who loved sturdy napes, this new beloved neck surging from his black collar floated in my hand. The phone rang: I immediately recognized the voice of the managing editor, who in practice I had never dealt with, I was ready to disdainfully defend the veracity of my statements, but he was calling me to congratulate me. I hung up, disheartened. I still wanted to daydream about P. but his image was disintegrating, in my hand all I had was the painful feeling that was the absence of his neck which, barely a hundred hours earlier, had swum there.

— 1983

Singular Adventures

A Kiss for Samuel

In April 19—, I left on my own for one week in Florence to photograph the figures at the anatomical wax museum. I came on Sunday. The museum was only open for a few hours on Saturday afternoons. It rained for those six days I waited.

I had little money. The tourist office had suggested a guesthouse on the via Martiri del Popolo, on the fifth floor, at the end of a courtyard where a movie theater was screening a Bruce Lee film. The room charmed me, despite its modesty; the water from the tap had a bleach taste that I didn't dislike; the inside of the closet smelled very much like the inside of a closet; the sheets were worn soft; the thin brown wool duvet reminded me of the one at the preschool dormitory. I paid seven thousand lira per night. The guesthouse closed at midnight.

Solitude immediately forced me to perceive more actively, more meticulously, to dissect the smallest things. My gaze paused at everything, but nobody paused at my availability. I looked at myself too much. T., who at the very last minute had let me leave on my own, became a safe haven of an idea, a point of reference, from which I could wander: should I seek out suffering?

I did not visit any museums. I saw myself meandering through the streets, coming back to the places I had gone with him two years earlier. I came back to the same foods, to the oily, hot bread from a bakery on the via dei Cerchi, but the store had been renovated. I took the same photos again, the children's graves, the medallions and mausoleums of the big cemetery, probably composed in the same ways. I did not come back to the Boboli Gardens where, two years earlier, walking behind him, I had suddenly wanted to use all my force to hit the back of his neck with the heft of the camera hanging by a strap around my wrist. It was an unhypnotic pilgrimage.

I was no longer sure whether I should talk to myself, or whether I should find someone to talk to, seal an envelope. There, not only was I sleeping alone, but I was exclusively alone, I only talked when ordering meals, or changing bills for the photo booths. If an idiot wanted to accost me, I didn't say that I was a foreigner, or that I didn't understand, I simply said: "I don't want to talk." I did not travel on any buses, not even the most important ones, I went by foot. My socks had holes where the heels were. I was no longer shaving, no longer washing my hair. I didn't have any writing implements on me, and I tore out the pages of my book one by one, I borrowed a pen to write. The photo booth became my most frequent hobby. The photo was guaranteed to be indestructible, imperishable for twenty years. On the machine was written that the photo was meant for passports, ID cards, driver's licenses and gun permits, someone had added "narcissismo." I went into these four-hundred-lira photo booths several times. I didn't know whether these images that came out of the appliance were reinforcing my isolation, or freeing me from it. With one of them I went in a store and ordered my headstone portrait.

I came back twice a day to the terminal station. I took this underground passageway monitored by a blind watchman who was begging endlessly. I paid attention to the chaos of movements. As travelers in the waiting room dozed off, a man in the Catholic chapel set his tartan hat and his imitation-leather bag on the pew in front of him, and kneeled to pray, women waited in line for the confession booth; twenty meters off, in the bathroom, men flaunting strips of pinkish flesh through the half-open doors. I slipped a hundred lira into the shoe polisher, and lazily set my loafer beneath the huge brush that had started spinning. But a man went up to me and pulled back my leg, he showed me the machine where *marrone* was written, then he pointed at my shoes which were decidedly black, and he seized the last few moments of the brush's turning to slip in his brown-colored shoes.

I came back later, drunk, to these stalls, my stomach rubbing against the damp tiles, the flush went off of its own accord at regular intervals, I got fucked by the first guy who came. The last night, I still hadn't talked to anyone. In front of the toilets, a young boy came up to me and asked for ten thousand lira to sleep with him. I had that amount, and even a bit more, in an inner pocket of my jacket. I also had five thousand lira, half of what he was asking for, in an outer pocket. So I got the idea to lie to him. I told him that I didn't have the money on me, that I only had five thousand lira, and that I would give him that, just for a kiss. This proposition seemed to delight him, flatter him. His name was Samuel, he was from Palermo, he was nineteen, he talked to me about his girlfriend who lived in the north of France, in Marcq-en-Barœul. We went out in search of a place where we could kiss. We walked down the quay, then we went down the underground passageways, where bodies swaddled in blue and pink nylon jostled on the ground in search of sleep, which at moments asked us, through the narrow gaps of their duvets, for the time. No opportunity ever arose for the kiss. There was always a traveler or a porter going by, some footsteps that kept us from stopping where we were. We crossed the entire length of the station, then we came out at the last quay, which was deserted and dark, and we walked its length to where the rows of tracks disappeared, far beyond a hall where men in overalls were moving huge boxes, we finally found ourselves alone, and we stopped, we turned toward one another, but a man crouching in the shadow of a locomotive shouted at us and ordered us to skedaddle. I said: "Promenade," and we left again, we went back through the underground passageway. We had been walking for twenty minutes, finally he turned to me and we kissed each other without paying any further attention to the traffic, at the bottom of a stairway. The exchange of money swiftly followed the exchange of saliva: as his tongue infiltrated my mouth, I pulled the five thousand lira out of my pocket and inserted them into his. At first it seemed that he had hair on his tongue, but it was a strand of licorice that he was chewing. The kiss lasted. Samuel laughed and said: "Your teeth are beautiful." He kissed me again, several more times. He said while laughing, in French, as in the song: "Voulez-vous coucher avec moi ce soir?" He asked me if I'd already seen Alain Delon, as I saw him, measuring the distance that separated us, and I started to describe him, because I had actually seen him, and my description suddenly struck me as deceitful in its stereotypes. Then he told me that he was hungry, and he invited me to the train-station café to eat some spaghetti with him and drink Coke. I hesitated to tell him that I had lied, and ended up letting him pay. I had to go back to my guesthouse, because it would be midnight soon. He accompanied me a short way out of the station, his hand on my shoulder, and when we said good-bye, he put five hundred lira in my hand "to get back to my place."

The next day I went to the anatomical wax museum as soon as it was open. I had awaited this moment for so long that I started taking pictures hurriedly, without actually looking at anything.

The museum was still empty, I could have taken as many photos as I wanted without being noticed, considering it was forbidden. But after the third photograph, the flash stopped working, the batteries were empty, and the space was so dark that it wasn't possible to take pictures without a flash. I went out to buy batteries, all the stores were closed. I would have to wait four hours. By the time they opened again, the museum would be closed. I checked out of the guesthouse room and put my bags in the station lockers. I still had a bit of time before my train. Samuel wasn't there. I went into the basements of this hygienic facility, which included a barber, restrooms, and Turkish baths. I shaved off the beard that had already grown after six days, and left the place, my cheeks reddened with blood.

I took the train to Siena. In the garden of the Palazzo Ravizza, the blossoming tree was already pink. I heard the muted hubbub of the rainstorm while the slow trickle of warm water filled the bathtub. The Tuscan countryside was just as Yvonne had described it, farther off stood the cemetery's crosses. The spirits supposed to inhabit my bedroom, on the top floor of this deserted palace, did not establish any hostile or mischievous presence around me, just a soft embrace. In front of the window I scratched my head insistently, until my skin flaked off onto the notebook, where I wrote: apart from the persistence of my fecal matter stuck to the enamel, there are no more points of reference.

The Trip to Brussels

I only saw him once, at this photography school I had been asked
to stop by. He was the tallest boy, with tousled, short, black hair in
cowlicks, he talked with a German accent, that's all I knew about
him, all I had to explain this attraction.

His image remained static for months: I couldn't bring myself
to forget it. When, at last, it seemed to be just about to disappear,
he called me on the phone. I told him: "I want to see you." He said:
"Come right away, I'll cook for you," hanging up before I could tell
him I wasn't free. I called back, but he was gone already.

I turned up at his place, at the top of a small, filthy staircase.
He lived at the far end of Paris, in the eighteenth arrondissement.
He opened the door for me the way one might open it for a friend
finally returning after years of absence (these years would have
been those of our ages, twenty-three, twenty-four). He flung
diced onion, banana, and ham mixed with oily rice into a pan on
the fire. We sat facing each other in the small, unlit kitchen, and
I immediately felt within his physical presence a sense of eleva-
tion, adventure, freedom. The words he had said had nothing
overtly erotic about them, but they suddenly, mysteriously had
my penis swelling.

Two things should have offended me, but I accepted them
calmly, as part of a harmonious suite of events: first he turned on the
bare lightbulb hanging from the ceiling, at the very moment I
thought I had come to relish to the darkness we were within, and

this new illumination weighing harshly upon our faces did not change anything in our gazes or our words. Then one of his friends rang the doorbell, holding in his hand a sandwich bought at the Arab's corner store, and this comical (because this boy was the sort who told funny stories) intrusion somehow didn't bother me: I had faith in every moment. The wine was bad, but that didn't matter at all, it simultaneously became, in our mouths, top-notch.

Finally, right before he left, the boy started recalling stories of danger: the neighborhood wasn't safe, he had already been attacked, he asked for a cab to be called to take him home. I still planned to take the métro, and once his friend had gotten into the cab, he offered to walk me to the métro stop. We rounded the corner of a street and came face-to-face with boys in black leather pissing on cars and yelling. One of them said: "We're gonna kick their asses." I shuddered, thought about backtracking, running, but he sensed my fear, and he set his hand on my shoulder, at the exact moment we walked past them, and they stepped away to let us through when he told me, out loud: "There's nothing to be afraid of, you're with me." I didn't turn around, when we said good-bye in the métro station entrance he wished me safe travels, as if to someone leaving on a very long cruise, putting some wind in the sails.

He gave me the photograph of a man holding a dead owl at arm's length. He laughed as he opened his mouth and pointed out a gap between his teeth, right in the middle, on the bottom, when he was a kid he'd gotten into a fight and the tooth hadn't fallen out right away but had ended up rotting. He had stuck the x-ray of this missing tooth to some of his photos. This delighted way of imme-diately revealing what other people might have wanted to hide made me contemplate the endeavor, with the first kiss, if there would be a kiss one day, of slipping my tongue into the space of this missing tooth before someone had filled it in. I could have taken his hand and run it over my chest, so that his hand might slip, as if on a cliff's edge, as if on a steel-jaw trap covered with leaves, so that his hand might vanish . . . but I didn't.

On the phone, we decided to go away together, I was the one who said Brussels, he had said Chartres, or La Roche-aux-Fées, he wanted to take me to sleep under a space he had discovered between two menhirs where cats slept. When he was a child he had been fat, but he hadn't lost weight, in this way he had gotten very thin because he had gotten suddenly, inordinately taller: he was taller than me, but I didn't know him yet. He was eight months younger than me. German, born in Fribourg. He had to go there soon to celebrate his father's seventieth birthday, and if we wanted to leave together, we had to leave quickly.

He had brought some tincture of myrrh to soothe his gums if they hurt. As for me, I had filled my little bag with all sorts of different pills and capsules, I had imagined all the possible varieties of suffering, and I had a remedy for each one, just as we were leaving I had methodically drawn up this catalog (I would have secretly liked for him to suffer so I could soothe him), everything meaning stomachaches, headaches, insomnia, nausea, and even extreme exhaustion. I hadn't brought any books, or any clothes, apart from a spare tee-shirt that was red.

Just as we were leaving his place, he had suddenly opened his photography bag again, and in front of me he had taken out his pajamas, he had said: "No, I'm not going to take them." But he purposely hadn't washed in several days so that his smell would protect him by erecting an armature around his body, a barrier that I would have difficulty overcoming (the same way citronella is recommended against mosquitoes).

He had put on a leather jacket that a truck driver coming from Hamburg had given him several years earlier and that he had had lined with sheep's wool. A few days before we departed, I had noticed, inside his ears, the yellow, waxy cerumen, and I'd thought to myself that this particular disgust it aroused in me would be a test of, a challenge to, my desire, like the obstacle in a tournament. But on the day of departure the yellow matter had disappeared. And this shabby black leather jacket, with its belt, became an all-too-evident bridge for my desire, an all-too-effective conductor thereof.

He chose a train that took six hours to reach Brussels when we could have made this trip in three hours. It was a train he could get a student discount for, a train that Portuguese immigrants coming back to work in the Netherlands took, it stopped in Amsterdam. There weren't any bunks, but most of the travelers were sleeping across the seats, shivering under heaps of clothes. We tried to stay awake by talking, the words would only amount to the tones they imprinted upon our ears. The train waited in a station for an hour, for no reason, it was already two in the morning and the man pushing a food cart up and down the platform tapped on the windows periodically, against the crushed faces of the sleeping travelers, just to wake them up, taking advantage of an illusory right that his job as a cart-pusher granted him, even though he didn't have the least hope of making a sale (maybe it was also because he was used to not selling any beer or any black dishwater that the man knocked on the windows this way, to disrupt non-drinkers' sleep . . .).

The train waited for another hour at customs, this time we had fallen asleep, he'd covered himself with his jacket, when I wasn't sleeping I was playing with his zipper, I didn't dare to turn to the side to look at him. A fat man with a Belgian accent woke up the entire compartment with his loud, drawling voice: "Who does this red suitcase belong to? Is it yours, sir? Yours, sir? I need to know who this red suitcase belongs to, otherwise I'll have to put it on the platform." After some twenty minutes had gone by in individual queries where these words, red suitcase, were repeated endlessly, the man decided to put the suitcase on the platform. As soon as it was set on the ground, the suitcase exploded, and the man was torn to pieces. They rummaged through our belongings, they took our papers, all the travelers were questioned.

The train came to Brussels late. It was five in the morning. The currency exchange would only open at seven o'clock, and we didn't have a single Belgian coin. Dawn barely broke, as he had hoped. The wind was very cold, the signal poles blinked in front of the mauve sky. We crossed the street and went into the nearest café. We asked the woman at the counter if we could pay her in French francs, we gave her ten francs for two coffees. We sat on a seat next to the unplugged jukebox, in front of us was a woman just about ready to sleep, nestled up against a man, her red-painted fingernails stroking the locks of his hair.

We were waiting for the currency exchange to open and as we walked we got further away from the train station. We went into a second café, off a small square. A man was ready to leave for work, a bag at his feet, looking freshly washed as he drank a beer. He asked us if we were British. He told us that he listened to French radio every morning, and he started singing the theme for a broadcast.

The Musée des Beaux-Arts had no Rembrandts, and the paintings at the Wiertz museum, which was hard to find, were crude, with coarse colors and pompous proportions: they were better viewed as postcards. The sun rose in the garden bordered by the greenhouse. Against the stairs, facing the wall, his back to the people walking up, a man rocked back and forth silently while kissing the wall. But the camera was utterly unable to transcribe this unity of movement, pose, immobility.

We came back to the same restaurant under a covered passageway three times, and we ate the same food, shrimp croquettes. An eyelash fell across his cheek, and I picked it up with my moistened fingertip to set it on my tongue, I swallowed, and that embarrassed him. We drank a white wine from the Jura. He talked to me about the walks he had taken as a child through the woods around Fribourg, about the Sunday lunches. He was the eldest of four boys. When his sister was finally born, he was seven, he had said: "I'm going to marry my sister." "Even today," he said, "when I clutch myself, I dream that I'm hugging her."

When we left, I was upset by how the icy wind, pushing my hair back from my forehead, left my face bare. I wasn't bundled up enough, I was cold. The long, narrow bedroom was poorly heated, with a sink at each end and two simple beds separated by a partition, he didn't shut the door. He got undressed and his tee-shirt rode up over a swath of slightly heavy, thoroughly white belly. I stretched out under the too-cold sheets, and I held my breath, we said good night to each other from opposite sides of the partition, our heads should have practically touched, we were each almost the opposite of the other, our two bodies were probably just as stiff and unmoving, I was suddenly seized by an overwhelming desire to orgasm with him, to stroke our two cocks together within my fist, I wanted him to come join me in my bed, and, without a word, lift up the covers to slip in, I knew quite well that his feet were as cold and damp as mine. He got up, I heard him walk, he was naked in the cold, dark space, naked in front of me, he was holding his leather jacket on his hand, he lay it on my bed so as to cover my feet, he just said: "You must be cold," then he was gone again, and had gotten into bed again, sleep finally swallowed us, but which of us first? In the morning he woke me up early.

We were supposed to go down to get a key from the front desk for the shower. The woman had insisted that we pay for the room in advance, because we had no luggage, nothing but these school-boys' bags. This time it was a man who was at the front desk, we had just eaten breakfast. I asked him for the shower key, and once again we were asked to pay in advance. In front of us, he went to find two towels in a cabinet, and I saw quite clearly, in the moment of hesi-tation that made his hand pause, that he had intentionally selected from the pile the two thinnest, most frayed, most rundown towels. I took the towels and I let him walk all the way back across the lobby. Once he was at the front desk, I gave him the towels and told him that I wanted other ones, thicker ones, in a tone that insisted on his compliance. He came back with one of the two towels changed, and, to humiliate me, he said: "My word, you're real young girls," and in a very calm tone I said: "Yes, we're young girls." He didn't reply, and we went up the stairs. I willingly gave him the thicker towel, and once again, like the swallowed eyelash, this atten-tion paid to his body seemed to unnerve him.

A brass band was playing in the square, and people had gathered there, some were taking pictures, we were watching them with a feeling of incongruity, of pity. We need to take the train back. He hadn't found what he had been looking for in store after store, the unobtainable, detachable section, perhaps of a weapon, of a barrel.

We took a streetcar to its terminus, without any idea of where it was headed, and, sitting in the same seats, we came back to where we had started. I took him to drink one of those sour cherry beers in a café that someone had pointed out to me, "La Mort subite."

Sitting side by side on the bench, people looked at us, and there, in my fervor, I said lines to him that were not recorded.

On the train back, he leaned toward me to kiss my cheek. We said good-bye to each other in the métro station, standing on the platform I saw him disappear behind the bright glass, he was going back to Marianne. I did not see him again.

I came back emptied out. The next day I rediscovered idleness, barely had the energy to read. Over the phone I woke up a voice that wasn't his, and I thought, without any sadness: he's warming Marianne's feet under his jacket, he's right beside her. But summer was already here. This girl's voice I had been confronted with seemed to be dozing, and I imagined his apartment, during his absence, like a huge dormitory. She said: "No, he hasn't left for Fribourg yet." I tried to talk in German, I almost gave up on writing to him.

The words we spoke made an apocryphal story that was perfect: faded, singed, written in invisible ink, buried and unexhumable. Nothing could reconstruct these words, they were like a treasure lost in the depths: intimidating, undetectable.

Over these few days, in this emptiness, in this time spent doing nothing, writing nothing, absolutely nothing, I was sure he had stolen my soul, but he had become my inspiration . . .

(Six to eight months passed between the two texts, the first one abandoned, unfinished, unconnected. I sent him the letter three months late, hoping that it would fall flat, in this lack of any relationship, as embarrassing as the loose eyelash or the too-wet towel. Then I happened upon this already-written fragment of text, and it was this same feeling of adventure that came back to me. I had to overcome forgetting, I had to rely on memory.)

The Desire to Imitate

I took the train from the L. station on Friday, December 26, 19—, at 6:50, toward R., a stamped ticket that I had long forgotten in a pocket serving as evidence. I hadn't taken anything in this golden crocodile-skin suitcase that I still have and that I had bought with my first paycheck, apart from essential toiletries, and a few changes of clothes, a present that was an empty photo album with thick black pages. I was careful not to bring my diary, out of fear that it might be read, opened in any case, and maybe stolen, maybe just struck through, I knew by heart the sentences that could have irritated her.

In the dining car, a man asked me for a light and imperceptibly, for just one second too long, or even less than that, kept his fingers on my hand: he was of Calabrese extraction, one year older than myself, and his cheekbones were prominent and his hair shaved, his voice low-timbre, the pores of his skin open, almost pockmarked, as if pinched repeatedly to squeeze out pus. His name was F., and when I asked him what this first name meant, I was reminded of lava, of the fire that flows from volcanoes. He offered to have me come stay in his hotel, a proposal that struck me as sleazy considering that he had all the makings of a robber, and in the morning, on the platform, as everyone got off the train, I didn't wait for him.

The driver was waiting for me, unblinking and all in gray, already old, with a somewhat crass elegance: he had a photo of his mistress at hand. Without a word he moved to take my suitcase and led me to the silver-plated Mercedes. The Rolls Royce had been sold ten years earlier. He asked me if I wanted to sit in the back or up front and I got in the front. Even though he was a valet of sorts, I felt shabby next to him, and I watched a chilly landscape go past under the sunlight, shifting abruptly from antique remains to industrial developments, unusual for R., or rather unusual for the image I had of R.

The car's movement reminded me momentarily of the train's movement. I was alone then and I'd started reading one of the two books my parents had given me for my birthday: Stendhal's *The Red and the Black* and Dostoyevsky's *The Adolescent*. I took in the foreword to *The Red and the Black*, which I'd never read. The foreword writer was explaining that Stendhal had been inspired by a real-life event and had barely changed its details in developing it: a young man shooting a woman he'd fallen in love with inside a church; Stendhal, said the foreword writer, had simply developed the feelings that might lead to the facts of this murder, and as I read these lines another fact came forth: the aim of my trip to R. was to kill this woman who had summoned me, I hadn't thought about it before, to be honest, this wasn't even an aim, but a fact, a thing that, from this moment on, I couldn't escape. But the meeting with the boy, the meal, the constant ruckus on the train, the awkward, chilly half-sleep all distracted me from this idea. By the time I arrived, I had even forgotten it. I tried to say a few words to the driver. Contrary to her usual custom, his mistress had woken up at nine o'clock to prepare for my arrival, a breakfast was waiting for me.

The trip from the train station to the house seemed extremely long to me, and it seemed later on that it had been drawn out on purpose, and made worse by several segments, crossings, and dark driveways, to muddy my sense of how far we'd traveled and to deter my attempts to leave the house. In this way it seemed distant, and isolated, the endpoint of a winding labyrinth that I was now ill-prepared to make my way out of. And the driver was already suggesting that he would go to the train station each day to buy the papers I would be reading, and it would look ridiculous for me to come with him. Apparently there was no bus for the area. He parked the car in front of a door painted green. The lady was in the house's basement, busy with some covert work: tiny glasses rested on her nose, and when she saw me, she took them off and got up briskly, immediately covering her project.

I had made it a condition, should I come see her again, that I had to be able to choose the room I would sleep in: I wanted it to be very far away from hers, and I imagined it being very simple, small, all white, with just a bed, a table, like a maid's room. She took me through the house, having grabbed my arm, to show me the rooms. There were about thirty, none of the ones on the third floor were heated, they had clearly never been lived in, and they contained a welter of tapestries, horrid little paintings. The huge lounge itself offered a bewildering mixture of Spanish and Chinese styles, baroque and classical with Venetian chandeliers, Romantic landscapes, pearlescent low tables from the Ming era, the woman had, over the course of her career, bought whatever was most expensive without further thought. Her bedroom was on the second floor: all the hallways, lined with closets, held the dresses from her films and galas, all of which she had kept; a vestibule, with thick rugs, and extended by further secret closets, also housed her dressing table in a recess, and a sort of low couch for a masseur's or chiropodist's alternating treatments. In the bedroom itself, the bed was covered with white percale, a tortured, wooden Christ overlooking it, but it was the three tiger furs with gaping red maws that stood out, set geometrically on each side of the bed, the three wild beasts looking at one another and holding impossible conversations (nostalgia for the jungle). The bed, which could have been mistaken as perpetually nuptial, was in fact a virgin one, the husband having left it very nearly twenty years ago, and the wife, being wary of her help, having never dared to bring other men there.

I still hadn't decided on a room, each one seemed drearier than the last. Finally she led me into the basement, past her laboratory and her cold room, into a secret little apartment. It was the former cellar, which she had cleared out a few years earlier with the help of her nanny's son, chasing away rats and digging up human debris, bones, slivers of shields, shards of vases that she had had set on rods for her displays. We made our way, bending down slightly, through a set of beaded curtains and doors as low as they were narrow. Finally we reached the opulence of gold, gemstones, rows of mirrors reflecting elephants, goddesses with hundreds of arms, entire tusks, immense lascivious Shivas. This room, which she called the prayer room, was in fact her rarely-used *chambre d'amour*, the men she brought there were supposed to flee at dawn, before the gardener came. There, she burned incense from the Orient. A basement window, closed off by iron bars, was the only egress; a dimmer bathed each object in light and set fake flames flickering. This room was the one she had in mind for me, and it was also the one I believed I had chosen.

I was alone. Somewhat sweaty from the trip, I wanted to take a shower. I opened a cabinet: I found some dresses there that had been lost or specifically put there, crimson sheath dresses, see-through chest panels, or Spanish flounces of black lamé, I shut it quickly, but not before jostling the fabrics with a sweep of my hand. The bathroom, too, was covered in mirrors, but most surprising of all was the transparent bathtub, as deep as a well, a vase, surrounded by moray eels slithering shiftily through the aquarium that followed the bathtub's contours. The mirrors reflecting my body ad infinitum while revealing my monstrous profiles became a much too evident path toward suicide, and I turned off the light. All that remained was the green, translucent light of the aquarium, I glided with a shiver into overly warm water, among these sea serpents that no barrier whatsoever seemed to separate from me and that, in their dark movements, suddenly revealing their menacing white fangs, as petite as ivory pins, within their flat muzzles, coiled around my legs, became, in the glass's pale reflections, horrific necklaces around my neck. But the morays were sated; that very morning, the driver, who took care of the aquarium, had given them several of these live goldfish awaiting their end in a separate basin and they now milled around below my feet.

I noticed a goldfish in particular that was bigger than the victims, rather flat, its sides striped by a thin silvery band which always stayed in the same place, floating in a specific volume, in the upper right of the aquarium, utterly immovable: this fish's inertia was fascinating, I decided to test it several times. I looked away to give it time to slip away, but when I turned my eyes back to the aquarium, the fish was still in the same spot, although it was impossible to figure out, given the oxygen whirling upward in bubbles, the shimmering stones, or the fake algae, why it was so enviable . . .

The woman showed me around the garden. To go out, she had covered her light dress again with a long leopard-skin coat that she pretended to have just grabbed out of one of her closets. She took me to the tennis court, a gift from a producer, which was now sodden, overrun by vegetation and now-faded bister. I made her climb up on the terrace on the deserted court, absurdly, to photograph her, I always kept the little contraption in my pocket. Behind the ivy-bordered fence, the three dogs, German shepherds, two male and one female, were barking at the sight of me. As she talked to them from the other side of the fence, she stuck her fingers through, and they took pleasure in sniffing the powdery scent they knew so well. They had to be talked to in code, in German, because they had been trained by the German police. So this woman's voice could be heard saying to her dogs, in a halting tone: "Sitz! Platz! Auf!" and the dogs sat, lay down, got back up. Those were the only words of German that she knew, along with those of a Goethe poem she had learned in school, and which she still recited mechanically, without understanding its meaning.

She took me to the garden shed, which she had had retrofitted for her son and her governess's son. The door was open. Her son was studying there. He shook my hand, a bit coldly but kindly. We had already met in Paris, of the two boys he was the one who liked me more, the other only saw me as a schemer, a gigolo, and in all honesty a rival. She asked her son to offer us something to drink, there was just whiskey.

When we came back to the house, the governess was waiting for us with the mail, which she had already sorted. She only had her read the telegram from an American television anchorman, who was sending her his best wishes. The governess's son got ready to leave for the winter sports with some friends. He greeted me icily, just as I expected, and got into the sports car that she had bought him, the skis on the roof.

We were alone again. She complained about the young boys' bad manners. They hadn't even thanked her, even though she had loaned them her house in Switzerland, without even meeting them. We sat down in the dining room, where the table was already set. And the driver reappeared, in slightly dirty white livery that was imperfectly buttoned. He held out, on a magnificent silver tray, some cold noodles in tomato sauce. The lunch was very mediocre, the only sign of refinement, which must have been the remnant of former customs, was to put the half-cracked nuts in a basket so that we could easily extract the meat.

After the lunch, I asked to lie down a bit, and she in turn went back to her handiwork. I tried to write, without much luck, I didn't like these mirrored tables, all these reflections unnerved me. I picked up *The Red and the Black* again, and the story of the murder struck me again, I shut the book. I walked into the bathroom to see whether the unmoving fish was still in its place: I wasn't wrong. I decided that I would ask to go out the next day. I thought about F., the boy I'd met on the train. I felt sad at not having gotten his address.

In the evening, we had dinner early, and quickly: in the salon, a white screen had already come down from the ceiling. Because the governess's son usually took care of the projections, she had asked two professional projectionists to come render their services. We went together into the basement, and she opened the huge refrigerator that contained the reels for her films. She had me choose two: *Nuits de Chine* and *Le grand Saba*. Then she took a keychain and put on a coat to go into the projection room, set up in the garden and connected to the salon, through a sliding glass window at the back of a cabinet. The room hadn't been opened for months, not since the previous visitor. Rats meaning to gnaw at the projector's wires had eaten the red seeds scattered across the wood floor and their blood had coagulated in their veins, they lay at the bottom of the machine. It had to be coerced into working again: the motor wheezed, the light sputtered.

The governess had already left the house, leaving in the salon a bottle of champagne, a brioche, and some black nougat. On the screen, her image as a child reappeared shakily; her voice, replayed so many times, lost its gleam every time: she was the queen of the Orient, borne on a chariot by bare-chested slaves, cracked her whip, she took my hand. The two projectionists were staying in the projection room and watching the scene while eating saucisson sec.

The reels got mixed up: the end came right after the first reel, she died and came back to life, the passions were switched around, she kissed men she hadn't met yet and before passion came hatred. She translated the voices for me, adding her voice to her earlier voice, and as they were often words of love, she seemed to be using the image and the story to say them to me.

She accompanied me back to my room and went to the trouble herself of removing the fur that served as bedspread, took away the cushions, uncovering the white silk sheets. Then I turned her down. She pressed her lips toward me, once again I gave her a peck on the lips. I slept a full, deep night's sleep, without even hearing the dogs. I was awakened by her voice. It was already noon. She had just woken up as well; her governess was going to come to her room with her breakfast, she would have her come to mine as well.

The governess set down the plate, turned on the aquarium's lights, and came into the room. At her mistress's request, she inspected me: I was sitting on the bed, in underwear and undershirt, my hair was a mess. She brought a murderously black coffee, which I had to top off with warm water from the bathroom tap. When she returned to her mistress's bedroom, she who was the only one to see her upon rising, without her wig, without her makeup, she told her: "But he seemed totally normal, he was sitting on the bed, in underwear and undershirt, I promise you, I examined him carefully, he's in good shape." And she repeated this to me.

When I got up, in the morning, after my breakfast, I took a shower, then I went into the garden with my book, I checked to make sure that the dogs were secured, they weren't barking anymore when they saw me walking past. But they barked all night: as soon as they were let out of their kennel, they started barking, without pause, until the morning, they kept me from sleeping, I got irritable in my bed. The few naps I got were nightmares. I was left with the morning sun, my eyes looking up from the book, half closed against this bright winter sun. The gardener went by with his ladder, his pruning shears, waved at me from far off. I waited for her, I was never able to see her before lunchtime, she wasn't visible. I sometimes looked toward her window, hidden by the curtain, and I imagined that she was looking at me. I imagined her in her seashell-shaped bathtub, her scalp half bald, then applying her makeup for ages, white strips around her face, then putting on her wig. When I entered her room, all the utensils had disappeared, I stared at the shut drawers. "It's not *make-up* anymore," she said, enunciating the English word. "It's restoration." She had just suffocated her chest by compressing it in a far-too-thin dress with Spanish frills.

She opened her secret closet for me, the one that contained the siren engine, dashboard with hundreds of buttons that powered the magnetic surveillance circuit. She hid personal photos there, her jewels, her love letters, she even kept the magnetic tapes of the phone conversations she'd had with her lovers. She'd never posed in the nude for any magazine, she had been offered millions of dollars, and she'd never appeared nude on film, it was always a body double. For half-nude scenes, behind the bath towel that hid her body so ravishingly, she covered all her flesh, her breasts, and her stomach with huge strips of skin-colored band-aids so that if the camera attempted to peer past the limits established by the towel and a special clause in her contract, it would get caught. So there was no photo of her wholly in the nude, except for two Polaroids that she had taken herself in color, in front of the varnished door of her dress closet. She kept them in a sealed envelope, the wax seal stamped with her initials preventing its being opened, she tore it open, and showed me the photos that I was the first one to see, that she unveiled like a treasure. I looked at them fairly indifferently, she pinched me.

After the lunch, I stated my intention to head out, she blanched, then she said: "I'm coming with you." I said: "No, I want to be alone for a bit." She said: "Okay, the driver will accompany you." Her face was ashen. I couldn't claim that I would buy the papers, the driver could have gone to pick it up easily enough. I agreed to be taken to the train station, but let the driver return alone, I would take a bus back. I walked a bit: it was two days before New Year's, and the streets were full of people. In no time, the city wore me out. I wanted to go back. Night had already fallen. A bus dropped me off on the road to the house, but several kilometers away. There was no light along the road, the cars' headlights blinded me, they zipped past me, others deviously braked beside me, dogs barked behind garden fences, I slipped into potholes, I got scared. Finally the house appeared, I called on the intercom, the governess's voice came through, I thought for a second that the door wasn't going to open again for me. I had been punished for my desire to flee. I crossed the garden in darkness, numb, the fires in the sconces arrayed systematically on each side of the paths hadn't been lit for a long time.

It was the final night that the men from the city would come to project films, the next night they would be with their wives to get ready for New Year's Eve. I wanted to see *Les Nuits de Bagdad*, a sequel to *Nuits de Chine* and *Le Cirque rouge*, in which she played the role of a tightrope walker beloved by two rival animal trainers. I remembered that my father had, when he was younger, fallen in love with her: when I was little, he had often described her to me as the most beautiful woman in the world. The governess had put out a new bottle of champagne, we were supposed to finish the brioche we had started the previous night, which had gone a bit stale, and the chocolate nougat. She started translating the dialogue for me again, and I asked her somewhat curtly to be quiet. For a moment, I couldn't listen to her voice anymore. I couldn't bear her dubbing, as a still-living person, of the slightly raspy voice embalmed by the film.

That night, as I slept, I was awoken by a door that squeaked slightly, followed by the noise of muffled footsteps. I didn't move, and kept my breathing slow. I thought about her, then her son, but it couldn't be him. An unfamiliar breath slowly approached my body. I held back from turning on the light, and pretended to be still asleep. Suddenly someone sat on my bed, then I felt the breeze of a breath huddling beside me, and finally lips touching my neck. Then these lips bit me violently, as if to draw blood. I screamed and turned on the light. At lunch we got into a fight. She called Pasolini a pornographer, she insisted that she was for the death penalty, I called her names, but our words were merely a pretext.

That night, as the projectionists weren't coming, I wanted to take her to the city. She resisted. It had been months since she had gone out. The governess took a dim view of this, as she had to watch the house herself. I insisted, and suddenly a burst of happiness made her accept. She found this screenplay she had had written ten years earlier, and which she wanted to be her comeback, she called a friend who was a producer. He was hosting a party right then, everybody there would be delighted to see her. I wanted to eat alone with her first before going to see these people. She took quite a while to get ready. The driver had parked the Mercedes in front of the entrance to the house, he sat and waited in the rumbling car. The son stood beside me. Finally she came out of her room and made her way down the immense wooden staircase, in a showy gold sari. The son whispered to me: "This house is beyond the world, beyond all reality . . . it's just like this film . . ." He didn't dare to utter the name. I did: "*Sunset Boulevard?*" "Yes, that's it . . ." She stepped into the car beside me and the son shut the door.

In the car, I told her about my desire to photograph her, upon our return, in front of the white screen in the salon, and in the ray of the projector's light. I imagined a sequence: first she would be holding a white towel in front of her, to hide her nude body, as in this film that had sparked a scandal; then the towel, pulled by strings, would fly away, and would uncover her body, her breasts, and her stomach, covered in band-aids; her wig would fly away as well and uncover her head wrapped in white bandages; then I would appear, first my shadow on the screen standing out against the device, I would be wearing the wig that had just flown away, and also one of her dresses. Once I had taken her place in front of the screen, her body would slowly vanish as if in acid. She didn't see the implication of murder, and I didn't either, she just said: "But you aren't my lover, I'll do these photos when you're my lover."

The restaurant I wanted to take her to was closed for the holidays, she took me to a restaurant for actors, not far from the train station. But she was worried about photographers: whenever she went to a restaurant, the owners called the papers so they could get a bit of publicity. "After all," she said, "I don't care that you're seen with me, I love you after all." But no photographer came, and we paid the bill. With some disappointment, she said: "These are decent people."

The driver took us to the producer's place. He was a playboy who had been the exclusive photographer, and the lover, of three princesses and an American film star. He had married the star's secretary, a young and rather crude Frenchwoman. Plenty of French ladies, former prostitutes who had married businessmen, were at this party. It was already winding down when we arrived. I was struck by the gaudiness of the decorations, smoked glass, weathered mirrors, and golden trinkets set on the plexiglass. She found a former booking agent who had become the general counsel for a huge American company, he said, dispiritedly: "You haven't changed," she gave him her script to read. While they were talking to each other, I got bored, the French women tried to distract me, because they spoke my language. They asked me: "What are you doing?" I answered: "Can't you see? I'm her slave," I asked to leave, she let me. Once we were outside, on the doorstep, the master of the house said: "Don't touch her, she's one of our greatest monuments."

One night I was woken up by the ringing of the house phone, she was calling me. She had come to the basement, where she often went in the afternoons, to devote herself to her covert handiwork, and she said: "There it is, I've just finished it. It's a surprise . . . but I can't keep quiet until tomorrow . . . guess what it is . . ." I couldn't imagine what it might be. My head was wholly empty in the presence of this voice that was so distant and at the same time so close (putting a name to this voice, her own name, was already totally surreal and fantastical for me). She said: "I've done your portrait in red chalk, life size, but I'll show you tomorrow . . ." She hung up. I went to urinate in the bathroom. I turned on the aquarium light to make sure the goldfish was still in its place.

The next day was New Year's Eve, the projectionists wouldn't be back until the day after, we had to find some activity for our evening. She said: "We can always go to a party, we've been invited to Prince V.'s, but you were disgusted by last night's people, you might not like the ones there and we'd be stuck. I've given the driver leave for the evening, and the prince lives in the outskirts. Here's what I propose: we'll go there this afternoon, on pretext of a visit, and if you like these people, only then, we'll go back tonight." We ate quickly, then we left. It was bright and sunny, and the industrial outskirts of R. unfurled like a long strip, muffled, cushioned, through the Mercedes's windows. The car glided gently, the driver peering ahead, we could barely hear the engine's noise, she took my hand, and she leaned toward me to speak quietly. I listened, seized by some sort of torpor. Out of fear of being depressed, she had taken some uppers, her rushed sentences broke up the countryside's calm:

" . . . When I came to Hollywood, he hid me in one of his houses, nobody was able to find me, I had my hairdresser, my dresser, my secretary, I didn't have anything to do, I waited, there was a solarium and I tanned all day long, one day I was on the terrace, a gust of wind slammed the door shut, I was all alone in the house, I called the gardener, nobody came, there was no shadow no matter where I stood, finally I dozed off in the sun, when I woke up it was almost night, but I was red as a lobster, my skin was peeling off, someone came to open the door, I gathered up all my skin, I put it in an envelope and mailed it to my son, every day I sent him something, he was five years old . . . He was a very odd man, nobody had ever seen him naked, he was ashamed of his skin, he couldn't be touched, his skin was very dry, like an old man's, I slept with him and I nearly grazed his shoulder, he said: 'I beg of you, don't touch me,' as soon as he had intercourse with a woman he made her wash up first, and he went right after to wash up, he had a very long, very thin penis, when he was in the bathroom I took the opportunity to check his jacket, he always wore the same one, he had set it on a chair, I turned it inside out, and I saw the tattered lining, which was unraveling, he was a multimillionaire but he always wore the same suit . . ."

These were stories she had already told me several times. I couldn't listen to them anymore. I couldn't even listen to the sound of her voice. It felt like each of her words had a materiality that was physical and not just acoustic: tactile, like swells, like waves of stench that broke against my face. At first I turned my face away, and stared determinedly at the countryside, I tried not to hear her voice at all. But she kept on talking, and squeezed my hand even more tightly. The facts of the murder came back to me, but this time images weighed on me with terrifying specificity: if I spent New Year's Eve home alone with her, I was sure to kill her. The actions of the crime were imprinted across the gloomy strip of the landscape.

We were both in the house basement, near the refrigerator with its motor the car's rumble, we were drinking champagne, she had just shown me my portrait, and it had become clear that it was my funerary portrait, if I didn't want to die she would be the one I had to kill. She wanted to kiss me, I pushed her away, so violently that she fell backwards, her head hit the back of the aquarium. The goldfish was still in its place and I saw its immobility as an order to kill: I got on top of her limp body and grabbed her throat, the pearl necklace broke, my hands quickly closed in around her crushed neck, a spurt of blood from her mouth was spat into my face, I went on shaking her head, then I let go of her, and she sagged like a huge, stupid doll. I pulled off her wig to see her scalp at long last: I saw the white bandages, the gauze gripping her skull while revealing some sparse hairs pasted down. Finally, despite the morays slithering maliciously, I went to wash my hands in the aquarium's turbulence.

The trickle of burbling water dispersed a cloud of blood that finally made the goldfish stir. I took care to roll up my sleeve.

Suddenly I said: "Stop, I can't listen to you anymore. I can't bear your voice anymore. I'm asking you, please stop, I'm having horrible thoughts. If we stay home alone tonight, I'm going to kill you, I know it. We shouldn't be alone." She let out a huge laugh: this idea charmed her, being killed at my hands thrilled her. I told her the details of my storyline, she accepted it. But I begged her to prevent it.

The Mercedes braking in the château's courtyard set the chickens fluttering in fright. In the dusk, it was a site of immense sadness: ringed by ramparts, the fenced-in former swimming pool now served as an outer courtyard, an empty pond was crisscrossed by lines of string for hanging clothes and sheets to dry. Prince V. welcomed us with his arms wide open: he was a half-ruined noble-man who had kept his castle by some secret maneuver, traveling so often that she suspected him of being a spy for China or Russia. He had married a young Eurasian woman, a former model forty years younger than him, she had borne him a daughter, a noisy, braided little monster, a fireball that darted throughout the château's chilly rooms and destroyed everything in her path, but there were few things that hadn't already been sold or stolen. It had been a long while since they had heated it, when they were inside they pulled tight their coat collars while moving around. Long low tables held bottles of alcohol from all over the world, another way for them to heat themselves. But what made the prince proudest of all was his kitchen: it was immense, and equipped in the old style, furnished with the earliest electrical machines which rumbled like archaic robots, the ice machine, the huge ovens had been bought from the reserves of run-down palaces. Long black eels moved slowly in water tanks, the little girl irritated them with the tapping of her fingers. He had had them flown directly from Greenland, he claimed that doing so was cheaper than buying them here. A Chinese cook, his hair lacquered and knotted, a small flat toque on top of his head cut where the braid went, was meticulously chopping ginger and rice leaves to make a cake. Pointing to his Chinese cook, the prince said in French: "That's my last indulgence." He had us drink a quince liqueur. As the party they were setting up had a white theme, she would have to go change. But the young Eurasian woman said something unfortunate: "My guests would be so happy to see a celebrity." In the car back, she said: "I've had enough of being on display, that's what I've been all my life." She decided that we wouldn't return for the party. We stayed home alone.

When the car had reached the entrance again, we saw, through the windows, the governess and her whole family returning to their house: so the housemaid had agreed to let the governess spend New Year's Eve with her family while she and I watched the house. She merely pretended to ask what I thought, fearing I would be irritated. I would be home alone with her tonight, wholly alone, and the thought of murder returned, with the piercing frequency of a blinking eye.

We wanted to walk around the garden as night fell. For me, she had already changed, she had put on a sheer, silver-encrusted evening gown of skintight muslin that she had sewn herself ten years earlier for a charity gala in Las Vegas, she had barely gained a pound since. I opened the gate to the garden, she went in front of me, two of the three dogs immediately rushed at me. She shouted, but they didn't stop, as if the governess's son, in his mountain, was remote-controlling them so they would carry out his murderous plans. I barely had time to shut the gate again, the dogs barking behind the glass and baring their teeth, the salmon pink of their chops, now I could mock them at ease. They wouldn't touch her, but she wasn't able to get them back into their enclosure. The third dog had been tied up by the house, in a ground-floor hallway, in case we needed it as a defense.

We were alone again in the house, unable even to leave. If I killed her, I would have to overpower the dogs. It was only eight o'clock, we had to while away the hours until midnight. A plate of lentils, traditionally prepared each New Year's Eve to bring more money in the new year, cooled in its pot; she opened a preliminary bottle of champagne. She tried to kiss me, and she responded, laughing an almost cruel laugh: "No humidity," her eyes got wet, the laugh hid her sadness. We watched television to the point of frustration, the soccer players got mixed up with anchorwomen, then she had the idea of going to find her photos. Her sister had organized them in sheaves up in the attic, under the house's eaves. We went up to the top floor and there, in the bathroom, she took an unplugged outlet that she inserted into a partition, a mirror pivoted, we found ourselves under the roof where thousands of photos were piled up. We took packets of them to carry into the small salon, where we looked at them one by one, sliding them from one knee to the other. She said: "I don't remember anything, it's as if nothing had happened."

We let the hours go by, we were brought back to reality by the fireworks being shot off in the neighboring villas, the sirens going off on their own, the dogs barking even more. We rushed to the kitchen, reheated the plate of lentils, and opened a new bottle of champagne. We kissed, like two friends. The photos had reconciled us, the idea of murder had gone up in smoke. She sat by the phone. But nobody called. The wait got more and more worrisome. An hour had gone by already. Finally the phone rang. She waited to pick up. She anxiously said: "That must be my son . . ." But her son was snorting cocaine somewhere in town. It was a man's voice, an unfamiliar name, a voice that came from far away, crossing continents, underwater depths, cyclones, hurricanes, all to say, a bit imperfect in calculating the time difference, but shaking with feeling: "Madame, you're the biggest of all the stars." This wasn't a joke. This was perhaps the only person in the world who had thought of her in this moment, and who had thought that she might be alone. But this year she had managed once again not to be. She didn't answer, she hung up.

Later in the night, she said:

"You think my mouth smells like powder, like flesh, like mucus, or maybe that it smells like wine, smells like vagina, smells like death. You say my mouth disgusts you, my mouth reeks, it reeks of death. This house is like a bank. I don't sleep. I'm alone and the dogs are going around. Don't leave. The champagne is warm, too bad. Cheers. Happy New Year. Stay here a little longer with you, will you please?"

The next day, the first day of the year, I checked that the gold-fish was still in its place in the aquarium, and, all of a sudden, I wanted to leave. I packed my suitcase. I said: "I'm leaving," and she didn't try to keep me. She wanted to give me one of her Etruscan vases, I said no. With the driver, she accompanied me to the train station. On the way there, she asked me again to tell her what had happened in Vienna with these two boys, I hadn't ever wanted to tell her the particulars. She prodded me again: I had told her too much, and not enough, she wanted details. I said: "But it was a spiritual relationship." She said: "I trust you, I showed you myself naked. I showed you those photos nobody had ever seen." She insisted.

Finally I took a pencil, a sheet of paper, and started drawing the erotic positions we had enacted. The driver watched this exchange through his rearview mirror, he saw that she folded the paper in four and that she slipped it, as in the stories of yore, into her bosom.

When she came back home, the bedroom was empty. She knew I wouldn't come back. In her bedroom, she unfolded the paper, and she scrutinized the poses, her fingers spread apart the lips of her crotch. Finally she found a new envelope, because she had torn the one containing her photos: on it she drew a skull and crossbones, put fifty dollars in it as well as a note where she begged the governess to tear up the envelope if she ever died. In another envelope, she inserted her photos, and enveloped them within this paper containing the erotic positions of the three boys. There, all alone, she started laughing.

I saw her again in New York two months later. I bought a plane ticket on an impulse, I'd never been to New York. I was suffocating in Paris, New York was the last chance I had, it was make-or-break for me. For her, too, New York was her last chance: the R. house swallowed up millions each month, and as she hadn't worked in ten years now, she got her money from progressively selling off the shares she had in Switzerland, and the funds were running out, soon she would be forced to sell her furniture, her rugs, her jewels. She was too proud to sell them: even to thieves or fences, and at reduced prices, she knew that these sales could not remain anonymous. She had the idea of launching a collection of bath towels, bed coverings, pillowcases, or tooth glasses featuring her clumsy drawings. She came to New York to sell her name, her brand, which she had always refused thus far, when she had been offered millions of dollars. But now her name had lost its luster and she was muddled up in matters of percentages, managers and lawyers, she signed papers that were switched at the final moment with other contracts not in her favor.

The day after I had arrived, we went to see a play on Broadway: it was so boring that she fell asleep on my shoulder and to fend off my own boredom I started writing the review on a small strip of paper. We wanted to be the first ones out, before the applause, but we found ourselves under the theater awning, facing an unrelenting downpour. I flagged a cab, it drove past, it was right when all the theaters were letting out. Everyone else came out and gathered around us under the awning. The rain made a practically impervious bulwark. She was wearing her apple-green mink, she had her sunglasses on, and by chance she was right beside an Asiatic dwarf, who was mistaken for her devoted admirer. The people who recognized her stared at her in shock: how could a woman like her have ended up in the same situation as them, reduced to this pathetic wait? A man positioned himself right in front of her, set off the blinding flash of an Instamatic in her face, and turned away without even saying a word to her. Behind her sunglasses, I could see tears. She said: "It's so stupid that I left this phone number at the house, I could have called my friend, he could have sent us a limo." But I knew there was no friend and no limo. I ventured into the rain to get us a cab and I came back unsuccessful. Despair had fallen upon us and soaked us.

Finally I suggested that we walk in the rain. For half an hour now she had been stuck among these people looking at her like a monkey, there was no other solution. She unfolded the program above her wig and set off beneath the waters. We walked for a while before stopping under the awning of a movie theater that had just switched off its marquee. People were running in all directions while screaming, the cabs were honking relentlessly. Two cops were off to the side, with their walkie-talkies, under the same awning. One of them, the younger one, looked at her, went red, and, after a pause, walked up and spoke to her like a true gentleman: "Pardon me, ma'am, I'm sorry to bother you, but aren't you Madame X?" At that moment, despair seemed to fall away from her, she came back to, those words of recognition brought her back to life, like a suicide revived with a few whiffs of oxygen. He said: "I see, ma'am, that you and your friend seem to be inconvenienced by the rain, may we call a car for you?" He turned to speak into the walkie-talkie, as if he didn't want to bother her even more with such a trifling thing, half a minute later an enormous police car came to a stop in front of us and opened its doors for us. The cops put on the siren, they said "We are so honored to assist Madame X," they didn't even ask for photos or autographs. The car stopped right at the doors of the restaurant where she had reserved a table for two.

A wondrous moment had passed: being in New York, at night, in a police car, with this practically divine woman beside me, I was intoxicated by the siren's noise and the car's speed, the cops' closeness, their respectful silence; as if I were basking in the glow of her fame and I alone had the ability to confer it upon her, I took her hand and kissed it.

At the moment of paying the check, we saw two new cops at the restaurant entrance asking the maître d' if Madame X and her friend would do them the honor of being accompanied by them to a place of their choice. She accepted warmly. But this time the cops asked for signed photos, she didn't have any with her, they would have to come up to her apartment. Talking to the doorman, because she was worried that she would be mistaken for a guilty woman who had been searched and arrested, she explained: "These gentlemen have been kind enough to accompany us back, and as thanks I would like to give them signed photos." She had a new lease on life. The two cops shyly entered the apartment, they were delighted to see just how much this apartment looked like what they had expected, with its smoked mirrors and all its ostentatious bad taste. They had kept their walkie-talkies with the wires dangling from their ears, because they weren't supposed to give the impression of being off duty. I photographed the two of them framing her, so much smaller than them both, in front of her bed . . .

Epilogue

There was a break that lasted several months, several years. We got upset with New York. Then one night, years later, she called me, once again, and her voice struck me as an apparition from the hereafter. I still hadn't moved. And I hadn't killed myself. I was crying, sitting on my bed. On my own continent, it was three in the morning. She said: "Are you asleep?" and I said "No, I'm crying." She wasn't on my wavelength of sadness, she said: "Don't cry, when a pope dies, they find a new one the next day." She was calling me because she had found the paper where I'd written to her (the only one I'd sent to her) by copying my diary: "She said that she had touched herself when she thought about me last night, to the point of drawing blood. I took her hand so she could touch my chest, so she could measure this emptiness that hollows out my sides, and she said: you have a heart . . ." She had torn up this paper, out of fear that her son might find it after her death. She said: "In this impossibility of love there will have been all the same a little love . . ."

Mauve the Virgin

Mauve the Virgin

One night Mauve danced with a fat woman, he pressed up against her and felt her massive belly against his body, through her clothes, bouncing and furrowed, rippled by their dance into waves, like unpredictable magma that might surge and graze him as he swayed; in the same way the woman felt his thinness.

Mauve saw the woman again a few years later, he couldn't remember the music they had slow-danced to, but he remembered precisely this impression of overflowing, all-encompassing flesh. But this memory had grown unreal because the woman, during this time she had been absent, had focused on losing weight, to seduce him, him or someone else, all her fat had melted away and so all around her stomach and thighs were tubes of twisted skin that a surgeon had then skillfully trimmed away. Mauve looked at the woman with a sense of well-being, of recognition. Seeing her new, tender skin on her bones, especially around her shoulders which a low-cut dress had left bare, he felt like he was the holder of a secret that put him in the catbird seat. Indeed, as if she were a diva, the woman had taken great care to destroy every photo of her as a fat woman. But Mauve had kept the image of her heft close to his own chest: her thinness merely had to be flaunted for him to be reminded of the fatness of the woman he had embraced one night.

Mauve had become friends with a small bit of awkwardly-knit wool too shapeless to be a scarf (and which would have been a truly mischievous handkerchief because the angora it had been stitched into would have set him sneezing anew), which he kept shut away in a box hidden like treasure deep within a wardrobe and which he took out each night when he was alone, turning off all the lights out of fear that his neighbors might, peering through their jalousies, notice him. He spoke to it. He would have happily dreamed of gloves or briefs but such a dream was too insidious, too intense, too absurd for him to even be able to imagine hands on this earth that might willingly carry out this work for him, should his request one day no longer be unspeakable. No, there were no silky, voluptuous gloves or briefs, it was nothing more than a rag, an unfortunate cast-off that he defiled doggedly.

Another woman gave Mauve a nail and said: keep this, it will bring you luck, and Mauve immediately knew that this nail would bring him misfortune. How could what had pierced the palms and the feet of the Christ possibly bring him happiness? In front of the woman, without her realizing it, with a deft sleight of hand, Mauve let the nail slip out of his hand and abandoned it without a sound—and that was the real art in his action, because nails clink—in the nearest gutter.

That night, for the fifty-first time in his life (he hadn't counted them, but his biographer is perfectly capable of knowing this number), Mauve returned to the "Las Vegas" and jumped over his shadow; usually, these stays dissolved in the silence of his observation. Nobody here knew his name, he was hungry only for faces, and he waited patiently for incidents, words, brawls, standing at a particular spot in the massive carpeted slot-machine room, like an off-center pawn from the billiard table set in the middle, he always walked back out alone, feeling sated. For the first time, he took a step forward, he came up to a boy. The Turk said he was named Ali, he was lying, and he cracked all the joints of his knuckles one by one, he said: I know how to crack all the joints of my body like that, pay me. In the street the boy was silent. In Mauve's apartment, as soon as they had entered, the boy stripped down and lay on the bed. He spread his toes and cracked them one by one, all nine of them because one had been shorn off in an accident. The night deepened the silence, Mauve stood a few feet from the bed. The boy stood up and grabbed his left jaw with all his strength, as if he wanted to unscrew his head, and after a great deal of effort a single crackling sound could be heard from his neck. The boy, on a roll, cracked his arms and forearms, then his legs, his kneecaps, his hips, his wrists, his shoulders, his shoulder blades, and finally his ankles, each note was different and the specific service seemed to have been determined in advance. All these flashes of sound affronted Mauve endlessly, they disgusted him like the smell of heated leather, at the same time these noises electrified his lower back and warmed his crotch, he hadn't taken the time to get undressed and stayed where he was, still a few feet from the bed, everything fell away in silence. The boy braced himself in a particular way, tensed the bow of his spine, and after a few seconds without moving, he could hear the incredible sound, the thunderbolt of his spinal column giving way under the contraction. A play on words occurred to Mauve, it's almost as if he wants me to jump his bones!, but he didn't have the time to say it, he could feel his semen spreading in his underwear. The boy pretended not to see, he turned onto his stomach and said to Mauve: Will you do me a favor? Take off your shoes, I won't make you pay. Mauve removed his shoes and his socks, the Turk asked him to walk up and down his back, he groaned happily. The two boys said good-bye once the work was done.

It's a square courtyard with its center taken up by a hostile, black, bluntly blocked-out mass even though it's in the center of the city, which could house those enormous rats that gnaw at the toes and knuckles of the idiots or bastards that come and do their dirty work there. A slanting ray of weak light rakes this space and illuminates, in the distance, a multicolored cloth that's barely visible (cloths are so lucky to be multicolored) that betrays the presence, on the other side, under the front steps, of a body on the lookout. This single light comes from the caretaker's lodge, it's rundown, and at this hour it's unclear whether they're asleep or even existent, whether the light is just a nightlight. On the street, Mauve followed a guy, it's the first time he's done this but ever since his adventure the other night, with the Turk, this virgin boy has become emboldened (he'll get younger from one episode to the next). The guy is wearing a blue-and-white fisherman's sweater and has noticed that Mauve is following him, before going in under the archway he turned around one last time and Mauve couldn't be sure whether this was a conspiratorial sign of sorts or a threat. But there, at the end of the courtyard he's crossing, is the other boy, not moving, waiting for him, wearing the same striped sweater: but he's smaller, and this can't be a twin. Still unsure, Mauve keeps going, and the boy pulls away from the other to swoop in on him, this time thoroughly menacing. He speaks to Mauve, not bothering to whisper because now the other one is too far away to hear, and he pulls Mauve by the sleeve out to the street, he says: I'll meet you any night and any time, but not tonight, go on, leave us alone or I'll break your head open, I've got a billy club under my arm. But that's the only night Mauve wants to touch this boy and he knows that on another night, at another time, he'll have forgotten him. He ends up alone on the street, one of his shoelaces undone but as he now knows that he's in his dream (in a later episode, he's been killed off weeks earlier, but at night he haunts the author with his own features), he doesn't take the trouble to crouch down to retie it, an undone shoelace in a dream cannot really make him stumble. This is where he's lying: there weren't shoes, he might have even been barefoot, yet the dark space that he had to cross, a few minutes earlier, and its jagged rubble have never bothered him. He's now daydreaming while thinking of a way to retell this story, it's five in the morning, he's coming out of a bad sleeping-pill-induced sleep (which should dull his stitches, his itching) and if he gets up he'll be too cold to write. The components of the story get mixed up in another dream, a more boring one that erases it. He loses the story.

When he was old, like so many others, Mauve left for the desert. He didn't go into the city of Ghardaïa, where the houses are blue. He headed away from the encampment, he hated the men, and carried his sleeping bag, he stopped where he thought he was directly below the moon. In March, the snakes and scorpions were still in their nests, but he tied plastic bags around his feet, he had heard that these animals that sting men dead are drawn to the smell of their feet and are intoxicated by sweat in socks. Once the moon had disappeared from the sky he was still asleep, he saw four Fulbe Mbororo ahead of him, two young women and two young men, he saw them coupling rather strangely and his semen made his belly cold. In the morning the encampment was broken down, he tore up the plastic bags so he could never protect himself again, he came across a Fulbe Mbororo asking for water for her baby, the German jeeps never stopped, the man who was making the same trip by bike had jury-rigged a device to pedal in the sand, the madman showed him the dollar he always kept in a pocket and which garnered him some offerings, the other madmen said that this man had a festering congolo, he wondered what state his own might be in. The men from the encampment, which had moved, were cooking, he was always fleeing them, his own hatred astonished him, he'd never felt it so intensely, it made him want to kill, he went off with his camera. He walked until he saw a mountain shaped like a comb: this land had never been described or transcribed on a map, and the comb was too big to unknot any hair that wasn't the goddesses'. The comb hid a basin with various heaps of rocks that the sun's crimping had set ablaze from behind; because of the glare he couldn't photograph anything. There, while biotechnologists in Japan were making giant crabs, accelerating hens' growth and creating diabolical sustenance from microbes and algae, Mauve started singing something inchoate akin to a bel canto. He decided that someday he would bring an orchestra, singers, and an audience there. His song couldn't reach anyone but if God was anywhere at that moment, He wouldn't be there immanently but deep within Mauve's heart.

A year before his son was born, not suspecting for even a moment that he might have a son, Mauve's father started painting a fresco. He was in front of a blank wall, the recesses of which seemed to define the frame of a painting, and he had brought back from a trip to Poland a discount art magazine published in the Soviet Union with several images that he liked. He couldn't have invented a design himself, not for lack of imagination, because his mind was teeming with scenes, but for lack of faith in his hand, which his wrist could barely hold until his pleasure was gone. He could carry things while doing things at home, his mind emptied out and he had the stiffness of a server. What he was incapable of, he believed, was laying hands on someone else, or carrying a child on his back, he would have collapsed. There was a virginity to his actions that ennobled him, despite himself, even when those around him were stuffing their faces, even when his wife was parting thighs with her hands: a vertigo turned this sturdy man's fingers into butter or wax. He chose one of the images and started gridding it with a ruler to reproduce it in precise proportions, he didn't have that set of jointed bars, a pantograph, that could copy a design and enlarge it; besides, using such a thing would have bothered him. The process of making the fresco gave him actual fevers, dreams, a zeal that lasted five days. The plastered, cleaned, sanded wall was covered with the dark lines of a lead pencil which the paint would obscure. The Soviet magazine was opened to the page with the image, lying on a trestle, the fold of the cutter divided the reproduction in half, the other, perpendicular line slipped away and spread across the full length of the wall. It represented a horizon, defined by a bank where the outlines of three bodies had just sat down, facing away, still nude for the moment, followed by the slightly complex bulk of a seaplane taking flight. The arm of one of the three seated bodies, the one on the right, whose massive back seemed to result from a deformation, was outstretched to point it out, and it was almost possible to see, if the copy had gone a bit further—just a week would have been enough—a small sliver of his face. But this character never had any eyes or mouth on this wall that Mauve stared at without realizing it for all his childhood, as if this anomaly, in the form of such insidiously familiar banality, had slipped, through his eyes, which had always seen it, to lodge somewhere inside him between his head and his heart, like a disgusting nook, a cavern of awkwardness that refashioned, or rather reerased, all his inner being, like an unseeing specter of incompleteness. On the sixth day of his labor—this task required all his strength, he could not do anything else—once the shadows of the design were drawn, with still no hint of their skins, Mauve's father went to get a paint box with some colors that were nothing more than dust, and which had to be wetted heavily for him to make a paste. Only the blues were reliable. He diluted them and started smearing it over the expanse of the sea, because that was clearly what it was about. But this blue was so slight that it faded and time made it hard to remember that there had been paint there. Young Mauve, over all these years of observation, still saw the sea there, the massive sea with its waves, its tempests and calms, its changing blues, its betrayals. His mother came to the restaurant where the father, the cowardly artist, ate alone in the Latin quarter, she shot a bullet in his back. She knew that divorce would take her child away and she wanted to keep him, she proudly made herself a prisoner. She had cheated and the father had asked for a divorce. Before Mauve was born, long before being cut down, this man had gone looking for a deep ultramarine blue that he had long been fiddling with on the palette, the sea had disheartened him, but once he had the color in hand, even though it wasn't in the original painting, he had been in a rush to apply it, without trying to even it out, in thick, clumsy streaks, on the right corner of the painting, within the limits established by this cliff's edge circumscribing the horizon. Then he left everything in disarray, the paints stuck together again, their grains colorfast, and the two clasps of the paint box started sticking again under their varnish; he never opened it again. Often his wife, who was waiting for their child, said: you should get back to that old fresco, you should finish it before he's born otherwise it'll scare him, it'll obsess him. One time, seeing how reluctant he was, she decided to apply a layer of white to the panel, specifically did so in front of him, unafraid of getting hit, and so slowly that it seemed like she was just waiting for his hand to catch her wrist; he twisted it harshly, did not raise his voice, did not explain, did not apologize. The child was born and the intense blue of the cliff's corner resisted the dust, the sun's bleaching, the sponge's stealthy wiping. And this useless, artificial blue entered the child's soul through his wordless, stubborn watching. During the domestic disputes that he evaded, in all the pains of his young heart, after being scolded or shamed, in fever or in boredom, Mauve resorted to this fresco, so accustomed was he to it that he didn't even notice it anymore, but as he determinedly examined it through its smallest details, the shameful anomaly that it represented. He stood in front of it for hours, he adored it and he cursed it, it was his prayer, his reading, his confidant, his friend, a yearning for dreams, for softness, for the laziness of schoolchildren just as much as the forcefulness of imagined adventures, of lies. He never forgot that it was his father's hand that had woven it, even if he had signed it with his spinelessness, and he submitted to it as he would a branding iron, a blazing stamp. When his mother was imprisoned, he stayed all alone with the fresco. It seemed like the woman, the aunt who cooked his meals and washed his clothes, read his report cards, didn't exist, was merely a puppet, while the fresco ruled the apartment, his father's soul was embedded in the insidious blue of the cliff, he saw everything. He dreamed or often fantasized that he was rubbing it with filth, that he was spitting in its face, that he was emptying the trashcan on it, that he was scratching it with his long nails that he didn't want to cut, it was still a way of adoring it. He sucked at drawing, in front of every sheet of Canson paper his hand froze up. Whenever he wanted to draw a house or an animal, he was convinced that the brush, despite himself, as if animated by a devil, would go back to emptying the empty squares of the fresco and, instead of a window or some fur, would give eyes and a mouth to this empty quarter of a face that haunted him. His hand hovered and he was seized by a shiver that often drove him to tear the sheet. Because of these bouts his aunt made him dispense with drawing, she put him in front of a psychologist who linked this difficulty to his mother's actions. Mauve didn't need to travel, to move at all, the fresco unfailingly represented all the potential abstractions of escape, night fell over the painting and he very clearly saw his three characters shivering, he wanted to be able to cover them, make them drink something warm, he wasn't attached to any one of them in particular and hadn't given them names. The day came when his aunt's indiscretion revealed that his father wasn't the author of the fresco, that he had simply copied it and stopped short. He only liked it all the more: even though he couldn't explain why, this information brought him closer to his father. But he wanted to find the original, compare it, and maybe, who knew, continue the fresco, finish it. His father had hid the magazine deep within a closet: Mauve unearthed it, but the page that the painting was on had been torn out, thrown away by Mauve's father. The discovery of the mangled publication drove him into torpor, into stupid, pointless, spiteful rage: flies were all that he could crush in his hand. As he ate, his back teeth bit into the insides of his cheeks. All this while, in prison, his mother was knitting sweaters that he only wore once a week, the day he came to visit. After seven and a half years she was released and in a book she talked about the murder, the trial, and her time in prison, she gave interviews, went on television. Mauve was going to turn eighteen. On the street, he saw one of his mother's acquaintances and he leaped energetically onto the man, madly begging him: the man next to him hadn't recognized him, Mauve asked him to come forward and tell his mother to stop all this ballyhoo, which exposed and humiliated him. But the man was afraid of this woman and, on the street, he felt an unspeakable attraction to this man which his fear thwarted, and he left him to fend for himself. Mauve didn't stare at the fresco anymore, he couldn't do so anymore, his mother wanted to move out, the subsequent tenants deemed the fresco a blemish. It saddened Mauve to think that his father's only artwork would be covered with a new color or some shiny wallpaper. He wanted to go to sea and signed up for a sailing school. They were trying out a new concept: each student went out on a boat, alone with an instructor. The students, who paid for their training, were supposed to choose their guides. There was a cabal against one of the instructors, just out of prison, who, rumor had it, had once murdered a man. Nobody wanted to sail with him. Mauve openly shunned the scorn: his own mother, too, had just come out of prison, where she had been for more than seven years, for a murder (he intentionally did not say that it was his own father she had killed), and he called the group of apprentices petty-bourgeois, chicken, bitter. They had to trust this person who wanted to reintegrate, like a righteous person, into society: as such, he would be the first one to sail with him, he wasn't afraid. When Mauve was alone with the man on the boat and he realized that the man wanted to kill him, his conscience slipped into such distress that he prepared himself for blows and didn't feel any. The murderer didn't really have a motive: he could have made him his companion or his wife, but he didn't touch him, he didn't even think of stripping off his clothes before throwing him into the drink. He hadn't contemplated this murder before embarking, he just knew that he would steal the boat, but everything in Mauve's bearing, especially his gaze, cried out for murder. And it seemed that in killing this innocent man, that this repeat offender would add new luster to his future. In breaking his head with one of the skiff's oars, he didn't say anything, not even: I'm going to kill you, not even an insult, not even the beginning of a prayer. Mauve was kneeling on the deck, he was letting some seawater into a bucket to rinse a jar of vegetables, he heard a creaking behind him. As he turned he saw the man, who he had gotten along with so nicely on land, the whole night before, with the paddle in his hand. Time stretched out, his sight blurred, now he could only hear the roar of the turbines, the lack of wind having forced them to set off using the motor. At that moment, universal memory recorded the greatest vertigo that any consciousness had ever experienced. No man sentenced to death nor executioner, no victim nor exterminator, neither God nor even the devil when they were still men, had discerned such a perfect logic in their fate. Mauve's soul, bursting apart beneath the broken bones, went flying toward the fresco.

Flash Paper

Fernand came to Rio, spectral, accompanied by an admirer. But I'll say these words to him in that order, and he'll reject them: no, not an admirer, a friend, a drinking buddy. This first line, in fact, is doubly deceptive: that Fernand was spectral is perfectly evident, I could have said wan or pale if I weren't tired of those words, I could have also said jaundiced if I'd liked him less. I hadn't been expecting him, I'd left him this phone number by chance, not thinking that he'd use it, only to hear his voice, so close, telling me: I'm on the island. Because that's the original deception: it would be reasonable to presume that this Rio is de Janeiro, in Brazil, but it's the name of a village on the island of Elba. I say to him: but where on the island? He says to me: I don't know. I say to him: but at which port? He says to me: I took the boat from Italy. I say to him: yes, of course, but where did you dock, I need to know that to come find you, at Portoferraio, at Porto Azzurro, at Rio Marina? He says to me: I'm going to ask, I'll call you back. We go to find him at Portoferraio. He's sitting by the port, in the sun, hunched over his baggage, and it's there, on the other side of the window as the car backs in, that there bursts forth, as if by a negative reflection, his white, muted pallor from an archaic era. His companion, by contrast, is reddish and his complexion drives me to offer him, quickly, perhaps spitefully, perhaps also out of sympathy, a glass of wine despite the early hour that would only bring another small blush of red to the crevices of his rosaceate nose. I stop there: it's goodwill that I'm looking for. Fernand swiftly evinced a coruscating, demonstrative, unparalleled cruelty. We were sitting on the couch, a wild child, Fernand, and me, I was between them. Fernand had, without uttering a sentence, plunged into a book on sign language. The child horsed around with me and with every move he almost knocked me onto Fernand, which I avoided doing. I warned the child with some wryness. But he crept up to Fernand, and pinched him, very gently, softly, ever so slightly inconveniencing him as he read. Fernand bellowed and we saw an astounding thing: his face suddenly seized and swollen by a burst of spitefulness that had him pouncing upon the child, twisting his arm to get control, methodically pulling up his sleeve, and, patronizingly, with his two fingers curved threateningly like horrible pliers, squeezing his skin until he drew blood and the child was writhing in pain. Then he picked his book back up, placated, leaving us there stupefied by such an extraordinary expression of cruelty. We went out to an abandoned valley, the summer residence of the noble family from the village, a slumping stone archway, two tall symmetrical cypress trees at the entrance, a chapel now adorned by goat droppings. Fernand caressed the trees, his eyes full of emptiness, his palm moving back and forth along the bark. A black goat with curved horns had caught itself while tightening around a tree its length of rope: very slowly, without talking to it, at the risk of getting gored, Fernand freed the weak animal, making it step over the multiple coils of rope. Then he chomped on an amanita mushroom that he'd just picked, saying he would have to eat several to be poisoned. In the cemetery, I saw him leaning over a funeral urn, absorbed in intense, senseless contemplation; I glanced over his shoulder at what he was scrutinizing and finally made out a drowned aphid. With Bernard we talked about the huge Milanese and Florentine cemeteries: about those stone bodies, life-size, with their uniforms, erected above the graves, and about these protruding forearms, these imploring hands, and about the monumental mausoleums, the pyramids, the marble palm trees bowed by tempests. Fernand said that he'd never seen a tempest at sea, he'd taken his first voyage at twenty-eight years old. Bernard described the grave of a mountaineer who had fallen while climbing a peak: they had placed a huge rock encircled by climbers atop the headstone, and above it an eagle bearing the hero's replica to heaven. I asked Fernand what sort of grave he might be dreaming of (he was shocked that the dead of this land were set not in the ground but rather in compartments aboveground), he reflected and responded: with a bit of sand, and an anthill. Sitting right beside him again on the couch, once the child was gone, I sensed that there was no getting closer to him; he'd immediately look up from his book to give me a glare like a furious animal in its cage. I imagined that he had been raised in a zoo. But he had been raised among his brothers, by the slag heap where his father, a small yet honorable man, worked. Now, every time he saw him, his father cried. I told Fernand just how much the child had been affected by the malice of his pinch: when he left, he rested his elbow on the car's hood, looking at the sea, and recalled it as a supernatural, magical flash of an event. Fernand started looking piously repentant and said: it was just because I wanted to play your games, but I didn't know how. At night we contemplated a walk. Fernand said he'd take one with me. I took him to a place inaccessible at night: a craggy mountain on the edge of a cliff. We didn't have a flashlight, I was always scared climbing up, but a bit less than going down. To cross a small stream in the afternoon, he'd presented me, like a squire, with a clenched fist at the end of his outstretched arm: I'd leaned upon it, and I'd felt a rising pleasure that we were reenacting this pair of painted plaster figurines that, when I was a child, had made me dream of the Middle Ages. As we climbed upward we sank into darkness: we could barely make out the curves of the path. In the distance, I heard Fernand stepping away to get closer to the gulch. I pulled him near and grabbed his arm. We made our way up the path this way, clutching each other like two blind men, hurtling happily, trusting each other entirely too much, toward peril. We both saw at the same moment a shooting star tracing a horizontal line nearby. The edge of the woods was no longer reddening like the last time I'd climbed this: no warm breath nor crackling came down in waves that caressed our hair and bathed our lips, bearing dragonflies with rasping wings that were fleeing the fire I had been describing to Fernand. We had reached the summit: the esplanade razed by the wind overlooked the island's two coves, revealing further down bays of bluish fog that made the lights wink. I felt an intense sensation of physical joy, of keen coldness, of exaltation: our heads were raised to the heavens. I stepped closer to Fernand, wavered at kissing him; at the moment I decided not to, my mouth said despite myself: may I kiss you? He said: you may. Our mouths were warm. I was happy and there was no longer this melancholy distance between joy and its representation, feeling and its expression, the present moment and eternity. Fernand kept his eyes open: when I saw this, in opening mine, I saw before me, sunken within the deep shadows of his upturned face, a shaky yet steady eye, midnight blue, carved within a carnation's violet crinkles, hazy and mad, unforgettable, beseeching like the miserable, reeking eye of the rhinoceros emerging from the straw. Out of the extended, warm pleasure of the kiss came other visions: we were two animals that had met on the terreplein, each from our own half of the forest, two horned beasts, two giant snails, two unhappy hermaphrodites. We kissed each other exactly as I kissed with my sister when we were little, sticking our tongues out of our mouth to rub our tips together, then he slipped his tongue into the quivering space between lip and gum, exploring the frenum of my tongue like that of a penis. And so we became two madmen escaped from an asylum, committing a final insane act before the nurses in white shirts, lying low in these bushes which had caught fire, came out running from every corner to restrain us in strait-jackets yet again. Then pleasure won out over caprice, and the kiss stretched out. Two days earlier, after nightfall, we had come by car with Bernard to this promontory to set off fireworks that shot up with humanlike cries, Japanese-style ones that exploded into bouquets. These fires, these works had become wishes. We came back down the sharp slope at a run, hand in hand, jumping over the ruts just as we flew in our dreams. I was happy and writing this a week later, refusing to believe the power of secrets, is painfully vertiginous.

I took Fernand to the café, I who usually feel so cowardly, so ill at ease there, I was proud to show off my darling to the waiters and the village drunkards. One of them, almost a dwarf, elevated to nobility by a drunkenness that made him dance in homage to all the world's striptease dancers, who had called me a dead man just two days earlier, grabbed Fernand's sleeve and called him a mute man. He asked what he did for a job. I said that he wrote, he didn't want to believe that, he repeated: tell me the truth, what does this boy do? He tried to sell Fernand to a little blonde bed-wetter walking past. We drank some Strega, the witch, a liqueur of heady herbs that married the chosen ones but sometimes doomed them.

I went down into the alcove where Fernand had set up his bed, I had hesitated to go down, I hesitated to stay. With sexuality we were at risk of falling into commonness. For hours we kissed without even the curiosity of our crotches. His wide-open eye had awakened mine and did not leave it: we had become insects. Fernand now bore several masks depending on whether I was near or far away, in a public place or a private one, and I struggled to connect all these aspects, his round-mouthed princess aspect, his hick aspect, his haughty aspect, and his frenzied aspect. He had the hands of my first love, staggeringly beautiful hands, and he had his skin, he had his torso, he also had, a little, his sharp features and his long blond hair. As before, I'd taken off my clothes to get into the bed. He stroked my torso and talked to me about his beloved brother, the youngest one, Maurice. He was a ruddy brute, always in a bad mood, always drunk, who he fought with, fished with for the pure pleasure of chopping off eels' heads. He squandered their father's money on nights of drunkenness: Fernand remembered the time when the five brothers would come home early in the morning full of beer, finding their worried, muttering father in the kitchen headed off to the coal mines. I bragged about having the same name as this favorite brother. Fernand seemed delighted to tell me that Maurice hated me, that he talked about me like a devil. I dreamed about monkeys that had climbed on top of each other in a doorway to form a pyramid. I went to look for my camera but when I came back to the site of that scene, it had collapsed. In the depths of the darkness, the unruly monkeys bit my feet and I showed those wounds to my father.

The night of New Year's Eve, the neighbor's fat little daughter wanted us to come to the ball that the communists had planned in the school basement. Black curtains had been hung over the gym windows, garlands were strung between the fluorescent lights. On a makeshift platform six village boys were pretending to be musicians, the instruments merely seeming to be extensions of their costumes. The room filled little by little: the old women had gathered in a corner while the old men in holiday dress were walking around with their hands in their pockets; the virgins were giggling in the corner opposite from their grandmothers, the suitors did not come, most of them having gone to celebrate at a classier, pricier party or at an actual discotheque. The music here was old-fashioned and sublime: waltzes, cha-chas, polka dances, paso dobles, twists. For Fernand I'd put on my Spencer jacket, my red pants, a white shirt, and a bow tie, I'd trotted out my musketeer's black shoes with buckles once again. We drank grappa, a local pomace brandy. I told Fernand, sitting beside me like a shy little girl, that I wanted to kiss him, French him on the dance floor. I asked our host, who only lived half the year in this village, for permission to do so, and he refused categorically. I was sad: I told Fernand that the two of us would go and dance together outside, on the other side of the black curtains, all while enjoying the muted music, like two poor shameful animals. I took his hand and examined his nails: they were unusually beautiful, strangely thick, apparently varnished, of a noble pink, clipped in such a way that they seemed to have been chiseled into his flesh. I especially admired the nail on his left thumb, which was far more beautiful than all the others. I made him admire it. He pulled his knife out of his pocket and started to cut away his nail to give it to me, not so much as a sign of love as much as an old ritual to rebuke all excessive laudations. To punish or to congratulate the flatterer, but above all to prove his own humility. I pounced on Fernand to pull away the knife which had already started, little by little, to pop off the nail. The rhythm of the music was frenetic, completely unsuitable for dancing. We struggled. I dragged this fight onto the floor in order to turn it into a dance. Our bodies straightened, hand in hand we jumped without glancing at anybody or anything other than our dangerous momentum. We danced like two spider crabs being boiled, destroying everything in their path. The orchestra gradually stopped playing: the musicians set their instruments down on the floor, some pairs stopped dancing. We kept on as we were, I was in such a state of shame and pride that I couldn't stop myself anymore, since we had already lost face we might as well wait for rocks or jeers to be hurled at us. But in the group of old women, one of them began to clap, followed by the rest of them. The musicians picked their instruments back up one by one, and the looks we traded as we went to sit down again were those of recognition, our mouths dry, our hearts pounding. Donatus and his brother had arrived. I let Fernand know, he hadn't seen them yet but this sentence excited him. Donatus, obviously, would be the name of one of his characters. Donatus had changed: he was no longer grimy and no longer stank of the garlic he chewed a fresh clove of every morning to cleanse his mouth and teeth. He had cut his hair, which he was starting to lose, and at the same time there was in his gait a momentary acceptance of his smallness which made it all the more touching. He was smiling at us. His younger brother, Uriel, was a big fellow with thick, tousled hair, his waist which he often ran his hands over was molded by a black doublet that accentuated the contrasting cloth and striking color of his sleeves, which had likely been puffed up to stand out from this seemingly armor-plated finery. I asked Fernand to join me for a slow dance, holding him tight, almost hugging him, my stiffness at odds with the lithesome upstroke of his arms. A city man making a country man dance. I whispered:

tomorrow we'll find owls nailed to our door. Our host, who had congratulated us during the first dance, disapproved of this. Fernand complained about my stiffness. I urged him to invite the two brothers, which one would he pick? He blushed as he said Donatus. I went up ahead of Fernand and bowed in front of Uriel who laughed and pulled me into a waltz mixed with a carmagnole, a dance of two drunken pillagers, two savages flayed by shame, the joined fists held out like a club, two sodomizing knights. I noticed Fernand getting up behind me and shyly making his way to Donatus, I looked for him among the more dignified couples, they were dancing a bourrée. In the middle of the dance Uriel stopped, took my wrist to position my hand within his, and then, once our fingers were intertwined, went back to dancing. With the obese young girl who had accompanied us acting as go-between, the village's girls invited us to dance with them one by one, a beatific smile on their lips when they managed not to burst out laughing. While I was dancing with Fernand again, an old man cut in, put a brush in my hand, and dragged a baffled Fernand away. I presumed it was a gesture of humiliation and, unsure how to retort, danced alone with the brush. Then I went up to Fernand and the old man to embrace them both from behind, stroking the man's bald head with the brush. But the livid man made it clear that I was playing the wrong game: I was supposed to pass the brush to another couple to separate them and cut in. I went and chose the butcher. But the brush kept coming back to Fernand, and he complained that everyone wanted to separate him from his favorite dance partner, who wasn't me anymore. I asked the fat little girl to a slow dance with me, Fernand claimed to have watched us and told me that he had never seen such a sad dance in his life. The music grew sultrier, I suggested to Fernand and the two brothers that we dance the maniacs' dance. The communist mayor walked up to our host and asked him if it was true, as rumor had it, that I was a dancer at the Opéra de Paris. Of course, said our host. If he's really a dancer, the mayor said, then he's a third-rate one. When we left the ball, two old men from the village were dancing together. A turntable stood in for the orchestra. We invited the brothers to the house. Uriel was wearing a wedding ring, I asked him who he was married to, and he said, to the light. I fell asleep in sodomy.

Fernand and I were woken up by Donatus's son. It was early, we had only slept five hours, the two brothers were dragging us out for a walk. We went up to the terrace for breakfast, the sun was harsh on our faces. Donatus's son was flipping through the program for a circus and bursting out in laughter every time he came across the photo of the little girl training ponies. We started walking. The partygoers hadn't woken up yet. We left the village and descended into a valley, crossed several streams, tramped through the mud or over trunks and boards to avoid doing so, all the while Fernand held his fist out to me. We came to the small house that Donatus had renovated and where he would be living for two months with his brother in order to build a patio and shore up a seawall wrecked by the last flood. In the wash house, Fernand caught a toad. He told me that he would make me eat it alive, and I couldn't chew. But instead he kissed the toad on its lips, the animal became the fat little girl who had taken us to the ball. We leaned over the basin to watch, in the greenish gleam, an enormous, swollen female toad that a male perched atop as it drained itself, emptying itself of its semen. Fernand's arms had come out of the water to catch the toad, I started massaging the veins up to his heart. The two brothers were sitting side-by-side on a wooden plank, their faces bisected by the sun, their hands magnificent. A mongrel dog had followed us and was running around furiously, jumping on us, getting mud on our pants and biting the child. Fernand started hypnotizing it, holding its jaws shut between his hands, until the dog fell down, immobile. A fire broke out: at first it was just a caterpillar that was chewing away at the tree above our heads, then a woodpecker pecking at the trunk of a distant tree, and finally flames started fanning out just above the hill. We wanted to go lend a hand but it was just a controlled burn that some horrid thieves had started.

They had to leave, to catch the boat. On the quay Fernand's companion mentioned that he had forgotten his red scarf at the house, and so he was offering it to me. He had found it himself on a coat rack, as he was leaving a *terminale* classroom, and he adored it. Fernand was no good at goodbyes. But, as the boat pulled away, he unwound his silk scarf from his neck and tied it to one of the poles so as to let his profile linger, through its movements, for a while longer in my sights.

As soon as we got back we found the scarf and threw it into the stove, contemplating the cremation of the red wool until an acrid, synthetic smoke chased us out of the room. Fernand had told me that he would write a story that would be titled "Donatus and His Brother," I had yelled at him on the boat to send me a copy once he'd finished it. I, in turn, took five pages of notes for a story that would be called, I haven't decided yet, "On a Few Moments of Grace" or "Magnified Observation." But I'd presented this title to Fernand, because he was struggling with his own observation, and he'd found it hideous. More than a story, what I wanted to write to him was a letter.

Fernand was gone, and even though I had told him that I would sleep there again, I left our bedroom cold and dark. Glimpsing it through the ajar door as I went into the bathroom, I avoided it. Fernand was gone, but grace remained, and his absence had made it all ever so slightly more melancholic. We went to say good-bye to the two brothers, the light had disappeared from the countryside. I wanted to take a photograph of Uriel with his face blindfolded, his hand held out for his brother to place a toad there. But we did not go back to the wash house, and other photos evidently had to be taken: Uriel painting in the valley, in front of the nobles' summer residence. He put away his equipment, Chinese pots of flared black stone that tinged the water, the paintbrushes that he rinsed and pinched between his lips before wrapping them in straw, all his small containers of nibs or erasers that he tied shut with his teeth, and finally his black watercolor set with his wash drawing taped to the cover. Seeing him enact these gestures was a reason to be over-joyed. I thought as I watched him: he had once been a little boy who always came into the house and observed things from a distance, drawing them or not doing anything. We had brought a white table-cloth, some cold cuts, and a rare wine from Moselle, made from a varietal that was picked grape by grape, pressed by clean hands, and which we hid from our Fernand who wanted to teach us the art of betrayal. Donatus had found a spot for the picnic, we had to start walking again. Uriel handed me the small case where he put his drawings and my palm experienced the pleasure of touching the wood exactly where it had been carved by his own, and proudly returning it to him somewhat warmed. We found ourselves seated on each side of the cloth, we toasted and we set atop our piled-up hands the dog skull that Uriel lugged around with him everywhere. In the clearing, toward the setting sun, the muted roar of the electrical tower reached us like an offering. Were we taking part in this beauty? What seemed supernatural to us seemed ordinary to those who brought it to us. Were we now agreeing to present what was ordinary for us as what was supernatural?

Fernand's thought nagged: for me, love is a voluntary obsession, an unsure decision, one I haven't made yet. That night the two brothers came back to say good-bye to us, Uriel had brought his notebook of drawings to show them to us. The faces he had drawn were full of antipathy and we preferred to discreetly aim our gaze at the fingers that were turning the pages. It was his flesh that was beautiful, not the paper on which it had perspired, and which would remain once his flesh had become nothing. I caught Donatus's eye as his brother was admiring his drawings: a generous absence, a superior sort of modesty. He had given up being an artist and this hadn't in any way been a defeat. He would take up astrology.

For an entire afternoon, when I was alone again, I wandered through the zoo in Rome, looking through all its cages, its ponds, and its enclosures, for Fernand's eye. It was nowhere to be found. I sent him a postcard. Upon returning to Paris, I got it in my head to write this story. It was mad to use this past tense that too quickly became posterior; projecting myself into this posterity was a mortification. Once again it was the letters that I imprudently wrote him each day that took over the story. They were the true story. But, in making it linger, the letters exhausted the sentiment. And I knew that Fernand could throw them out without opening them, or fiddle with them to make wads or origami or paper airplanes, as if they were simply made out of blank flash paper. Flash paper, which can be bought at the pyrotechnic store, is basic folded paper that can be thrown at one's enemies, or at small children to rile them up, that catches fire with a vivid gleam and burns up without leaving a trace. We wasted it all for this New Year's Eve. One night, for the first and only time, I called Fernand. I asked him if he had received my letters. He said, very calmly: yes, I received them, but I haven't read them yet. In spite of his coarseness, I had wanted to reappear before him, disguised as a lover, standing halfway between declamation and secret.

Joan of Arc's Head

In December or November 19——, the paper sent me to do a story behind the scenes at a wax museum. I was greeted, in her office which also served as the staff library, by the director, a suspicious yet affable young lady. As she was telling me about the history of the museum, I examined the room: a reading desk with music scores, several violin cases, a metronome, a dark stuffed bird, the bookcases' glass panes seemed not to open anymore, none of the titles were familiar. The director led me into the museum's workshops, where cardboard outlines were boiled in vats then plastered over, where workers inserted the hairs one by one in the warm wax then painted the faces; she opened the drawers of eyes sorted by hue, with their iridescent globes blown out of glass mounted on curved stalks or bundled together in pairs with rubber bands. She unwrapped boxes of different clumps of natural hair, such long shocks that they could easily have been stolen from women in prison, but no lice jumped out of the crates, each wad of hair was gleaming, straightened, numbered. Finally she opened the door, which was always locked shut, at the back of the makeup room, to a storage room where disused heads were kept: swaddled in thick plastic bags, set in rows and packed tight on the shelves, often unrecognizable, they were the heads of men and women that current affairs had rejected, killed, or aged far too quickly: chiefs of state and champions, singers, overly resplendent young actresses: they stopped at the neck; their arms and hands, if they had been revealed, had been melted down again or modified on a rotating assembly line; the cumbersome bodies had been thrown into the junkyard. Sometimes, for a new diorama, an anonymous or secondary character had to be modeled, and a worker opened the storage room again to choose, somewhat at random, from the dozens of heads, lifting the plastic up to the lips, an obsolete character that could do the trick, that could be done up a bit, freshened up, cleaned up, dolled up, plucked or fattened a bit, to alter the caricature's features. I asked the director, somewhat at random as well, because there was so much there that it would have been thoroughly rude to stare at them as much as I would have liked, to unwrap a few of them. And so I saw Brigitte Bardot and Mao Tse-Tung, whose immediately recognizable physiognomy had escaped being recycled, a realistic singer whose hair was moth-eaten, a champion who had died while saving a child. On the lowest shelves entire torsos could be glimpsed, and I unearthed young fauns with thick-fleeced rears, flute players, horned half-beasts with crooked smiles. Before I left, since I couldn't bring myself to, I asked, at the risk of annoying the director completely, to see just one more head, one last one, that one. She had to be careful while handling it because it wasn't mounted on one of those wooden supports that fit within their forms, and its pose was, strangely enough, so off-kilter that there was no way to keep it balanced, it had to be supported on both sides at the temples, or else it could break. But we weren't there yet: there was no label on the plastic, it was knotted tightly with a cord. At last a face could be made out in its dusty chrysalis: at once a girl and a boy but rather without any sex or imbued with every sensuality, it was not so much a face as its sublimation, in a supplicant pose, beckoning either the flames of the stake, or the voices from the hereafter. It was Joan of Arc. Why had it been removed from its scene? One ear was badly nicked, maybe that was it, but there were other scenes she appeared in, a tomboy in the countryside, then a saint climbing up to her sacrifice; apparently there was no copy of this head in the current scenes—in principle each character had an imperfect copy that maintained the illusion during the rush to dust, wash its hair, and redo its runny makeup—and a number of heads had had to go to the museum at Rouen dedicated to the saint. Maybe the head had been the one that had, when the museum was built, been on the monumental white horse, in the atrium, Joan in armor bearing the standard, but no pins for the steel gorgerin had been imprinted in the wax, and the break in the neck was less marked than what could be seen in the old photograph. I immediately wanted to hold up this head and kiss it as it commanded me to; it was impossible, I was being watched, I sensed that my fascination made no difference to them. Was it possible to acquire this head so I could adore it tranquilly? No, the museum would not sell any of its creations, they needed this head in case a new scene had to be erected in a hurry—I shuddered to imagine the massacre—and should they ever agree to sell it, the price for it would be considerable. As such, it would have to be stolen. But it wasn't the time for that just yet. Could I at least come back to photograph it? That much was kindly granted to me.

Standing a second time in front of the head, in this difficulty, I took a photo that was a kiss. But I could only kiss once: a worker, holding the head, was my supplier, but brought me back to my senses at the same time, her calm, amused gaze cut short all my declarations, all my warmth. I immediately had the single photo printed which, on the contact sheet, seemed to be high in contrast: it was struck all the way through. On the negative I saw the same cruel, almost inexplicable, stupid strikethrough. It was then that I went to see a retoucher, the same way one might see a soothsayer or a disenchantress. She produced a masterpiece for me. A paltry masterpiece in light of the inimitable original, whose purported longevity offered not reassurance or comfort but only middling anger, atrocious doubts.

I had to consider how to save the head: the storage room had another entrance, in the back, which led to a control booth where, amid ropes and beams, an old man in a smock summoned up the luminous, flowing effects of a funhouse's mirrors, one hand on a button, the other on a lever, running over a walkway to pull the thread of the luminous butterfly that had caught its wings in the veil of the forest, and that the viewers down below were already trying to catch; when it was all over, he sipped some soup, and slept on the edge of the gap, bundled up beneath his coats, curled up under the light board, his hand clutching a dustcloth. Might he be the one who had to be convinced, exploited? Wasn't it really the director who had to be seduced?

My article came out and I set to work. My descriptions had delighted her, I talked to her flatteringly, mischievously. We saw each other again, she opened up her heart. She was the grand-daughter of the museum's founder, her mother still came and prowled around there, regally, despite her advanced years, presiding over the workshops, and destroying everything in her fits of pique, disfiguring an old mirror by having it lacquered with a vile gold paint, fixating on exact recreations in the style of royal tableaux found in *Points de vue et images du monde* and frantically ripped apart the compositions with ghoulish grace. Having grown up among wax and its bland smell of boiled tallow candles, she hated it, sprayed her clothes heavily with perfume to unshackle them. She especially detested wax in its most remarkable instances of imitating human flesh, a recognizable head would give her a horrible fright, and she used the least talented sculptors so that they would make shoddy caricatures. She held the handiworkers' wrists so that they would redden the cheekbones properly and cover the scalps with fiercely modern hairstyles, she dreaded nothing so much as the cadaver that suddenly appeared in a wax figure. She had all the basement rooms demolished where immensely striking reconstructions of the first Christian martyrs had been displayed.

She had been living alone with her daughter ever since her husband's death, she also had a son who she had named director and who ran the business exactingly, with the cold, sharp, cagey face of a young man who had grown up too soon. His emaciated, restrained profile in his sole three-piece suit made him a perpetually absent yet omnipresent shadow. Between this regal mother and this thin-lipped brother, the daughter, who had had to grow up too soon as well, without a lover, had remained brash and bumbling, which irked her family endlessly. Accordingly, everyone called her eccentric, but secretly kept an eye on her check stubs, her travels, her friends, and they had spoken with their lawyer so that her portion of the inheritance would be paid directly to her nieces and nephews without passing through her careless fingers. She had, in fact, had a late, extravagant romance, a handsome young man who pretended to be a musician, and who had been the start of her ruin, from cruises to musical seasons, until her brother caught him by the scruff of his neck. She read novels and practiced violin. Her eyesight worsened. Her brother upbraided her so she would stop her performances, which he considered ridiculous, where she appeared dressed up as a marquise on the stage of the museum's small theater, among the wax replicas of famous people, playing the violin until the ribbon encircling her neck snapped under the tension of her veins.

Ever since I was a child, one of the museum's tableaux had captivated me, to the point that I bruised my stomach on the iron bar holding me back; it depicted Louis XVII in the Temple prison. The waking nightmare made his body rear up on his grubby camp bed surrounded by rats, his throat bared and his white shirt torn off, the protruding cloth of the sheet cut through the shadows where, as if seen through peepholes, there hovered the profiles of bearded heads, executioners, and bearers of bread that the rats were better positioned to steal. The ice of the iron bar slowly made its way through the Breton kabic and the sweaters to touch my stomach.

One morning, when the director had taken me inside the closed museum, and abruptly hid me behind a column so that I would avoid inspection by her mother whose steps she recognized, having found myself alone at last at the edge of the tableau, I stepped over the bar and went to kiss Louis XVII. I loved him so madly that I had nearly untied the strings attaching him to his hips of stone (the sheet had allowed them to cut him off at the waist), slipping my hand under the dickey, to carry him on my back and bear him away from his suffering, when a cleaning woman's bucket clinked on the tiles far too close by.

It was only much later, years later, to be very precise a few minutes ago, in writing that, that I realized that Joan of Arc's head and Louis XVII's were the same head, that they had been formed, a century earlier from the same mold of a young boy, an apprentice whose name I didn't know. This is why we couldn't find this Joan of Arc's head in any of the tableaux, whether they were demolished yet photographically preserved, or in the Rouen museum devoted to the saint. This head had to be the broken original or the copy of Louis XVII, some carelessness in labeling had led the child king into a meadow so he could hear voices, and made him climb the stake.

I did not stop lusting after the head and confessing my desire to the museum director, with whom I now had a lovely relationship. She always told me to be patient, her eyes didn't glower anymore when I steered our conversation toward this fixation. At first she wanted to make sure that the head's mold remained in the museum's cellars: its hazy cover, the internal wrinkles of which would someday produce its features if wax was poured into it again. All her efforts were in vain: the mold was one of the few to have disappeared (it must be recalled that she was looking for Joan of Arc at this point rather than Louis XVII). She suggested that I ask a caster to make an imprint of the head and then peel off a thin film of wax, like a mask. I refused. And I was afraid that one of the handiworkers might happen to choose the head for restoration, spruce it up, defile it. She acknowledged that my desire was so foppish and determined that it was reasonable for me to insist on her saving the head from such ruination: she gave specific instructions in a calculatedly indifferent tone, kept an eye on the schedule for recasting, and ended up completely hiding the head in the back of a shelf, behind several rows of colleagues. All the same, for good reason, I was still shuddering. I finally convinced her that the head had to be stolen, because her brother was curtly refusing her overtures.

She swore to me that she would have given that head to me immediately, if it were up to her, but there was the matter of her conscience, and her religious belief, she went every week to church, such an abduction wasn't an easy thing to confess. My covetousness intensified to the point of giving the head a sacred significance, and she attempted to deter me by offering me other heads that she happily purloined, but never that one, she was incapable of it. I realized that I could lead her as far I wanted to, up to the limits of that desire: one day when we were alone in the workshop, I calmly took a wax arm and broke it under her eyes.

As she mended the arm, she took responsibility for the error and the handiworkers gloated over it: they knew that her dexterity was what kept her from such a blunder. She put forward the prospect of a cruise, then a season in Salzburg; I declined these invitations as I had those to dinner. One afternoon when we were supposed to run an errand together, an unusual one as it was a matter of finding and comparing glass eyes inherited in a batch by two old skinflint brothers, I happened upon a conversation behind an ajar door: the museum's administrator was refusing to give her a blank check, she in fact did not have a checkbook, they made it clear that ever since the notorious incident they could only allow her a very limited sum of liquid money. The brothers weren't at home or, sensing that there would be haggling, didn't open their door: I set about telling her the story of kidnapping Joan of Arc's head. It was so plausible that she believed it and added some particulars to it.

We had to sneak into the museum one evening when the only person we might cross was the night watchman, who was on her side, who could be silenced with a bill. We would need a large bag to put the head in, and then that would be the occasion for a dinner. She reassured me so often and thoroughly that we would carry off the head that I very quickly bankrupted myself at an antique dealer so I could offer it the handsomest of pedestals: a small black Egyptian stelette with pharaohs' death masks embedded on it. The antique dealer had just enough time to bring it to my place, and I rushed to the museum. It was already late. In the arcade surrounding the museum, I came upon the slender brother who pulled up the collar of his raincoat, recognized me, and waved unpleasantly at me. As a result he could testify that he had seen me at that time that night. The night watchman was perplexed: no, Mademoiselle wasn't there, in fact she had left a long while ago, and she hadn't left a message. Would she be back? That was unlikely . . . I waited an hour for her, walking back and forth under the watchman's eye among the fun-house mirrors of the hall where the visitors stood and burst out laughing. I was sad, all of a sudden the watchman decided I was an impostor, and pushed me out. With an empty stomach, I went to look at the small stelette bought too hastily and I embraced the void that it held up.

The next day, the wily cheat called me up: no need to be gloomy, it was just a misunderstanding, the whole thing would go off this very evening, in any case it was wiser for her to do it on her own, she would come to my place, yes, with the head of course; my impatience had become her favorite joke.

The head, which I hadn't seen for four years, reappeared as all around it fell a snow of torn-up paper that had protected it. Up to the final moment I was certain that I would be brought some other head. But it was that one, and it sealed, between us, with a smile, those four years of courtship in which she had been the prize, all while fortifying our affection. The director said that I would have to put all these five-franc coins that the end of each day would leave at the bottom of my pockets into a coin purse. Once the purse was full, she would deposit it at a church to pay for our sin. Today the head is very shakily balanced on its small stele in my living room. I haven't kissed it twice and its presence is so familiar that I don't see it anymore. But I do notice that it scares away dogs and bothers all visitors. I still haven't been interested in embedding it on the stelette's wood and just one millimeter really would cause it to shatter. I tell myself that this head won't have any history so long as it hasn't been destroyed.

A Man's Secrets

When it came to trepanning, the specialist said: I could never touch this brain, it would be a crime, I would feel like I was attacking a work of art, or hacking at perfection, or burning a masterpiece, or flooding a landscape that needed to stay dry, or throwing a grenade into an exquisitely structured termite mound, scratching a polished diamond, ruining beauty, sterilizing fertility, tying off the canals of all creation, every cut of the blade would be an assault upon intelligence, thrusting iron into this divine mass would be an auto-da-fé for this genius; only a barbarian, an illiterate, an enemy would commit such a crime! The enemy existed. Sarcastically, examining the three lesions spreading across the scanner's images, he says: how could such brilliance be left to rot? We have to open this. This intelligence had pierced him, personally, not by name, but by condemning all the deceit in his system, in several books. The man of the mind had castigated the man of law: the doctor, the judge; the philosopher had ultimately accused his ancient predecessors of abuse of thoughts; in their texts, he tried to find the exact moment when the thread was lost, imperceptibly but insidiously, when the right words, drawn from the right thoughts, slipped ever so slightly, were recovered maladroitly, and turned into wrong words, oppressive words. The surgeon took pride in assailing such a fortress, especially considering how he called his prestige groundless; a man's head, he said to his assistants, is nothing more than a bit of flab, of cured meat. But when the orb was opened, he was astonished by the powerful beauty that matter exuded; his disdain was as mute as his tongue, and his stylet fell from his hands; all he could do, now that he had been converted, was contemplate. The brain was no longer a simple, tender walnut with manifold, indecipherable convolutions, but a luminescent, teeming terrain as yet uncongealed by anesthesia, and every fiefdom was busy working, gathering, connecting, charting, drifting, damming, rerouting, refining; three strong-holds had collapsed, that was easy to see, but all around the moat kept golden thoughts and laughter flowing. The most noticeable veins carried along all sorts of nasty old ruined things, prison tur-rets, torture vises; but the whips seemed to gleam royally like scepters, and the gags were woven like finery. Exposed discourses glittered on the surface, opened up to derision; their reek of arro-gance was absolved by their aroma. Digging just a little revealed corridors full of savings, reserves, secrets, childhood memories, and unpublished theories. The childhood memories were buried deepest of all, in order not to clash against idiotic interpretations or poorly woven veils that were meant to be enlightening but which instead shrouded the work. Two or three images were buried in his vessels' depths like vile dioramas. The first one showed the young philosopher led by his father, himself a surgeon, through a Poitiers hospital room where a man's leg had been amputated, that's how the boy's manliness gets shaped. The second revealed a typical backyard the little philosopher was walking past, which was aquiver with the recent news: right there, on a straw mattress, in this sort of garage, was where the woman all the papers were calling the Poitiers Prisoner had lived for dozens of years. The third retold the beginning of a story, wax figures coming to life through the machinery hidden beneath their clothes: in high school, the little philosopher, who had been the top of his class, was threatened by the sudden and seemingly inexplicable invasion of an arrogant band of little Parisians who were sure to be more talented than the rest. The ousted philosopher-child came to hate them, insult them, hurl all sorts of curses upon them: the refugee Jewish children in the area did disappear by being deported to the camps. These secrets would have sunk in the Atlantis ever so slowly, ever so sumptuously chiseled, suddenly shattered by lighting, had a vow of friendship not raised the vague and uncertain possibility of their being passed on . . .

Each of these strongholds were threatened, one by one: the cache of proper names emptied. Then it was personal memories that were very nearly ruined: he fought to keep the scourge from winning out. Even the existence of his books vanished: what had he written? had he even written? Sometimes he wasn't sure at all. The books there, in his hands, could have borne witness. But the books weren't himself, he had once written that and he remembered it still: that the book wasn't the man, that between the book and the man was the labor that had dissociated the two, and sometimes drove them apart like two enemies. But was that actually what he had written? He hesitated to return to the text itself, he was afraid to find himself locked out as an idiot. So he wrote and rewrote his name on a piece of paper, and underneath he drew rows of squares, circles, and triangles, a ritual he had taught himself to verify his mental integrity. When people came into his room, he hid the paper.

He had to finish his books, this book he had written and rewritten, destroyed, renounced, destroyed once more, imagined once more, created once more, shortened and stretched out for ten years, this infinite book, of doubt, rebirth, modest grandiosity. He was inclined to destroy it forever, to offer his enemies their stupid victory, so they could go around clamoring that he was no longer able to write a book, that his mind had been dead for ages, that his silence was just proof of his failure. He burned or destroyed all the drafts, all the evidence of his work, all he left on his table were two manuscripts, side by side, he instructed a friend that this abolition was to continue. He had three abscesses in his brain but he went to the library every day to check his notes.

His death was stolen from he who wished to be master of his own death, and even the truth of his death was stolen from he who wished to be master of the truth. Above all the name of the plague was not to be spoken, it was to be disguised in the death records, false reports were given to the media. Although he wasn't dead yet, the family he had always been ostracized from took in his body. The doctors spoke abjectly of blood relatives. His friends could no longer see him, unless they broke and entered: he saw a few of them, unrecognizable behind their plastic-bag-covered hair, masked faces, swaddled feet, torsos covered in jackets, gloved hands reeking of alcohol he had been forbidden to drink himself.

All the strongholds had collapsed, except for the one protecting love: it left an unchangeable smile on his lips when exhaustion closed his eyes. If he only kept a single image, it would be the one of their last walk in the Alhambra gardens, or just his face. Love kept on thrusting its tongue in his mouth despite the plague. And as for his death it was he who negotiated with his family: he exchanged his name on the death announcement for being able to choose his death shroud. For his carcass he chose a cloth in which they had made love, which came from his mother's trousseau. The intertwined initials in the embroidery could bear other messages.

As the body was collected in the morgue's rear courtyard, masses of flowers lay all around the coffin: in wreaths, in rows, from editors, from the institute where he had taught, from foreign universities. On the coffin itself stood a small pyramid of roses among which a band of mauve taffeta revealed and concealed the letters of three names. The bier traveled the whole day, from the capital to the rural village, from the hospital to the church and from the church to the cemetery, it passed from hand to hand, but the pyramid of roses, which the florist had not stapled or taped to the wood, was never knocked off the structure. Several hands tried to move it. Either those hands were immediately caught in a moment's hesitation after which they reconsidered, or other hands reached out to stop them. An occult, imperious order bound the pyramid of roses with its three names to the coffin. When the coffin was gently set in the pit, the mother was asked what should be done with this spray of flowers, and she gestured, she who was not crying, to leave them on the coffin. Nobody got rid of the letter that someone had left when the body was collected, or worried about whether it contained love or hurt, the cut flowers buried it. A tall young man with bare shoulders, in a leather jacket, sunglasses, stood in the distance, accompanied by an old crooked man who seemed to be his father, or servant, or driver; from the capital to the village, from the morgue to the church, from the church to the cemetery they had traveled in an elegant sports car. I had never seen this young man and when he threw flowers into the ditch after me with his sunglasses still on, I suddenly recognized him and I went up to him, I said: are you Martin?, he said: hello, Hervé. I said: he always wanted us to meet, and now we have. We kissed each other and perhaps we kissed him at the same time over the grave.

The Earthquake

On March 4 at eight forty-five, I'm alone in my workshop, with the wood of a paintbrush the wrong way around I tap a sheet of gold onto an icon, a sound like thunder and the sheet of gold crinkles, slips from my thumb, shrivels up into a ball and nothing in front of me could catch it, the first tremor lasts several seconds, the icon is thrown against the wall, cracks it, it opens onto the garden, I'm unable to reach the door handle, it slips away from me, the floor slips, the workshop shrinks, breathes, the moment I'm in the garden the four-story building that usually faces me collapses into a column of dust, the sky is red, I try to step over the barrier, it takes three tries, finally I hug this crooked tree that wouldn't let me, I wrap my arms around it and it twists on itself, the second tremor throws us more than a yard off our feet and roots, I don't wait for the end of the third tremor to brush off its seeping back, the cherry tree that's slumped over behind me could have flattened me as well, I go and cross the city to see whether Vincent is still alive, I walk calmly, my head raised to assess what's still standing, my eyes on my feet so they don't veer away from the crevasse, at first I don't see anyone then people come out of their houses, buildings have crushed buses and cars, there isn't any crying to be heard, a father comes back from work and all he finds of his home is his son's pillow which he clutches dumbly without complaint, gas pipes explode, fire surges upward, the glowing dust still hasn't floated down, the day is gone but the night is delaying its appearance, dogs prowl, I hold out hope that a fourth tremor will wipe away everything and me as well, my legs are unexpectedly surefooted, I don't even imagine Vincent's face, I don't imagine his death or survival, my steps seem to record the path usually taken by cars to bring me his body, loudspeakers that can't be seen proclaim a state of alert, looters will be shot on the spot by militiamen, but they're already there, they're crawling and breaking, they're sneaking in, they rummage in the rubble, they fill their pockets and bags, people curse them weakly, they're unreal, they're looking for precious stones and are ready to pull them off corpses, they're not even masked, they're shameless, these are angels, the bridge that was supposed to connect me to this end of the city where Vincent lived doesn't exist anymore, I have to make a long detour through neighborhoods, some devastated, some untouched, to get there, the city is like an off-kilter theater stage set framed by a frieze of little houses, I sink into an ever-slicker horror, bunches of stunned corpses clog the gutters, petrified, the animals are mad, they flee and shriek, they mate thoughtlessly, hyenas try to mount dragonflies, Vincent's building doesn't exist anymore because the neighborhood it was built in doesn't exist anymore, it's an abyss of whirling dust, men in work overalls are crawling out, a dumpster arrives, an excavator sorts the rubble, and the gypsies skulk around with their huge bags, I look up to try to reconstruct in space the fifth floor where so many embraces took place, I walked all night without realizing it, the bars are closed, I didn't see the night, it fell and went away again, and the morning sun seems too strong on the brazier of the ground, the earth's heat has only increased, I reach the morgue, there's no space left in the refrigerated rooms or even in the hallway or the administrators' offices filled with corpses, a huge tarp had been stretched in the garden where scattered members had been put, arms, legs, feet, bare or decorated limbs, dressed, amid which this horde is trampling in search of likenesses, clues, reunions, this horde that I slip into and that, like me, wants to recognize a name on a bracelet, a cloth, a scar, a wart, or simply a silky softness, and steal the appendage for no reason, wrap it in a bit of newsprint to go broil it or devour it somewhere far from prying eyes, it's starting to stink terribly, an odor of sugary shit, of caramelized blood, of praline offal, the sun pounding on the tarp has a barbecuing effect, the odor nips at both sides of my throat and pulls my knees out from between my thighs and my calves, morgue employees come with phenol canisters to spray the corpses, I know that of all these members I won't be able to recognize anything of Vincent's and if I suspected that I recognized something I'd spit on the limb in question and go on my way, but I'm being pushed, I'm being pressed on all sides, and I have to keep trampling through, I could also force my way out of this horde and leave, but this walk has all the sensuality of a dream, the sun becomes almost caressing, the stench almost delicious, appendages have spilled over past the tarp and these elegant little girls' and boys' giblets lie on the cool grass, it's next to them that I'd like to kneel down or faint, it's those that I'd like to tread on as if by accident so as to carry something under my shoes; as they meet in the interminable labyrinth the two unruly lines of the horde crash into one another, curse at each other like two enemy ranks, stepping on each other's feet, ignoring each other while jabbing each other, it's at that moment that I'm sure I see Vincent's face laughing so close to mine.

The Lemon Tree

I surreptitiously admired the wiry strength of his hand. I had never stroked it. Sometimes I shook it, harshly, briefly, like a good friend's. Our hugs were more frequent when we'd had several beers, we kept up with each other, we ended up each having eight half-pints, sitting side by side, while Bob watched us, flabbergasted, his excuse was being too poor to pay for his drinks, he couldn't get us our seventeenth and eighteenth half-pints, and Jeannot, the bartender, cut us off. Jeannot was a funny old guy; whenever anyone shouted his name from one end of the room to the other, he yelled: "Drop your pants, I'm coming!" which was his favorite joke, he talked to the girls more respectfully. As for them, we only peeked at them through the mirror, whenever they weren't paying attention, Bob was a master at looking away at the very last minute, he balanced his cigarette on the table, said that the beer was making us glassy-eyed, somewhat gross. It was doing us good. Bob set off early, he was odd, he left us at one second or another without saying why, he must have sensed that his smiling little virgin face made us want, after our fourth beers, to hurt him, lie to him, mess with him, he was so innocent. We weren't in good shape for geography class, it would be much better to skip it. With a thump of his palm, Cistou showed us one last, dangerous triple flip of his beer coaster, then we emptied all the coins out of our pockets. Jeannot took them one by one in his hand while telling us that the place didn't keep open tabs for drunks like us. Jeannot was all too happy to play with Francis's fingers, he was so infamous for his jokes that nobody guessed he was gay. But I was shaking in fear at the thought that my Cistou might suspect my attraction. When I was drunk like that, I buried my hands deep in my pockets. But Cistou was so affectionate, once we were out of the café he rubbed his forehead on my shoulder, he gave me friendly kicks in the butt, he pretended to push me into the ravine so he could catch me in his arms. Sometimes I was sure he saw it all, and that his playful mischievousness was what drew him so close to me like a shadow or a twin.

I noticed the splendor of his hands the moment he broke his wrist playing basketball. Within his plaster bracelet, his left hand had become an unconscious, offered-up woman. My gaze seized it. Its paralysis gave it a feminine unconsciousness and slenderness, without diminishing its strength, the bluish vigor of its veined tracery, but rather putting them to sleep, like pure anesthetized beauty fighting against its sedative, straining for stable supports or loose pocket-bottoms so that softness wouldn't betray itself in a peasant's hand. Bob had refused to write anything on the plaster, he insisted it was as unhealthy as exchanging blood. But I didn't have to be asked twice to write, lightly, in green ink: "To my good old Cistou, hoping his wrist will be back to rendering its usual services soon." I kept up the big talk, but I was a hypocrite: I wasn't the least bit interested in his hand being freed from its case or its vise.

Several months went by. Cistou rushed into my room, livid, sweaty, he was hiding his hand behind his back, he stammered:
    "The old hag . . . from the intersection . . . the crazy one . . . who yells at me like a madwoman whenever she sees me walking past her fence . . . like I'm a black dog . . . a devil's dog . . . I've got a score to

settle with that old girl . . . so I cooked up a little surprise for her, all on my own . . . a nice firework—to give her fence some color, since it's starting to fade just like her . . . it didn't take a lot of thinking: a big banger, two or three bolts, a cord that's long enough, won't hurt anyone . . . I didn't want this little grenade blowing her vagina apart to clear off a bit of her stinking virginity . . . just a little shot to the heart—but I was the one who got the blackout . . . the bitch grabbed my hand . . . it tore off my hand, and the crazy old thing was just looking at me and smiling behind her window, and I saw her watch my fingers go flying off, it made me feel like hell . . . so I ran off . . . but first I had to look for my fingers . . . two of them were goners . . . all the rest, my hand, were just mush, but the three others were still holding on, not really together, but they were still hanging, and they were wriggling on their own, and I told them to stop . . ."

"You're lying, show me your hand."

For a few seconds, I was scared his hand was hiding a weapon to threaten me.

"All right, I'm lying to you . . . The old girl didn't see a thing . . . And that's the worst part . . . She didn't see my fingers go flying off, that wasn't even going to give her a proper nightmare . . . She won't need to try to forget them . . . I wasn't able to get her, that revenge was all for nothing, and I feel like hell . . . I was alone in the shed, patching up my machine . . . the fingers flew off in the wood shavings, not in the grass . . . it's gross, live skin and muscles buried in the sawdust . . . I pulled them out, went to wash them outside, under the pump, nobody could see me, and then I came back to the shop floor to find newsprint and pack them up, I already had the idea in my head, but before that I wiped my two fingers in my hand-kerchief, they got cold in the water, and I was blowing on them, but it was no good, those bastards weren't going to get warm again . . ."

"But what did you do with those fingers? What did you do?"

"Calm down, Lulu. And don't ever tell anybody this story. It's between you and me. Because I don't want anyone to know what happened."

"Well, tell me, tell me . . ."

"So I had my little package: a little handkerchief shroud, you know Muslims have themselves wrapped up in a sheet, right on the ground . . . I went into the forest . . ."

"Let's go, Cistou, let's go there right now! You have to take me! I'm begging you!"

"What for, Lulu? Why are you getting all worked up? It's ancient history to me. I've still got eight. Enough for polishing my pole, and too many for a whore's hole . . . And the two I don't have anymore, you can figure it out for yourself, it's easy to see that there's something missing in the middle of the cast, but you know, I can still feel them, they're going crazy, a delicious tingling . . ."

"Which of the two forests did you go to?"

"The one where everyone gets lost . . ."

I finally talked Cistou into taking me there. Once we were there, I got impatient and asked:

"Where was it?"

"Over there . . . I don't really remember . . ."

"You don't recognize any of this?"

"No, not really, it's all a bit the same . . ."

"But where you buried them, do you not remember that?"

"I scraped up some dirt under a heap of ferns . . ."

I lost it:

"Ferns? That's all there is here! You didn't see any landmarks? An intersection, a cross, a tree, anything?"

Cistou got angry:

"Let's get out! I don't need to be here . . ."

"No, wait! We're going to find it! A heap of ferns? That's easy . . . We'll find it . . ."

"I don't know why I followed you . . ."

I got nervous. "You didn't lie to me, did you? You didn't burn them, did you?"

But Cistou wasn't paying attention. Suddenly he seemed to recall: "A lemon tree . . . I buried them under a lemon tree . . ."

Had the explosion wrecked his head? Or was he messing with me? I was scared to press him.

"A lemon tree, around here? You're sure . . . a lemon tree?"

He hadn't been dreaming. Five minutes later, we were kneeling on each side of the lemon tree, as if it had grown under our steps. I clawed at the earth. I was so happy:

"If we don't find them now, we can come back! We'll come back at night! We'll come back every day, until we find them again!"

Cistou looked worried:

"What do you want us to do with my fingers?"

But I wasn't listening to him anymore. I was rummaging around on all fours, I was pushing away the underbrush.

"On this side, you think, or that side?"

"Probably there," Cistou answered.

He wasn't sure anymore.

"There? Wait . . . I've got it, I have it . . . I've got it!"

I'd just pulled out a small package full of dirt. Cistou was shaking. I held out the package. "You unwrap it."

"No, you do it. I can't touch them anymore. You're scaring me."

I peeled off the newsprint, then I undid the handkerchief's knots, I was ecstatic.

"What a wonder! What a treasure!"

Cistou grimaced. "They're already brown, wet, wrinkled. Ugh, drop it! It's worthless now . . ."

I took one of the fingers and put it in my mouth, and started chewing it. Cistou grabbed me and shook me.

"Spit that out right now! You're going to poison yourself!"

Something came over him, I was in a hurry to swallow it, I pushed him away harshly.

"Get away! Leave me alone! It's none of your business anymore . . ."

We were fighting. Once the finger was all the way in my throat, I felt an immense calm rise up within. Cistou let go, in his eyes the deed had been done. He wanted to mess with me. He picked up the handkerchief with the other finger and hid it in his pocket.

"Now, this one," he yelled, "I'm not going to let you eat this, you pig! Unless . . . You'd really have to deserve it!"

He danced around me, teasing me. I ran at his pocket. We were tussling like children. Cistou burst out in a happy laugh: "He's mad! I love you! You're mad!"

While still pushing me away, he covered my head with quick little kisses. I had his filthy taste in my mouth, and I heard him saying that he loved me. I had him inside me, I had nothing else to say to him.

Acknowledgments

This collection is the result of five years of research and translation, and it would not have come to fruition if not for the support of many colleagues and acquaintances. The two guiding lights at the outset of this endeavor were Marie Darrieussecq, whose passion and steadfast support were a balm at the thorniest moments, and Nathanaël, whose labor of love in translating *The Mausoleum of Lovers* paved the way for my own work. I am grateful, too, to Agathe Gaillard and Christine Guibert, whose work in safeguarding Hervé Guibert's legacy has been formidable.

This project very literally would not have happened without Hedi El Kholti at Semiotext(e), who very bravely took on this strange project and became a fellow journeyer through Guibert's works. It was many years ago that I first shyly mentioned to Sophie Langlais that I was curious about the prospect of translating Guibert's stories into English; I am endlessly indebted to her for remembering this detail and sharing it with Hedi. At Gallimard, too, I want to thank Anne-Solange Noble and Margot Miriel for their attentiveness, resourcefulness, and patience as the project metamorphosed into its final version. Valerie Borchardt, similarly, has been a true ally in representing Minuit and allowing Guibert's stories from that publishing house to be included in this collection. The jury members for the 2016 PEN/Heim Translation Grant were an invaluable vote of confidence in the project's early stages, and I am still grateful especially to Sara Khalili for her insistence that I not compromise on this project's most essential aspects. And I would be remiss not to mention Jean-Pierre Boulé, whose *Hervé Guibert: Voices of the Self* remains a definitive text on the author's œuvre two decades after its original-language publication and whose answers to my emails have always been so swift, so incisive, and so thoroughly helpful that I wish I were able to repay all the favors he has done me.

Guibert's stories have not been easy to translate, especially his earliest ones, and as I worked to decipher his most recondite sentences, David Ferrière was my first port of call. There is something deeply French, in my mind, about the idea of intellectual friendship, and I'm grateful to him not only for his many answers, suggestions, ideas, and bon mots, but for teaching me what such amity can look like. Other friends answered smaller questions along the way, including (in alphabetical order) Christopher Austin, Jean-Pierre Boulé, Sean Gasper Bye, Jean-Baptiste del Amo, Amanda DeMarco, Arnaud Genon, Steve Goldhaber, Charles Lee, Nathanaël, Nell Pach, Alta L. Price, Clément Ribes, Kit Schluter, Edmund White, and Frank Wynne.

To honor the real-life external sources quoted in "The Static Electricity Machine" from *Vice*, I have quoted Arthur Goldhammer's original translation of Otto von Guericke's words from *Grand Street*, Summer 1995, and commissioned a translation of Reveroni Saint-Cyr's words from Patricia Worth, the consummate Englisher of George Sand's *Spiridion*.

This entire endeavor is the result of two editors at *The Offing*, Amanda DeMarco and Geoff Mak, asking me to translate "The Knife Thrower" from *The Sting of Love* in the fall of 2015.

An early version of "Flash Paper" from *Mauve the Virgin* was published in the first issue of *Tinted Window Magazine*; my thanks go to Oscar Gaynor and Alex Bennett for their support and to Andrew Durbin for thinking of me. "A Man's Secrets," also from *Mauve the Virgin*, previously appeared, in earlier versions, on the PEN web site, and then in the final issue of *Animal Shelter*. "The Sting of Love" was published as part of a chapbook honoring 2016 recipients of the PEN/Heim Translation Grant.

Hervé Guibert (1955–1991) was a writer, a photography critic for *Le Monde*, a photographer, and a filmmaker. In 1984 he and Patrice Chereau were awarded a César for best screenplay for *L'Homme Blessé*. Shortly before his death from AIDS, he completed *La Pudeur ou L'impudeur*, a video work that chronicles the last days of his life.

Jeffrey Zuckerman is an award-winning translator from the French, most notably of Ananda Devi's *Eve Out of Her Ruins* and *The Living Days*, the diaries of the Dardenne brothers, and Jean Genet's *The Criminal Child*. For his work on the stories of Hervé Guibert, he was bestowed with a PEN/Heim translation grant, and his other translations have garnered him the 2017 Firecracker Award in Fiction and multiple French Voices Awards. An editor at *Music & Literature*, his writing and translations have appeared in *Guernica*, *Harper's*, *The Los Angeles Review of Books*, *The New Republic*, *The Paris Review Daily*, and *Vice*.